THE WARRING *Soul*

Blessings

Kristin Wells

Eccl 3:11-15

Kristen Wells

THE WARRING Soul

TATE PUBLISHING
AND ENTERPRISES, LLC

Scripture quotations marked "NIV" are taken from the *Holy Bible, New International Version ®*, Copyright © 1973, 1978, 1984 by International Bible Society. Used by permission of Zondervan Publishing House. All rights reserved.

Scripture quotations marked "MSG" are taken from *The Message*, Copyright © 1993, 1994, 1995, 1996, 2000, 2001, 2002. Used by permission of NavPress Publishing Group. All rights reserved.

Scripture quotations marked "CEV" are from the *Holy Bible; Contemporary English Version*, Copyright © 1995, Barclay M. Newman, ed., American Bible Society. Used by permission. All rights reserved.

The opinions expressed by the author are not necessarily those of Tate Publishing, LLC.

Published by Tate Publishing & Enterprises, LLC
127 E. Trade Center Terrace | Mustang, Oklahoma 73064 USA
1.888.361.9473 | www.tatepublishing.com

Tate Publishing is committed to excellence in the publishing industry. The company reflects the philosophy established by the founders, based on Psalm 68:11,
"The Lord gave the word and great was the company of those who published it."

Book design copyright © 2012 by Tate Publishing, LLC. All rights reserved.
Cover design by Matias Alasagas
Interior design by Joana Quilantang

Published in the United States of America

ISBN: 978-1-62147-841-6
1. Fiction / General
2. Fiction / Christian / General
12.10.19

Dedication

"But I see a different law in the members of my body,
waging war against the law of my mind and making me
a prisoner of the law of sin which is in my members.
Wretched man that I am! Who will set me free from the
body of this death?"

—Romans 7:23 (NASB)

For all those who are struggling to fight the war that wages within.

Acknowledgments

To my heavenly Father who helps me fight my war every day. And to my "cheerleaders," thank you for always believing in me and loving me without judgment.

Prologue

I should have known from the moment I was born that my life would go against all odds. Now some may see this as a blessing, and I would tend to concur if only they were the right odds. My parents used two forms of protection to *not* have me, and I was still conceived. That 1 percent chance became reality for them. They were devastated. Then to be born into a family that does not want you—well I had a 20 percent chance of that, so my rates were a little higher. As I grew older, my parents' feelings toward me never changed, so the abuse began, which lucky for me, 14 percent of kids also went through. Yet I had a 14 percent chance that my mother would cheat on my dad, and I had a 3 percent chance that out of the five affairs she had, one would be with the guy I liked in high school.

I had a 4 percent chance of becoming anorexic or bulimic by the time I reached junior high school—lucky for me, I became both. Mostly because my mom wanted to use me as a way to get "to know" people, so she entered me in a lot of different contests—of which I had a one in twenty-five chance of winning—yet didn't win any because those would be odds in my favor. She wanted me to be as pretty as I could possibly look, which meant trying everything to get me to look like her and not me. So even though I was born a brunette, which seemed odd considering both my parents were blonde, I often had blonde, auburn, or black hair. My eyebrows were often different shades and shapes, and I was pushed into the gym more hours than I was actually at school. Although instead of trimming down and toning up, I just bulked up, and given my five-foot six frame, I looked more like a wrestler than a beauty queen—much to my mother's chagrin. I must have lucked out and got my dad's build. Thus, I turned even more to throwing up the little food

I actually ate in hopes I could counteract the bulk from the muscle and appease my mother.

Yet my childhood wasn't all bruises and shadows; I had friends. I lived for my drama class so I could escape to be someone else, and I loved to ride horses. I had a strict curfew, from parents who didn't care, which again seems to go against all odds, but I made the most of it. I grew up in a small town where everyone knows everyone else's business, and our idea of a good night was dragging the dimly lit main street eating breadsticks and ranch dressing from our local pizzeria. I didn't really get into a lot of trouble—except for the occasional party thrown while I would housesit for a neighbor—and I got over a 4.0 GPA thanks to the local community college where I gladly spent some extra hours. I could accept the trauma at home because I knew someday I would be gone, able to lead my own life away from all of the insanity. I worked hard knowing that day was nipping at my heels waiting to bring me into a world that was full of growth and opportunity. I dreamt about my prince charming waiting for me somewhere out there, even I knew the boys I dated in that small town only wanted one thing. And I was not willing to give it to any simpleton who drank too much. I was waiting for my dream job as a cardiac surgeon saving people's lives, then coming home to my loving husband who would rub my feet and tell me how beautiful I was. I admit I read way too much in high school. It was the only way I could live—thinking one day I would be empowered, like Elizabeth Bennet from *Pride and Prejudice*.

College

It was my first day away from the horror that was home, and I couldn't be more excited. It was a gorgeous August day, and I was standing in the doorway of my new home at the University of Santa Barbara. It was twelve hours away from home and full of sun and potential. I was ready with my list of courses—the usual freshman classes plus some extra chemistry and biology thrown in there to get me pre-med ready. I had my parents help me throw my stuff in my new nine-by-nine-foot home, and with a quick good-bye I was off to my orientation meeting. They talked about sticking to your studies and not letting yourself get too distracted by this "new world" we were entering. They jabbered on and on about illegal drinking and partying. I heard passing words of "date rape" and "sorority and fraternity initiations" while I daydreamed about the fact that as I looked around no one knew me. No one knew that I was a battered kid or that I came from a freakish home. I was just Katerine Isabella McDermott—freshman. I decided that I would introduce myself as Kate. I was Katy back home, and I wanted to get as far away from that as possible.

I turned to the girl next to me, and with a fake smile and a shaky voice said, "Hey, I'm Kate. What dorm are you in?"

"Hey, I'm Samantha, but most people call me Sam. I'm in Silvermont. What about you?"

"Me too! What floor?"

"Second."

"Oh, I'm on the third," I said with slight disappointment.

"Cool." Sam laughed, and just like that I had made a new friend. We walked around the campus getting to know where our classes were—not one of them together but close enough that we could walk together. We then went back to the dorm to unpack and promised to meet up for dinner. How nice it was that we didn't have to eat alone our first night.

When I got back to my dorm, I realized that I hadn't met my roommate yet, and I got extremely nervous. As I cracked the door open I saw a tall, thin, blonde girl organizing her stuff.

After seeing her long legs and graceful movements, I immediately felt short and stocky. Yet, I strangely found myself sighing in relief, knowing my mother hadn't met her—this real-life example of her perfect daughter.

I walked in and introduced myself. She turned around and with a quick glancing me over she said, "Hey, I am Renee, but no need to get too comfortable with me as your roommate. I don't plan on being around that much."

"Oh," I said, "Well, it's nice to meet you anyway. Do you have family or friends around or something?"

"No, not at the moment, but on my walk up here I already got asked out on two dates, so I don't think it is going to be a problem."

Not only was she beautiful, she knew it. I decided not to push the conversation, knowing I would just feel worse about myself and turned around to start trying to make something of my side of the room. I met up with Sam about an hour later for our first cafeteria meal. After that experience it only took us a week to find the popular hamburger hangout, and the freshman fifteen had begun.

Classes were as usual. Professors seemed rigorous in my premed classes and a little too lenient in my general education classes, which made for a nice balance. I stayed in my room a lot getting my work done, which was what I was used to doing. I was a good student, and I knew if I wanted to be a doctor I would have to work for it.

The first semester flew by. Sam and I became inseparable, given that we seemed to be insanely alike, and finals were easy since we didn't spend much time doing anything but studying and enjoying the nearby beach. It was quickly time for Christmas break, during which I went home for a week and decided it wasn't worth it, so headed back to campus for the final week of break. There were few kids there, which I found relaxing and quiet. I ate alone, read a lot of books, and played a lot of solitaire. One day, I was relaxing on the beach, reading *Pride and Prejudice* for the fiftieth time, when all of a sudden a guy sat next to me on my towel. His hair was blond and shaggy; he was wearing only board shorts and sunglasses. His abs were wet and glistening in the sunlight, and sand stuck to his legs and feet.

"Hey there, what are you reading?" he asked.

"Uh, *Pride and Prejudice*. Have you read it?"

"In high school and only because it was required. You must have Mr. Hawthorne—he always makes his students reread the classics. Good for you for getting a head start," he said with a smirk.

"No, actually I don't. I just really like the book."

"Oh, I see. You are one of *those* kind of girls." He winked at me with sparkling blue eyes, and I found myself drooling.

"Is there a reason you came over here? Or did you just want to insult my choice of reading?"

"Wow…okay well, I saw you sitting here. I have seen you around the last couple of days and was wondering why you weren't at home for the break."

"I like it here better, let's just put it that way."

"I totally understand that one. I'm in the same boat. I'm Paul, nice to meet you."

"I'm Kate, nice to meet you!" I said with a little too much excitement. I nervously tried to suck in my stomach and straighten my windblown beach hair.

"Hey, so do you wanna go get a burger or something? I am starving!"

I tried to hide my surprise. "Sure, sounds like fun. I could use something to eat." Although, by looking at me that might be debated. Once I stepped foot on campus, not only did I change my name, but I vowed to change my habits. I decided to live my life without having to think I needed to be thin. Even though I wasn't throwing up every single meal anymore, it was still a daily occurrence. I couldn't remember the last time I actually finished a meal or even half of a meal, but it was a definite improvement. Of course, I thought about it all the time, and it took a lot for me to even eat a little bit without vomiting, but I was enjoying the fact that I could conquer something my mother had instilled in me.

Paul and I walked up to the boardwalk where my bike was tied up.

"Instead of us taking two modes of transportation to some dumb restaurant, why don't we just go grab a couple hotdogs from that stand over there and sit here at the beach? There is a picnic table over there. What do you think?" he asked.

"Sounds like a good plan." I was relieved I wouldn't have to get all sweaty from riding my bike.

We walked across the street where Paul bought us each a hot dog and a coke. He proceeded to pile his high with mustard and sauerkraut, while I left mine plain.

"Wow, I don't think I have ever seen somebody eat a plain hot dog before," he said.

"Yeah, well, that is not all that is different about me."

"I am starting to notice that."

Was it good that I was different? He seemed like the kind of guy who would drive up in a convertible with a bleach-blonde bimbo attached to the passenger seat. In fact I wondered if he had met my roommate yet; she would be perfect for him. We made our way over to the table and quietly ate our hot dogs—well, I picked at mine, but eventually managed to eat half.

"Not much of an eater?" he asked.

"Oh no, I am, I am just admiring the scenery."

"No reason to be shy around me," he said. He had mustard all over his face. We both broke out laughing, obviously a little too hard, because I ended up dropping the rest of my hot dog.

"So what is your major?" He wiped up the mess on his face.

"Biology. I am hoping to be a doctor one day, but it is probably just a pipe dream."

"Wow, that's great. I don't see why it has to be a dream though. You seem like the kind of girl who can make it happen. Reading *Pride and Prejudice* while relaxing on the beach still at school when the rest of everyone else is partying at home."

"Yeah, I don't know. I guess I don't have much faith in dreams coming true. What about you?

"Well, I'm a junior and a business major. I belong to Delta Sigma Pi, it is a business fraternity, so I must mean business."

"Hmm, they must not teach you a lot about comedy in that fraternity."

"Well, I tried," he said, laughing.

We sat there for the rest of the afternoon, talking about our dreams of the future and what we hoped to be when we "grew up." It was easy to talk to Paul. He was kind and sincere. His blue eyes sparkled in the sun. His blond hair now dried and out of control still looked shiny and gorgeous. He was irresistibly attractive in a rugged way. Yet I still couldn't understand why he was giving me the time of day.

Before we knew it, the sun was getting lower in the sky and a cold breeze was coming in.

"Wow, it has really gotten late. You must be freezing because I know I am." He winked at me and stood up. "It has been so nice to meet you, Kate. You are a breath of fresh air."

"Thanks." I knew I was blushing. "It was amazing meeting you! Thanks for being so down to earth. Not at all how I expected you to be." I cringed. Why did I say that?

"I now understand why I haven't seen you around before, since you are miss brainiac. You know college is more than just getting ready for a career. It is about meeting people and finding out who you are in the world. You should get out and explore more! I would love to help you out in that area if you are up for it."

"I guess I have been a little bit of a hermit. But I don't want to get distracted. Right before finals last semester some guy threw his couch out his eighth-floor dorm window as a practical joke. Not quite sure I want to go that far in finding myself."

"I get your point. Well, let's start slow then. There is a party at my fraternity this Saturday, kind of like a welcome back party, and I would love for you to come."

Knowing I didn't want to go to a party, yet undeniably wanting to see Paul again, I agreed. Sam would be back by then, so I knew I could talk her into going with me.

"Great, then I will see you Saturday. The party is at eight o'clock. Our frat house is on third street. We are the big, brown house with the Delta Sigma Pi signal on it. Can't miss it. See you then!"

We exchanged phone numbers, and then he was off, running down the boardwalk. Even from behind he was great to look at. Then, like a ton of bricks, it hit me. What was I doing? I couldn't go to a party. I didn't want to get swept away into that kind of life of fraternity parties and recklessness. I wanted to make something of myself. Yet I wanted so much to see Paul again. The fact that it was only Wednesday, and I had three whole days till I would see him again made me anxious. Sam would be back Friday night, but I couldn't wait. I hurried back to my dorm and called her. After much debating and promises by me to do her laundry for a month, she agreed to go. Knowing it was just a business fraternity, we were assured that this was not going to be a typical frat party.

Friday came quicker than expected, and I was excited to have Sam back. We talked all night about her break and her new car she got for Christmas. We fell asleep still contemplating if going to the party the next night was a great idea. By the time we woke up the next day it was already 1:00 p.m. So we grabbed a bite at the cafeteria and headed back to get ready. Sam grabbed her stuff and came to my room, for just as my roommate predicted she was never around. She actually didn't go home for break either but met some guy her second week in and was practically living at his house.

Which was kind of nice, like having a room all to myself. She would come for a "costume" change occasionally and to get her messages and return phone calls and then she was off. I had no idea if she was actually taking classes.

We got ready in record time. Sam wore her faded blue jeans with her seventies-inspired, flared sleeve, black shirt and a rhinestone belt. Her brown hair was curly and soft, and her makeup was smoky and sexy. She looked great. She was amazing at makeup, so I made her do mine as well, hoping it would help me stand out a little from all the other girls who were most likely going to be all over Paul. I put on a form-fitting black tank, dark blue jeans with a flare leg, and flip-flops. I had to admit with Sam's handy work I didn't look too bad.

We got to the party at 8:30 p.m. thinking we were being fashionably late to realize we really weren't late enough because the party had barely started. We walked inside and immediately I felt like all eyes were on us.

"Um, Kate, are we in the right place?" Sam whispered. I could sense her eagerness to turn and run.

"Yeah, this is where he told me. I know this is it," I said with a shaky voice. Right when I started to think he played a mean joke, Paul came striding in as gorgeous as ever. He was wearing a dark blue pullover and khaki pants with brown loafers. His hair was messy yet controlled, and his face was shaven and smooth. He saw us immediately and with a huge smile on his face came galloping over.

"Kate! You came! I can't believe it! I didn't think you would!" He was as happy as a horsefly in a rodeo, and I didn't understand why. Immediately I was at ease as he came up to us and gave me a hug. "I see you brought a friend. Leave it to you to not want to come alone into the lion's den."

"Yeah…well, this is Sam. Um, did we get the right night? There is no one here."

"Well, one thing you will get to learn if you hang out with me long enough…parties don't really get started till like ten." Then he turned and shook Sam's hand. "So you're the best friend? It is nice to meet you."

"Thanks." Sam was blushing. I could tell that being around him made her just as nervous as me.

"So, this is my frat, let me take you around and introduce you and get you a drink."

"Okay great." I knew I was lying—this was not great, this was awkward!

He grabbed each of us a red plastic cup with something called "jungle juice" in it and paraded us around the room like some new puppy dog. I heard the same thing from everyone, "So are you a transfer student? You're not? Wow, how come we haven't seen you around?" It was like I was a mystery to all of them. In fact, at this party they passed out nametags, although you could put any name you wanted, so they handed me a nametag with "Third Floor Mystery Chick" on it. I was slightly flattered. We drank our drinks, which I could tell had a little too much alcohol and a little too little juice, and we danced and mingled. Paul would come and go to make sure we were okay and having a good time. I was disappointed by the fact that I thought I would be spending the bulk of the night with him, but accepted whatever attention I could grab from him. I really wasn't that surprised, for by 10:00 p.m. there were a ton of beautiful girls around who all seemed to be vying for his attention. By midnight Sam and I were definitely feeling loopy and knew we needed to head back to the dorms.

"I actually had fun." Sam laughed as we walked down Main Street back to the dorms. "I can see what you mean about Paul. He is mesmerizing to say the least and yet seems so laid back. I can tell he likes you."

"I seriously doubt that! Did you see the way all the other girls were all over him? He acted the same with me as he did with all of them. I am nothing special. But at least I get to call him my friend."

"You are so hard on yourself, and I don't get it. You must have some deep pain, girl, to think so screwed up all the time. If you are not careful you will drive him away just by thinking you are not good enough for him. If anything he is not good enough for you."

"Thanks, that is sweet, but deluded."

Sam sighed and let the subject go. "So when do you think you guys will see each other again?"

"No idea. He didn't say when I left if he would call or anything, so I don't know."

"Well, give it a few days then call him."

"I don't think so. Plus I don't plan on making this party scene a habit. It was fun for tonight, but I have school to think about."

"Yeah, but Paul is right. This is the time of our lives! I can see why there is a time for partying as long as we make a time for studying too. Plus it was cool to be the 'mystery chicks.' Enticing to say the least to have a little fun with it."

"Yeah, that was pretty cool. Made me feel wanted for once, but promise me we will keep it balanced. We will keep each other in check, okay?"

"Promise!" She smiled.

Paul didn't call for two days, but I was excited when I heard from him on Monday night. "Hey studious one…let me guess you are studying right now?"

"I could say no, but then I would be lying. Hey, thanks for the invite Saturday…it was fun!"

"Wow, you had fun? I am impressed. I have to say everyone really liked you…our little 'mystery chick.' So are you ready to do it again this weekend? There is a reggae party being thrown at Alpha Chi Omega this Friday. It starts at eight o'clock, but now you know what that means. So shall I see you there at ten?"

"Another one already? Umm I don't know…I have a lot to do."

"What do you mean already? It will be almost a week since the last one. Come on now, you know you had fun. Let loose. Studies can wait till Saturday. You owe it to yourself. Plus it would be fun to see you again, and a frat brother of mine Jay *really* wants to see you again. Say you will come."

And with that my stomach dropped. He was trying to fix me up with his frat brother? What about him? I thought *he* wanted to see me.

"Since when are you trying to pawn me off to your friends?"

"He is a great guy. I think the two of you will really hit it off. Come on. For me, please!"

"You really know how to play a girl don't you? All right, Paul, Sam and I will come, but we are not making this a habit. Okay?"

"Great! See you then." I heard a click on the line, and he was gone. I called up Sam to meet for dinner where I gave her the scoop.

"Wow, so he is trying to set you up with his friend? Why would you say you would come? And why did you include me?"

"Well, you are the one who said we needed to get out there didn't you? Plus I was thinking that if maybe he saw me with his friend he would get jealous or something, I don't know. Either that or it is just as I thought in the first place, and he thinks of me only as this little girl he is trying to "save" from a life of boredom. Anyway, it is worth a shot to find out. I figure I would rather be his friend than nothing at all." And with that we made plans to go Friday night.

The week went without a hitch. I got all my studying done and took a pop quiz in chemistry. I missed two questions, but that was just because I was distracted thinking about Friday—already this was distracting.

Sam came up at 9:00 p.m., and we got dressed in our coolest and hippest Jamaican-inspired attire, and Sam, once again, did my makeup Island-fresh this time.

We walked down to sorority row and found Alpha Chi Omega, which wasn't hard considering it was all lit up with tiki torches. We went around back and entered the blue tarp to find a reggae band and a horde of people drinking and dancing. How I was going to find Paul in there I had no idea. We walked around, grabbed a drink, and tried to find someone we knew. By 11:00 p.m. our drinks had fully taken effect, and we found ourselves dancing with perfect strangers. Feeling the sudden urge to have to use the bathroom, I grabbed Sam, and we headed inside. When on our way to find the bathroom we came across three couples making out and a girl throwing up in a paper bag. Lovely! We made it to the bathroom and freshened ourselves up. I opened up the window to get some fresh air and saw him. Down in the party with some guy, who I assumed was Jay, that I vaguely remember from his welcome back party. Paul was flirting with some blonde sorority gal.

"So I found Paul," I said.

"Where?" Sam tripped getting to the window. That girl could not hold her liquor. She pushed me out of the way and peered out the window. She spotted him right as he leaned in to kiss Blondie.

"Oh! Yeah. Okay. Time to go."

"What? What did you see? What is it?"

"No way, girl, let's go, this party is dumb anyway."

"Sam! Tell me."

"Oh, he just is getting very friendly with some chick down there, and you don't need to be a part of that."

My heart sank as I pushed her out of the way to peer outside. I saw them holding each other while swaying to the music.

"Oh. You know, that's fine, really. I am totally fine. Let's just go back and enjoy the party," I said, forcing a smile.

"Kate, no, let's just go."

"No, Sam, seriously there is no reason we can't have fun."

We walked back down to the party, and I found my way over to where Paul was standing, but pretended not to see him.

"What are you doing?" Sam asked.

"Just act cool, like you don't see him."

"Oh, brother! You are a glutton for punishment."

But my plan worked. Within two minutes I felt him come up beside me. "Hey, there you are! I thought you didn't come."

"Oh, hey, Paul. Wow, I totally forgot you were coming."

"Oh, well, it is good to see you are having fun. You remember Jay?" Jay came striding over with a funny little grin on his face. He was cute, not great, but cute. He had ash-brown hair and dark-green eyes. He was tall and thin, very business-like; I could see he fit the business frat very well.

"Hey, Kate, Sam. Good to see you again."

"Hey, Jay, nice to see you. Are you enjoying the party?" I said.

"I am now."

I felt like I was in some cheap bar. Sam was snickering at my side.

"And this is Brett," Jay said, introducing another guy we had never seen before. "He is my roommate."

"Oh, cool. Hey, Brett, nice to meet you," I said.

"Likewise," he said, offering a hand to me but staring at Sam. I moved out of the way and let him go to her. "Hey, I'm Brett. I have seen you in my poly sci class, right? With Mr. Douglas?"

"Oh, yeah. I thought you looked familiar. What did you think of that quiz the other day? Totally caught me off guard." And they were off in their own little world. I couldn't believe it. My best friend in an instant taken from me like a thief snatching a purse. I felt alone and yet I was surrounded by people. I decided to drift my attention back to Jay. At least I could have someone to talk to.

"So are you a junior as well?"

"Yeah actually, but I think it might take me two more years to complete my degree instead of one."

"I can totally understand that." Perhaps he should've partied a little less. Yet I found myself drinking more and finding him more appealing as the night wore on.

Finally at 1:00 a.m., I was able to pull Sam away from Brett and head back to the dorms.

"So I take it you had a great time," I said.

"Yes, it was great! Brett is great isn't he?"

"Hmm I don't know. I didn't really get a chance to talk to him. You were alone the whole time."

"Well, you seemed to get along with Jay."

"Yeah, he was okay. He is pretty good-looking, and he seems to know a ton of people. Something worth looking into anyway."

"You sound like you are buying a couch or something. Just relax and have a good time. So what if Paul doesn't work out? You are the one who said you would rather have him as a friend than nothing at all."

"Since when have you changed your story? Has Brett changed you already?"

"Let's not start, Kate. Seriously, I really like Brett, and it would be great for us to have dates once in a while. I am sorry about Paul, and I wish it would have worked out differently for you, but he could be a good friend to you, and Jay may be a great guy. At least someone to have fun with, ya know? Plus he and Brett are room-mates, which means we can double a lot!"

She was right, and I knew it. It would be fun to be dating guys who were roommates. For the next semester we somehow managed to hang on to our grades and date the roommates. I saw Paul every weekend at a party here and there, generally with a different girl each time, and we talked several times during the week. Sometimes, at parties, when he didn't have a date the two of us would spend more time together than I would with Jay. Which for some reason never seemed to bother Jay. It was almost like we liked having each other there, but neither one of us thought we were right for each other. I think Paul saw that too and took advantage of that whenever there wasn't someone better around. I didn't let it bother me, I just did what Sam said and relaxed. Sam and Brett, on the other hand, were very much an item. She adored him, and it really seemed that he adored her. I never saw him look at another girl in any capacity. He always had all his attention on Sam. I was happy for her, and I was happy to be able to share in this time with her since it was usually always the four of us going out. Occasionally

Brett and Sam would go out alone, but that was fine because I had my studies to keep me in order.

Everything seemed to be going great until the last week before spring break. Brett and Jay had come over to our dorm for a small birthday celebration for Sam and I. Our birthdays were two days apart, and we didn't have time to really celebrate because of studying for midterms. They brought beer and French fries and the new Katy Perry CD. We were a little nervous about the whole thing since we were not allowed to drink on campus, and I was underage. If we were caught we would be in serious trouble. At about the third beer we relaxed a little and started to enjoy ourselves. We kept the music low so that no RA or RD would suspect anything. We didn't worry about my roommate since she had come down with mono a month ago and went home to get well. They were letting her take her midterms over the break. As I got up to hit replay on the CD, I turned around to see Brett and Sam leaving.

"Hey, where are you going?"

"We are just going to go out and get some fresh air. We will be back." Sam turned to Brett, pulling him out the door, while Brett turned and gave a little wink to Jay. I knew then that this was not good. The door shut, and Jay looked at me with a smile on his face.

"Well, I guess it is just you and me. Come sit next to me." He patted the bed and put on his best "come hither" face.

I suddenly became very nervous. Granted we had been dating a little over two months, but it never really felt intimate. It was always a kiss here and holding hands there. I guess I never really thought of him that way. Plus I knew he was not the prince charming I was waiting for…at least I hoped not. So giving myself to him was not going to be in the cards.

I sat next to him and immediately he pulled me close, kissing me. He was rough and excited, and I could tell he thought this was going somewhere. I pushed him away slightly and told him that I wasn't going to have sex with him, after all it wasn't his birthday. He said he understood and said he just wanted to be with me. So I let myself give in slightly to the temptation to wanting to be wanted. He kissed my neck and moved his hands quickly over me. I was a little uncomfortable with it, but it felt nice, so I thought, *Why not?* Suddenly we were lying on my bed fully making out with him unbuttoning my shirt.

"Jay, slow down. This isn't going to happen," I said.

"Don't worry. I got the point the first time you said it. I won't take it that far."

I wasn't sure how far he would take it though, and I felt myself crumbling underneath him. I felt like I was ten again being beaten for the eightieth time by my mother, and there was nothing I could do but take it. As his hand started to reach up to unhook my bra, I pushed him with everything I had and said, "Stop! Seriously, Jay, I like you, but not that much! I don't know how far you plan on taking this, but this is far enough."

He looked at me, shocked that I had rejected him and hadn't given in. Screaming expletives at me, he stood up and grabbed his jacket. "Seriously I don't get you, Kate. You sit there dating me for two months with what in return? Paul was right. You are a girl you take home to Mom, but not one you have fun with. I kept up with this stupid charade thinking I was getting somewhere with you, and I was wrong. I am outta here."

He opened the door to storm out and ran into my RA. She had come to see what all the yelling was about. She glanced at me inside and saw all the beer cans. "What is going on in here? Kate, you know you are not allowed to drink on campus. I am afraid I have to report this."

"Well I don't live on campus," Jay said, "so I am leaving. Good luck, Kate." He ran off without even looking back.

Tina, our RA, came in. "Kate, not only are you not allowed to drink on campus, but you are underage. I assume your boyfriend there got you the beer?"

"He isn't my boyfriend anymore," I said, with tears starting to roll down my face. I was mortified. Not just by Jay but now by getting caught drinking. I was a good girl. This wasn't how it was supposed to go.

Tina left, and I called Sam and told her what happened. "Oh, Kate, I am so sorry you have got to be kidding me! I can't believe Jay would act that way." I could hear Brett saying something in the background. He sounded angry like he was mad at me, and not Jay. I could hear him say, "She is lying. He wouldn't do that."

"I will be right there, Kate. Just hang tight."

I waited an hour for her to come. I was getting angrier by the minute. Why wasn't she coming to my rescue? Was Brett turning her against me? Just then Sam came bursting in crying.

"What happened, Sam?"

"Brett and I got in a fight about what happened tonight with you and Jay. You better not be lying to me, Kate, or so help me!"

"How can you say that to me, Sam? You know I wouldn't lie to you. Don't you think this situation is bad enough as it is without having to lie to my best friend? Give me some credit will you!"

"No, I know I am sorry. I am just upset. I didn't mean it really! I am so sorry about what happened tonight. Sorry about Jay, sorry about Tina finding out. What did she say?"

"She said that she was going to report me, and it would be up to the RD to decide what would happen."

"Geez, Kate! And right before midterms too! This sucks!"

"You are telling me! And here I was hoping life would get better for me! I was just fooling myself."

We both sat on my bed and cried until Sam excused herself to go get some sleep.

Brett called her the next morning saying they needed to talk. We both knew that wasn't good. While she was gone, Tina and Adam, the RD, came to my room to tell me that I had to attend alcohol counseling for six weeks upon returning from break, and I had to do campus community service as well. I was mortified. I was depressed. I knew this feeling. I had felt it my whole life, and here it was coming back full force. I somehow managed to get through midterms, and I couldn't bear to go home for spring break. Sam was devastated by Brett breaking up with her during their talk, so going home sounded great for her, but she didn't want to leave me alone like I was. So, she decided we should hang together and get some solid beach time in. It sounded like a great idea.

Paul hadn't called me the week of midterms, which in someway I was glad about. I was a little angry with him for what Jay said. What did Paul mean by me not being a girl you could have fun with? Is that why he didn't want to date me? He wasn't ready for a girl who he could be serious about, or was it he really couldn't have fun with me? I blew off his silence to him being busy, but I knew he didn't know what to think. Who knows what Jay had told him? Yet, I thought we were good enough friends by now that he would at least want to hear my side of the story. I mean for the last three months we had seen each other every week and talked practically every day on the phone. Granted, it felt a lot like my relationship with Sam than anything romantic, but I now chalked that up to what Jay was saying Paul said about me. Maybe that is why he was trying to get me to party with him, to make me more fun. I thought I had been letting loose plenty, but maybe I was still too nerdy, as he put it one day. The thoughts of both of them made my stomach hurt. I just wished I could talk to Paul so I could figure it out.

Finally, the Saturday after midterms, our first official day of spring break, when Sam and I were about to go for our first beach jaunt he called. Jay told a fellow "brother" what really happened, and that boy told Paul. He kept saying how it was all his fault and he felt awful about it. I told him that I was glad to hear it and that we should set up a time to catch up over coffee. I still had a lot of things I wanted to talk to him about.

"Why not now?" he asked. "We could go for a burger."

"I can't right now, Paul. Sam and I are having girl time at the beach."

"Oh, great, are you guys staying for the break?" He actually sounded excited.

"Yeah, we decided it was cheaper than paying for a vacation and better than going home. Why are you still here?"

"I got an internship this past week, and there was no way I was going to be able to go anywhere. Sucks, but I guess since I am getting into my senior year next year I better start taking this stuff seriously."

"That is great, Paul, good for you! Why don't we meet at the Bayside Coffee Shop at nine?"

"Good, see you then."

"Bye, Paul."

I hung up the phone and grabbed my beach towel and sunglasses and walked out the door.

"Hold on, Kate! What in the world? What happened? That was Paul, right? What did he say?" Sam was running to keep up with me as I was rushing down to the car with a smirk on my face.

"Let's talk about it on the way." We walked the remainder of the way in silence with Sam pouting the entire time. I finally spilled the beans as she turned the ignition to her gray VW convertible.

"So he was apologizing for introducing you to Jay?" She lowered the top at the next stoplight. The sun hit my head with soft heat, while the wind whipped my hair around. It felt great to be out of the dorm in the gorgeous town, knowing Jay was away and not having to be home with my mom and dad.

"Yeah, we are going to meet for coffee tonight to talk more. But he really seemed shocked by the whole thing. But given Jay's reaction it didn't seem like he had come across too many girls who say no. So it is unlikely Paul really knows him this way."

"True. We all have our demons, I guess. That is what Brett said. He thought it was hard to believe Jay would do anything like that, but you never can tell with people when you aren't around to witness them in all kinds of circumstances."

"Has Brett called at all?"

"Nah, and I don't really want to talk about it. I guess he chose Jay over me, so whatever. There are a lot of fish in the ocean my mom always says! Plus it is not like we were in love or anything. It had only been eight weeks." Something told me she was lying. I saw the way they looked at each other and more so the way she looked at him. Either she was really good at lying or she didn't feel as strongly for him as I had thought.

"I am proud of you, Sam! That is an awesome attitude! You make me jealous that you are not harboring hatred toward him." I decided to test my theory of her lying and play the proud parent to see if she broke the facade.

"Yeah, well, I guess I didn't like him as much as I thought I did. Plus I don't think I have ever really had a guy I really liked. It is more about the chase with me. Plus I realized half the fun was just being able for us to double date all the time, and once that was gone I realized I didn't really want to be alone with him anyway." Her brown hair was flying around her face. She was laughing at herself for finally realizing her real feelings for Brett. I still had my doubts.

The rest of the day was a bunch of sun, sand, and relaxing while we read our own copies of *A Walk to Remember* and discussed the possibilities of someone finding love like that.

"Maybe, if there was such a thing as God, we would have hope that that type of unconditional love really exists," Sam whispered.

She had never mentioned anything like that before. For the first time, I could see her insecurities about how she felt about guys and love. She had never mentioned God before. We had never really talked about it. It wasn't something I believed in or was part of my life. I had gone to church occasionally as a kid, when my mom felt bad enough about an affair she had had or a beating she had given me. I guess that was why I never put much faith in God. I saw my mother struggling to believe in Him, and even when she did ask forgiveness she would return to hypocritical ways. And then I would always think if there was a God, He didn't care about me. If He did then why had I been placed in this situation? Why would I be given to someone who didn't want me? Now I got a glimpse into what Sam thought as well; she didn't believe either.

"Why do you think there isn't a God?" I asked.

"How could there be? Neither of my parents think there is anything out there, they have always taught me that science and personal power is the way. Although I am not sure I believe that either. I do see some things and people that boggle me. True love, kindness, caring, differences in certain people that seem to know something that I don't that is helping them along. But then again, there is the other side of the coin to think about…the ugliness of life. I think that it might be the survival of the fittest. Those strong enough survive, those with power make the biggest changes and impact. I don't think there is a *why* to anything—there just is. Every time I look for the *why* everyone seems to be looking for I keep coming to the same conclusion."

I completely understood what she meant. Yet I had never come to any conclusion. The *why* of life that made me who I was and made the decisions I made never seemed to figure itself out. It never seemed important enough to figure out because no matter the decision I made, everything always seemed to turn out badly. Except, so far, for Sam. I had never made friends that easily. I had friends, but I never thought they were lifelong friends, and of course, we had our problems of jealousy and spitefulness growing up. It felt good to talk to Sam about these things, knowing she had the same questions. It was like we were meant to be friends, like kindred spirits or something like that. She always seemed to be right there with me in everything, and it all kind of landed in my lap. The only thing that ever seemed easy in my life was my friendship with her.

We headed back to the dorms after grabbing a quick bite. I went to my room and got ready for my coffee date with Paul. I threw on my raggedy bell-bottom jeans and a red polyester tank. Sam and I had been getting back into the seventies look the last few days. I slipped into my flip-flops and ran out the door. It took me only ten minutes to ride my bike there, considering most students had darted out of there after their last days of finals. The weather was crisp and clear. A gorgeous Santa Barbara night. It made me wish we had decided to meet at the beach instead.

Paul was surprisingly already there reading a book and drinking coffee.

I casually strolled up to his table and saw he was reading *Pride and Prejudice.*

"Very funny!" I said.

He looked up and started laughing. "I actually thought about having the book upside down, but then I thought that might be too much."

"Real mature! I will be right back, I am going to go get my coffee." I went and ordered my small, nonfat mocha and went back to sit down.

"So where did you get ahold of a book like that? I know it isn't yours!"

"Actually no, it isn't mine. You are right," he said, with a frown looking down. "It is yours. You left it in Jay's room, and I grabbed it when I was there telling him what a jerk he was."

"Oh! I didn't even realize I had it there. So you were standing up for my honor, huh? That is pretty brave with a fellow frat bro, isn't it?"

"Well, considering I have been in the frat longer and I am smarter, he has to listen to me."

"I appreciate it, really!"

"Well, don't worry about it, I feel like it is completely my fault. I should have never set you up with him."

"Let's just forget the whole thing." Seeing Paul sit across from me now made me rethink wanting to talk to him. I didn't want to lose him.

"I hope this won't make you not come to anymore of our raging soirées." He took a swig of his black coffee. Again, thoughts of him trying to make me more fun popped into my head.

"Hmm, that will be a hard one for me. I don't really have any yearning to see Jay again, so we shall see."

"Look, Kate, don't let this guy ruin your college experience. Believe it or not, this really is a small school, and you can run into him anywhere. The best thing to do is to put it past you, and if you see him, just ignore him. I will watch your back okay?" He put his hand on mine and smiled.

Butterflies were flying in my stomach, and I could feel my face getting hotter. "Thanks, Paul. I can't tell you what this means to have you on my side. I promise to give the college life a good try still." The thought of partying didn't seem appealing, but I wanted to prove to Paul I could be fun.

We enjoyed the rest of the night just laughing and talking about absolutely nothing. We rode back to the dorms together…since it was around eleven at night, he wanted to make sure I got home safe. We hugged good-bye, although I was yearning for more. I went inside immediately to Sam's room and told her the whole scoop. She was happy for me that he was being so kind.

"I am telling you, Kate, he is so into you. Regardless of Jay, just forget him, you need to see Paul. I know he likes you. I can tell. Plus Jay was just a distraction for you from Paul and now that he is really showing interest, then you should totally go for it."

"Yeah, well, we will see. He did hold my hand tonight, and the fact he chose me over Jay—I think really says something. Oh, Sam, you should have seen the way he was looking at me it was like… amazing!"

"Okay, crazy girl, let's get some sleep."

I slept in Sam's room that night since neither of us liked sleeping alone in a semi-empty dorm. We spent the rest of the week hanging at the beach. Paul met us a couple of times, but he was so busy with the internship that I didn't see him as much as I had wished for. Soon everyone was returning, and classes were back in full swing. It took me awhile to get back to wanting to do school again, but I realized that I needed to apply myself if I was going to continue to change my bad luck. I didn't want to help it out at all. Paul called on Wednesday and asked me to a welcome back party.

What was it with these welcome back parties they always seemed to have? I talked Sam into going. Actually, she was more than willing and was talking me more into going. She said she had fully moved past Brett and could care less if she saw him. She let me borrow her slinky turquoise tank, and I wore my bell-bottom jeans again. The party was in full swing when we got there, and we had no problem finding a drink and blending in.

Paul was his usual self, friendly to me but always seeming to be with some different chick. I wondered what he clung to me for. Was he really interested or what? Sam kept telling me she could totally see it and just to hang in there for now. We enjoyed the party with no sign of either Brett or Jay, which I was thankful for. We crashed back at the dorms around 2:00 a.m. feeling very happy with our choice to go to the party. I felt like I was getting a hang of this partying school thing. We became regulars in fact. Parties on only Fridays turned into Fridays and Saturday, thanks to my longing to see Paul, since I didn't see him all week. We would talk on the phone here and there, but he was busy with school and internship, and I was busy with school and my new job of working part time at a toy store. It wasn't the greatest job, but with all the eating out and partying, I had to keep up with the money. I didn't want to ask my parents for any more than they were already giving me. Of course they had it, but I was lucky that they were giving me any at all. I think they felt a little pressure from the fact that I was their daughter, and they wanted to be able to brag to their friends that they gave me money. Of course school was paid with student loans and scholarships, yet they still seemed to brag they were sending me to school with their generous one hundred bucks a month—somehow that didn't cut it for me, so the toy shop was the only place that was accepting applicants. It was okay, though, because Sam got a job there too, so we would try to work the same shifts. Plus even if we worked on the weekends we were always done by 9:00 p.m., and parties never started till 10:00 p.m., so it worked out great.

At least I thought things were working out great. My partying, even though only twice a week, had turned more intense. Partly because I was still trying to impress Paul and partly because Sam had made some new acquaintances at the parties, who always brought along things to make the partying more interesting. I was unsure about these people at first, but I trusted Sam. First they brought along things like different types of cigarettes. I told myself that it wasn't like I was smoking every day so it was okay. Each week it escalated to something new and more involved. I was apprehensive, but Paul was there as well, and I felt somehow safe that he would keep me in check? Plus I was with Sam, so what would go wrong? And nothing did. Soon we got confident enough to try anything they brought. They never really told us what each thing was; they would just say, "You have got to try this." We would end up sick on the floor and completely hung-over the next day, and I didn't like that feeling at all. But Sam seemed so sure that everything was the way it should be and everything was perfectly safe. Slowly I could feel myself spiraling down to a place I didn't like. I began to dislike what I was doing and who these people were that came into our lives so mysteriously. My grades began to show it as well, and I knew that if I didn't do something soon I was going to be on the outs with the school and losing everything I was trying to work for. So I decided to stick to the smaller things, thinking that was going to be safe and easy. Sam wasn't mad; she did her thing, and I did mine, and we had a good time. We were having the college experience we thought we had always dreamed of. Paul had become a great friend—someone I really leaned on and sought protection from. Not to mention a great math tutor. I was falling for him more and more every day. I knew soon I would have to make a move since he didn't seem too apt on doing that himself.

It was three weeks before the end of the semester, and there was a buzz on campus. A high of freedom licking at our heels. We just had to get through finals. I knew I needed to tell Paul how I felt about him before we hit finals mode or else I wouldn't get the chance. His internship would be over, and he wasn't sure he wanted to stay for summer.

I asked him to meet me at the beach in the spot where we first met for a picnic before the end of the year luau at the Theta Chi fraternity. I wore my cream tank with sheer overlay and khaki shorts with my brown flips. I pulled back my hair into a loose pony-tail, threw on some lip-gloss, and headed out. Paul was entirely too prompt and was waiting for me when I got there. It fit his personality. I plopped down beside him with the picnic basket and pushed him with my shoulder.

"Hey, stranger, how was your week?"

"Hey!" he said, wrapping his arm around me. "Great now that we are sitting here together. What did you bring us?'"

I opened the basket and took out the sandwiches I had picked up earlier from Subway, two cokes, potato chips, and some grapes.

"I know it is nothing fancy, but with my budget from the toy store you are lucky you are getting more than just the chips!"

"Hey, this is great. I am just glad I don't have to eat what Joe is making back at the house…his famous chili, which all it is famous for is giving people the runs."

"Nice!"

We sat and ate our sandwiches, talking about our upcoming finals and which ones we were concerned about. The sun was beginning to set, casting brilliant pink and blue hues on the clouds and sand that spread out before us. It was the perfect moment.

I looked at him with his eyes glimmering in the setting sunlight, his thick hair blowing in the breeze and a sudden lump was in my throat.

Right then, he looked at me with his kind eyes and stared at me for a moment. "What, Kate? Why are you looking at me like that?"

"Oh, sorry, I was just noticing how handsome you look today."

He smiled and laughed. He wrapped his arm around me and looked into my eyes. "Thanks, Kate. You look great too. I would suggest something warmer for tonight, though, you don't want to catch cold before finals."

"Thanks, Dad, I will remember that," I said with a smirk.

"I didn't mean it that way. I just am looking out for you that's all."

"I know you are. You always are, and I am thankful for that." I could tell this was it. The moment I was waiting for. I reached up my hand and touched his cheek and stroked back his hair. "Paul, having you in my life has been such an amazing thing for me. I have never had someone who stuck by me the way you do. Your friendship means so much to me."

Paul's face slowly lost its smile, and his hand came up to softly take mine. He looked down at the space between us. "Kate, wow, I am so flattered, you have no idea. Your friendship is a highlight for me as well. But I am getting some weird vibes here, so before you go any further, I hope I haven't given you the wrong impression. You remind me so much of my little sister back home, that immediately I took to you. I see you as my sister, Kate, and nothing more. I am sorry if that is not what you are looking for with me. My sister, Ann, and I have always had to look out for each other, and it has been hard to not be there to help her out when she needs someone. I guess when you came along and you reminded me so much of her I felt like you were my surrogate little sis. I never meant to give you any other impression. Please forgive me if I have done that."

The burning sensation behind my eyes started again, and before I could compose myself Paul was wiping the tears from my cheek.

"Kate, please say something. I don't want this to affect our friendship."

I couldn't speak. Sam was wrong; he wasn't into me at all. His sister? I could feel my cheeks burning red, and I knew I needed to leave.

"Oh, right, of course," I said. "No, I wasn't thinking anything other than friendship here, Paul, I was just trying to tell you thank you. That's all. Wow. It is getting late. Please excuse me." I got up and ran to my bike with Paul calling after me.

I rode back to my room containing what composure I had left till I got to my room. As soon as I hit the bed I let loose. What was I thinking? I had read him wrong. He was just trying to be nice to me. Why would he ever like someone like me? I was an idiot to believe things would ever work out. When had they ever worked out for me? Sam suddenly came to mind. At least I had her. With that thought I wiped my face and headed down to the second floor to find her. She was in her room reading her poly sci book. As soon as she looked up at me, I lost it again.

"Kate! Kate! What is going on?"

"I totally misread him, Sam. I made a move to show Paul my feelings for him, and he dissed me. I am a total waste of space." I walked over to her bed and collapsed my face down by her knees where she was sitting.

"Oh, Kate, he totally played you then, because I even thought he was into you. Seriously, something is wrong with that guy." She stroked my hair.

"No, there has never been anything wrong with anyone but me!"

"Stop it, Kate. I am not going to sit here and listen to this self-pity. Get up! Clean yourself up. We have a frat party to go to."

"What! You have got to be kidding me. Paul will be there. I am not going anywhere near another party."

"Don't be such a defeatist! The party is exactly where you should be. You will show him that you are no fool. That you are not going to be embarrassed nor be taken hostage by your feelings for him. Show him you can blow him off as quickly as he did you."

"I can't do that. I just can't. I don't think I have the strength to see him right now."

"Fine. Then I am going, and you can just sit here and sulk."

"What is your deal, Sam? I thought you were on my side here."

"I am on your side, Kate, that is why I am doing this. Now get up." Sam pulled my arm and yanked me off the bed. Throwing me an outfit out of her closet, she left the room to go put on her makeup in better light. I stood there unable to move. I realized maybe there was a point to what she was saying.

"You win, Sam. I will go get ready, but you better not be wrong about this," I said, as I peered into the bathroom. I ran upstairs and dressed in the short skirt and black-sequined top that Sam had thrown at me. I quickly applied mascara, blush, and lip-gloss and tossed out my hair so my curls would be full and shiny. Sam knocked on my door, and with a huge sigh and rolling eyes I followed her out the door.

We arrived to the party when it was already in full swing. The band was already playing, and red cups were being tossed around. We mingled for a few minutes noticing some acquaintances from our separate classes. As I was waving hi to the band's bass player, he was in my chemistry class, a red cup was thrust into my hands. I turned to see Jay smiling at me. With a jerk I jumped back and almost growled at him.

"Whoa now, tiger, I am just coming over to apologize. Don't get your panties all in an uproar here."

"I thought you didn't think you had anything to be sorry for, Jay," I said.

"Yeah. I know. I am a total jerk. Please, I understand that. But seriously, I am sorry. I should have never treated you that way. I am sorry it has taken me so long to apologize, but I didn't want to end the year this way with you."

"Why am I not believing a word of this?"

"Believe what you want to, Kate, but I am trying to make an effort here."

I looked down at the red cup still in my hands and back up at Jay. Maybe he was making an effort, or maybe he heard what had happened with Paul earlier and was trying to somehow make a fool of me. Sam could see my inner struggle and leaned over to whisper to me, "Stop with the self-pity and thinking the world is out to get you. I am sure he feels bad. Take the drink as an apology and move on."

"All right, Jay, I appreciate your apology and the drink. Have a good night." With that I turned around and headed toward the food table. I wasn't hungry in the least, but I needed to get away from him. I guzzled down the beer and grabbed another from the table.

"Okay, I made my appearance, and I don't feel any better. Can we go now?"

"No way, we just got here, give it a chance. Jay apologized. That was a good start. Now lets go find some cute guys and have some fun."

I rolled my eyes and followed her around to look at the inventory. Due to my keeping my head down most of the time, I didn't even notice when Paul came up to me. He grabbed my right arm while yelling my name over the screeching of the band.

"Paul! Oh...uh...hey!" I stammered. Sam, again, was wrong; this was a bad idea.

"Hey, look, I know I am probably the last person you want to see right now, but I saw you talking to Jay a second ago."

"Yeah, so?"

"Please just stay away from him. I promise you nothing good will come of you talking to him. I have heard some—"

"I don't care what you think. You had your fun with me, and I can take care of myself. Plus Jay is harmless, considering you told him I am not the fun kind of gal you date, anyway. So, Paul, when you are ready to take a girl home to Mom, you let me know."

"What are you talking about? I am just trying to look out for you. I should never have introduced him to you. Kate, look at me. I am sorry if I embarrassed you earlier, I was trying to save you from further embarrassment. I am sorry," he said.

Sam then turned around having been distracted by her groupie friends showing up.

"Oh, hi, Paul. Come on, Kate, let's go," she said, dragging me away. Paul's face was turned down in worry, and his eyes were filled with frustration.

Sam pulled me over to where her friends were getting drinks trying to talk to me about the nerve of Paul and how not to let it get to me. But I was starting to feel a little weird, so I wasn't paying much attention to her. Little did I know that would be the last thing I would remember of that night.

The Death of the Old Man

I awoke the next morning in a daze. I was cold, and I could feel my body was in an odd amount of pain. I pushed my eyelids open and found I was in my dorm bathroom with my head hanging in the toilet. How long had I been there? Why couldn't I remember how I got there? Where was Sam? I tried to get my mind to work to try to remember what happened. Sadly enough I wasn't unused to waking up in the bathroom, but usually I knew how I got there. All I could remember was Jay apologizing and drinking the one beer and a few sips of another. There was no way I had done anything else; I always remembered what I had done.

As I tried to get myself off the floor, I realized my bra was missing and that my clothes were ripped. I could feel my body tensing in pain with each movement I made. I clung to the toilet and pushed myself up over the bowl, trying to get my balance. I looked into the toilet where vomit still lingered and flushed it. I didn't even remember throwing up. I stumbled out from the stall and just made it to the sink before collapsing. The hot water on my face felt comforting and nice, but the pressure from my hands was agonizing. I looked up into the mirror to survey the damage. I knew there had to be damage from the way I was feeling; yet nothing could have prepared me for what I saw in the mirror.

The girl staring back at me was not me—it couldn't be. Her hair was a frizzy mess and missing in spots; there was a black eye and weird purple marks on her neck. There was a bloody fat lip and a cut on her eyebrow. I shook my head and tried again. The girl was still there looking at me. How did this happen? I started to panic. I looked down at my tattered clothes and started tearing off what was left. There were bruises everywhere. Trails of them leading every which way. I didn't remember even being in pain last night. Adrenaline started taking over as I started to realize what this possibly could have meant.

Don't freak out! Don't freak out! I thought. There had to be some logical explanation to all of this, but even as I was saying this to myself small flashes of the night started to come into play. Scenes of eating tacos with Sam, a basement of some sorts with distorted dark figures. Then a dark bedroom. Whose bedroom? I could hear the voice in my head of a man getting angry. Was that Jay? I tried so hard to concentrate and remember what was going on, what had happened. A flash of Jay's face staring angrily at me as he threw me up against a wall. Why was he so mad? I heard his voice telling me he was too drunk and couldn't get the job done and it was all my fault for taking so long for the drug to take effect. Drug? Drug? What drug? Was I raped? Did Jay rape me? I ran to the toilet again and surveyed my underwear, but there was no blood. I had heard the first time would hurt and that there would be bleeding, but there wasn't any, so something must have gone wrong for him. I hobbled back to the sink and tried to remember more but couldn't. Everything was so fuzzy and cold and dark. Anger started to stir my every nerve. Jay! He wasn't making apologies; he was trying to get what he wanted. I could feel it now, the verge of insanity creeping up on me. The feeling I was about to lose it and lose it big.

Tears started to roll over my bottom lids while my body started trembling uncontrollably. Just then a girl on my floor, Amy, came in. She didn't pay any attention to me at first because she dropped some of her shower supplies on the floor. As she bent over to pick them up I panicked. What was I supposed to do? I couldn't let anyone see me this way. I turned quickly with my clothes covering my chest and tried to get out and run down to my room, but as I was passing by she looked up. Fear was all I saw in her eyes as she looked at me. I couldn't just stand there, so I ran out of the bathroom and down to my room. I covered myself in my bed and let loose. The trembles, the uncontrollable sobbing. I couldn't stop. Suddenly a hand was on my shoulder, and I jerked with a scream and sat up. There was Amy with sadness and a knowing look on her face.

"Please, please, I am sorry to just come in, but let me help you. Can I help you? I don't know what is going on with you, but I can tell you need help. I don't need to know anything, but please just let me help you."

"How could you possibly help me?" I said.

"Well, why don't we just start with getting you cleaned up? I can tell you aren't moving very well and getting cleaned up will help. Please trust me."

As I looked into Amy's eyes, I could see understanding and compassion. We shared something. There was a light about Amy. One I couldn't understand or pinpoint. I hardly knew her, but I could trust her. We had said hi in the hallways before and had a quick conversation my first day, but that was all. As she grabbed my robe from the closet, I started to lose my anger, and the depression came back. Before I could answer her anything I let loose again. Crying uncontrollably. Amy knelt down at my bed and put her arms around me.

"Shhh, its okay, Kate, its okay. Everything will be all right. You will see. I don't know what has happened to you, and you never have to tell me, but understand it will be all right." After a few minutes I pulled away to grab a tissue to wipe my face. Amy sat back but still kept a hand on my knee to comfort me. I could tell she was really trying.

"I think that cleaning up is a good idea," I said as I started to get up to go to my closet.

"Okay, but before that do you mind if I say one thing?" Amy looked serious.

"Kate, is there any reason we need to get you to a hospital first? Are you hurt bad enough that we need to get you checked out? Or..." I could tell she was hesitating on the next part. "Or do we need for someone to check you out in a womanly manner or take pictures? If this is what I think it is...Kate, if you are going to want to do something about it, which I think you should, then we need to get you to a hospital."

Fear exploded through my body. Hospital? No, I could tell nothing was broken or bleeding internally. I could tell my injuries would heal, but I wasn't prepared to even think of other reasons to go to the hospital. Would I want to report something? From what I could remember nothing *really* happened. I was beat up pretty badly, but I didn't think he did anything else. Just then another memory hit—me running through some bushes. It was on campus, the bushes hurt, and it was dark. I was running from something and tripping every couple of seconds. I shook my head, *no, no,* I would not do anything. What if he found out? I had no proof; I couldn't even remember anything. There I was fitting the statistic again. Molded into the 7.7 percent statistic of girls who will be raped or undergo attempted raped by the end of their college days. I just wanted to forget who I was and what happened to me. There were only three weeks left of school; I could do it. Study, take my finals, and then… then…what? I really had no home to go to. I looked at Amy who was still staring at me waiting for a response.

"No, no, nothing like that happened. I am fine. I just need to take a shower and try to feel normal."

Amy took both of my shoulders into her hands and stared right into my eyes. "Are you sure, Kate? Once you wash away the evidence—"

I cut her off, "There is no evidence, Amy. From what I think I heard him say, he was too drunk to do it, and that is why I think I look like this because he got mad. I don't really remember, only flashes of memory that don't really tell me anything. But I think I would *know* if he had succeeded. I really just want to put this behind me and move on."

"Okay," Amy said, "I respect your decision because it is not mine to make, but know you can always change your mind even without a hospital report."

With that she reached into my closet and grabbed my shower basket. "Why don't you pick out something to wear, and I will meet you in the bathroom okay?"

"Okay, thanks." With that she was out the door. I peered into my closet and couldn't seem to find anything that covered me enough. I picked out a pair of black sweatpants and a long-sleeved black shirt.

I had second thoughts thinking someone would probably ask me if I was in mourning and decided to go with a long-sleeved dark-green T-shirt with white lettering that said, "buzz off"—that was perfect. Everyone just buzz off!

Amy got me all set up and said she would wait outside and to call if I need anything. Didn't she have anything else to do? Why was she protecting a stranger? I took my time in the shower. Scrubbing myself several times, rubbing myself raw. Crying in the shower seemed so pathetic, but I couldn't help it. So I gave in one more time and let my tears run down the drain, imagining those were my past and troubles. Hoping that once I got out of this shower I could start anew.

I got out of the shower and dressed. Now time to go look in the mirror again. With a clean face I looked a little better, but I would need a lot of makeup to cover all the damage. Just then Amy came in.

"Hey, I was just going to check on you. Do you need anything?"

"Yeah, sorry, I know I took a long time, I—"

"No need to explain. I brought my makeup case and thought maybe I could do your makeup for you. My sister is a makeup artist and has always used me for her guinea pig, so I do know a little about it."

"Oh, yeah, I was just thinking about how I was going to do this."

Amy walked over and set her case down and started to work. She then braided my wet hair back into a loose braid being careful to cover the two bald spots I seemed to have. While she was working, I was thinking to myself again why this girl who I never took time to talk to would be nice to me, or why I felt so immediately drawn to accept her help. She probably knew I was a party girl, and that didn't seem like her thing since I never saw her at any of the parties. She seemed to always take her schooling so seriously. How did she do it? Stay so concentrated on something?

"Why are you being so nice to me, Amy? I mean why are you helping me? Why are you helping somebody so different from you who never really gave you a nod of notice?"

"You did give me a nod of notice…I know you are a good girl, Kate. I think you have just lost your way. Your friends are so good at manipulatively getting you into terrible things, I think. I know the situation all too well. Let's just say you remind me of me a little during my freshman year here."

"Really?" Somehow the thought gave me hope. I could tell she had been through something like this just from the look in her eyes and the helpfulness.

"There. I am all done! You look great if I do say so myself. Maybe journalism is the wrong major for me," she said with a small laugh. "Kate, I would love to share my story with you. I think it might be just what you need. In fact I had someone help me when things were going awry in my life, and it made the choices I needed to make much easier. Why don't I take you to get something nice and healthy to eat? You really need some nourishment that will help to get whatever it is you had in your system last night out."

"Um, sure, I guess that would be okay," I said. Leaving my dorm was not really what I wanted at this point.

"Okay, let me go take this stuff to my room and get my purse, and I will meet you at your room."

I gave her a nod and a small smile, and she left. I apprehensively looked into the mirror to be pleasantly surprised at what I saw. I could hardly make out the bruises, and she lined and colored my lips in a way that didn't make the lip look so huge and out of place. There was no disguising the cut on my eyebrow, but it was cleaned nicely so that it wasn't so prominent. The marks on my neck where covered nicely as well, and I could tell I wasn't going to have to pull on a scarf to hide them. As I walked to my room I realized that even though the warm water relaxed my muscles, I was still limping and pretty sore, so when I got to my room I popped a few pain relievers to do the job. I wrapped my ankle with the ace bandage from my first-aid kit that I had found hidden in the depths of my dorm closet the first day. As I was loading some makeup supplies into my purse, Sam came bursting into the room.

"Wow, girl, that was a heck of a party. You were on fire! Way to let loose." She flopped herself on my bed wearing the same thing she had the night before and a stupid smirk on her face. Anger surged through my body again. Why was I mad at her? Was it because she wasn't there this morning? Or was it that she was supposed to be helping me cheer up last night and didn't do anything to protect me? Or maybe it was because I saw it as her fault I was at that stupid party to begin with!

"Sam! Where have you been? What in the heck happened last night? Are you just getting home?"

"Cool your jets, girl. Why are you so upset? We had a great night, and I am sure we succeeded in getting rid of your Paul favoritism forever."

"Sam, what do you mean? What happened last night?"

Sam then really looked at me. Her face turned from ecstatic and happy to worried. "You don't remember? You only had one beer, girl, and you only smoked out once…you have had way more than that before. Why don't you remember?"

"I think I was drugged by Jay last night, Sam. Seriously look at me! I have a lot of makeup on but you can tell. Wait…I smoked out? When? Were you there? Did I go with Jay somewhere? Please tell me what you know."

"Okay…okay slow down, Kate. What is the last thing you remember?"

"Taking the second beer and you saying let's check the inventory and then something about Paul." Thinking about it was making the depression seep its way back. Tears started falling slowly again. So I sat next to Sam, who was in deep thought with a wide-eyed doe look on her face."

"Seriously? You have got to be kidding me."

I shook my head.

"Well, we had the whole night ahead of us…I mean after that we danced with some guys. Yes, you even danced with Jay at one point I saw. We kind of split up a little when we were dancing. But then we went to the Taco Spot with a huge group of people after the party. When I came out of the bathroom I saw you talking to Jay again... he was part of the group. But you weren't upset with him. In fact you seemed quite relaxed, actually almost too relaxed...things are a little blurry for me too though, Kate. I had a lot to drink last night. You did keep saying you felt really weird and that is why you kept pushing away any offers of drinks. After the Taco Spot we followed a group of about ten back to the Theta Chi frat and smoked out with some of the guys. After that I lost you. I mean I was getting along with this guy, and we went for a walk. When we got back you were gone, but one of the guys there said you had left with someone who you knew, and it looked like you were in good hands. I didn't think anything of it, Kate, really! I am so sorry. What do you remember? Did Jay—"

"I don't know...I don't know, Sam. It is all blurry, dark, and flashy. I think I was in Jay's room. I remember lying down at one point, and he was angry. I remember being pinned against the wall at one point, but I don't remember if that is before or after. I don't think he did anything though...I mean I don't think he could. I think that is why he was upset..." I trailed off as another flash came to mind. "Wait...there was a phone call...in the middle of everything. I remember lying there not able to decipher what was happening... trying to get up...and there was a phone call, and he answered it. He said your name, Sam, your name! Did you call?"

"Okay, wait...wait...yes. I did call Jay at one point to see if he had seen you, and he said no."

"No, wait...he said, 'I am almost done, I am kicking her out in a minute.'"

"Okay, then it wasn't me on the phone, Kate. If I knew you had been there I would have come for you."

"Would you though, Sam, I mean really? You are the one that wanted me to get over it, remember? I think that if I would have gone off with Jay you wouldn't have cared."

"Okay now, Kate, just because you are upset with what happened to you last night doesn't mean you should take it out on me. Don't get all dramatic and emotional, I am all you have!"

"Oh, thanks for reminding me of that, Sam. But I am beginning to think Amy is right…my choice in friends is not the wisest."

"Who is Amy? What are you talking about?" She spit out the words in my face, as her cheeks were turning red from anger.

"Amy, the junior who lives down the hall…she found me this morning in the bathroom as I woke up hovered over the toilet covered in bruises and blood, without a clue to what happened to me or where you were."

"You mean Amy Snider, the Bible thumper down the hall? You have got to be kidding me. Since when have you been talking to her? Of course she is going to tell you that she is a goody-goody who believes in crap. Seriously, Kate, you are going to throw away our friendship because some Bible thumper tells you, you need new friends. Who has been here for you this whole year? Who has held your hand threw everything? *Me*—that's who."

"Where were you last night? Where were you this morning?" I screamed now, with tears fully coming down my face ruining the nice work Amy had done.

"*You* don't know what even happened last night, Kate. For all you know you fell down a hill or something."

"You know that's not true! Why are you trying to make this worse?"

"Okay, okay, you are right…please I am sorry. I just don't know what you are doing. Why are you trying to throw me out of your life? I haven't done anything but be your friend. Your first friend, mind you!"

"Thanks for rubbing it in my face, again!" I said, as I turned away from her. "I just can't make sense of anything right now." Just then there was a slight hesitant knock at the door. I had totally forgot Amy was coming. I opened the door.

"Hey, Kate…is everything okay? Is this a bad time? Do you want to get together later?"

I looked back at Sam who was staring daggers at Amy. I realized going out with Amy and talking to her was exactly what I needed.

"No, no, Amy, I really could use your advice." I grabbed my purse off the bed, and Sam grabbed my arm. "Don't do this, Kate, stay. We have a lot to talk about."

"Look, everything will be fine, Sam. I just need some time to figure out what is going on."

"Be leery of what she *counsels* you on, Kate. Remember who your *true* friends are."

I gave her a confused look and headed for the door. As Amy and I walked down the hall, I could feel Sam's eyes on us.

"How about we go to the Sunset Smoothie on the corner of Main? We can get you a good smoothie and a pretzel. That shouldn't upset your stomach too much but get you the nutrients you need," she said as we headed to her car.

"Yeah that sounds good. Um, I am sorry about Sam."

"No worries there, Kate. I am sure she doesn't want to lose her best friend." We hopped in her car, and I let the sun rest on my face as I eased back into the seat for the ten-minute drive. We got to the smoothie shop and ordered our drinks and sat out in the fresh air away from the rest of the crowd.

"This should help you stop feeling so lightheaded and nauseous." She handed me my drink.

"How did you know how I was feeling?"

"Like I said…I have been there."

"What happened to you?"

"It is still a pretty painful memory for me, for it was just two years ago, but I am stronger now. I don't mind sharing because I truly believe that God will work good through the bad things that happened to me, even if it is through me being able to help someone like you, Kate, who is going through the same things now that I went through then."

I got a pit in my stomach as she said the word *God*. Sam's warning started making sense. This girl is a Christian. No wonder she had been so nice to me. She was trying to win me over—help the sinner. I decided to keep my thoughts to myself because the thought of being with someone else who knew what I was going through was extremely comforting.

"I was a freshman like yourself," Amy said, "trying to find my own way in this world. You see, my dad is a pastor of a small church in Sacramento, and I have always been molded to live a certain way. Well, when I went to college I saw it as a time to go my own way. My family trusted me enough to pick my own school and not require me to go to the Christian college that they both went to and the one my sister was graduating from at the time. I picked here knowing that this was far enough away to be my own person but close enough to go home for holidays without too much trouble. Things were going great right from the start. I was excited to get my life going.

"I made a lot of friends and even joined a sorority. My sorority became my whole life, and the more of my life I gave to it the less I gave to God. I came to find out I don't think I ever really belonged to God. I just believed in what my parents believed in. But once you get caught up in yourself, it is really hard to think of anything else. But I was happy. I was happy without Him, knowing I didn't need anything He had to offer me because I had everything I wanted right where I was—friends, popularity, good grades, fun times, etc., etc. I was working at Macy's selling makeup even then because of my sister, I knew what I was doing with makeup." Her face turned serious and mournful, and I could tell we were getting to it.

"One night early in the spring semester we had a toga party at the sorority to welcome everyone back from winter break. I was playing waitress when one of the guys who I actually had a small crush on at the time told me it was time to, "ditch the tray" and get with him. I was ecstatic he seemed to be interested in me, although he already seemed three sheets to the wind. But I wanted so much for him to pay attention to me that I didn't care he was a little drunk. We began dancing and bobbing for apples, which might seem funny, but you don't bob for apples in water—the tub is filled with different liquors. It is pretty gross now that I think about it.

Anyway, we decided to go for a walk to a nearby park. He guided us to a little bench toward the back of the park and put out a blanket and a thermos. In the thermos was a drink he had made himself, he had said. I should have known then or at least suspected something, but I didn't. I equate it with watching a horror movie, and you are yelling at the girl on the screen, thinking she is so stupid for doing something that you know will get her killed. But when you are in the situation you don't know what lurks behind the corner.

"So I took the cup, and it was actually quite good. We spent some time talking. Suddenly he started kissing me and at first I was excited about it, but it started to become a little rough and exaggerated as he started trying to take off my clothes. I got up and said that this was getting out of hand and told him I would see him back at the party. For me that is really the last full thing I remember, and that is from the last two years of trying to recover my memory. I know at some point he dragged me back to that blanket. I also know I must have put up a good fight because I woke up very bruised and battered. In fact, I had broken a rib. I have flashes of a dark memory of me running and fighting at some points, but the memories that haunt me the most are the ones of me just lying there not able to fight. I get mad at myself then…" She trailed off, looking at the floor with tears in her eyes. I suddenly felt lucky, that my ordeal was not as bad as hers.

"Did he succeed at what he wanted?" I asked hesitantly.

"Yes. Unfortunately he took away from me something that I can never get back. A gift that I was saving for the man I fell in love with. Some things my parents taught me actually stuck. Even though I didn't care about my relationship with God anymore, I still held on to my physical virtue. I held it like a treasure."

"I understand that. I am the farthest from anyone believing in God, but I still hold onto my virginity like a gift. I am so sorry that is was taken from you without your consent. It is selfish of me to think that I feel lucky right now."

"I am glad you feel that way, Kate, that was a little bit of a goal I had…I guess, to show you that you shouldn't despair, for even then God was taking care of you."

"How can you say that after what has happened to you? I mean you seem to be even closer to God now, and you had this horrific thing happen to you."

"Well, it drew me back to Him. I believe in our darkest hours God carries us. He never left me, not even when I abandoned Him."

"But how does evil draw you back to God. He didn't protect you!"

"He did protect me. I am alive aren't I? I have the ability to help others. It made me stronger. I didn't wake up in a bathroom discreetly, Kate. I was found naked and beaten in the park by some of my sorority sisters. They helped me back to the house and helped me clean up. One of those girls came to my room that day and shared the gospel with me and counseled and guided me. I realized how badly I had lost my way from God and that all things apart from Him are evil and cannot be trusted. That I can only look to God for that which I was seeking. And she was right. The other girls in my sorority wanted me to keep quiet because the guy was well known and a liked guy, and it would just cause problems. Plus they painted a picture of that night for me and what I looked like. It wasn't pretty. I was so scared that I didn't turn him in. Unfortunately, he ended up doing the same thing to another sorority sister of mine a few months later. I felt really guilty about that, but she *did* turn him in, and I supported her and shared my story with the school, and he was expelled. I don't know what has happened to him since.

"But after this I started going back to church, and I let God heal me. I put my full heart and soul in His hands, and I am so much stronger now. I am almost thankful for my dark experience because without it who knows where I would be now. I don't know if I would be back in God's loving arms living for Him. My soul and eternity would be lost. I feel that I can love more now that I have been loved more. I have been forgiven of all my past transgressions and have been healed of my hurts by the love of the Lord. Understand something, Kate. We can *never* suffer the amount that Christ suffered for us. God in His loving mercy sent His Son Jesus Christ to be mocked, ridiculed, and judged even though he was sinless. Sinless! Think of all the sin you and I have committed, and then think of the pain we have gone through.

"Now think of Jesus and how in His perfectness He was flogged to the point of flesh falling off, then shoved a crown of thorns on His head, then made to carry His own cross to His death where He was nailed by His hands and feet. But this wasn't the worst of His pain. In order to take on the sins of the world He had to be separated from God. Jesus, part of God, God's son was separated from Him where He spent His time in Sheol to pay for your sins. He did this for *you*. He loves you so much that the pain you feel now He took on one hundred-fold just so you could have a relationship with His father and be able to spend eternity with Him. His love can get you through this, Kate. Please listen when I tell you I know so much of what you are going through and your only way through this is to turn to Him. He will give you strength." She grabbed my hands and looked at me with tears in her eyes. It was almost like she was pleading with me.

I had sat there listening to her. At first the rambles of God were dumb to me, but seeing her passion, her strength. I wanted that. I wanted to heal! I wanted to be someone else so badly. To forget my past, forget what I had done, and what had happened to me.

"I believe what you say you believe has truly helped you. I can see that," I said. "But I don't know what is right for me. How do I know God exists? Has He ever helped me? If only you knew my life, Amy. I don't come from anything good, and nothing good ever happens for me."

"But God is calling you, Kate, that *is* the best thing that can happen to you. There is nothing better than to be in God's family. Regardless of what you come from you can be a part of God and His family. He is taking care of you even though you don't see it. All things work for good to those who love the Lord. Evil will not win out in the end, Kate. Whose side do you want to be on? What people don't understand is that you cannot just be…there are two sides…God's side and Satan's. If you are not for God's side then you are automatically on Satan's whether you want to be or not. Choose God. Let me help you. Just come to church with me tomorrow. Just try to let yourself believe and see what you find. I won't badger you. I just want you to try. Believe me, once you open your eyes there is no denying what is right in front of you."

I hesitated, taking it all in. I needed so much right now, and she was offering it to me, but did I want to take it? To try it? "Okay, Amy. I will go with you tomorrow, but if I decide it is not for me, then you will need to not mention it again."

"Fair enough, Kate, fair enough, but really open your heart to it. Give it a try. Okay?"

"Okay."

She lifted her smoothie. "To new beginnings, to new family, to a new life."

"I will drink to that!" We clanked our cups, and for the first time I felt something. Something I never thought I could feel—*hope*.

I didn't talk to Sam for the rest of that day. She wasn't in her room when I returned, and I ate dinner in my room that night not wanting to face the cafeteria or a restaurant alone. I told her I needed to think, and she was giving me time. I wondered if she would reject me if I went to church. But I couldn't think that way. I needed to just get through what I was dealing with. If she couldn't stick by me, then she was never really my friend. But the thought of being alone haunted me.

I woke early the next morning and picked out my best trousers and blouse. I headed to the bathroom to once again try to make something of my mangled face. Amy was already in there getting her hair finished.

"Hey! Good morning. Look at you...you must be a fast healer. Your bruises are already turning yellow."

"Yes, I guess that is a good thing about me."

"Would you like me to help you with your makeup again?"

"Yes, that would be great. I am already feeling nervous. I don't need to look like a freak too."

"First off you wouldn't look like a freak, and secondly there is no reason to be nervous. But I do understand where you are coming from."

As we pulled into the church parking lot, I looked around at all the people; people talking while the young ones chased each other around their legs, people smiling and happy. I felt like I was in some other universe where everything was good and right in the world. The church itself was just in an office retail space, nothing snazzy or special, but there was still something about it. As we walked up to the front to enter the building, we were greeted by many happy, smiling faces. What were they all smiling about—seriously!

Amy was courteous in not making me feel awkward by stopping to talk to a lot of people. She waved casually to many but kept walking. We took seats in the back pews, and she handed me a small Bible from out of her purse.

"If you want to use it you can. No pressure."

"Thanks." I took the Bible and held it as I looked around the room at everyone talking. I caught a few conversations that all seemed very normal. Some about children being sick, books they were reading, catching lunch after. So far no conversations about the weird girl at the back of the room.

The music began to play, and it seemed everyone took that as their cue to get to their seats. The music actually was quite contemporary and filled with things that I could actually understand. Most music I had heard was always so slow, and I could never understand what any of it meant. But this was stuff I understood—lyrics about wanting to change and be held and loved and yearning to have strength in times of suffering. I could definitely relate to that.

Soon a pastor came to the front and instructed everyone to get out their Bibles and turn to the book of 1 Peter. Suddenly fear gripped me. I turned to the people sitting at my right as they flipped through the pages of their Bibles. One of which I caught had a ton of handwriting in it. Notes? I didn't know the Bible. How was I going to turn to the right book?

Suddenly I heard Amy whispering to me, "There is a sort of table of contents in the front of the book. That is how I find the books. It is hard for most people to remember where they are. I always sing a little song in my head that names the books of the Bible." I could sense a chuckle to her voice as she opened the front of my Bible to the table of contents.

"It's in the New Testament," she said.

I scanned down six books till my finger hit 1 Peter on page 675. I quickly turned. The pastor announced we would be focusing on 1 Peter 4, living for God. "Let us all stand and read aloud," the pastor said, and everyone started to rise with Bibles in hand.

I stood and looked briefly at Amy who was smiling. I looked down and read along. "Therefore, since Christ suffered for us in the flesh, arm yourselves with the same mind, for he who has suffered in the flesh has ceased from sin, that he no longer should live the rest of his time in the flesh for the lusts of men, but for the will of God. For we have spent enough of our past lifetime in doing the will of the Gentiles—when we walked in lewdness, lusts, drunkenness, revelries, drinking parties, and abominable idolatries. In regard to these they think it strange that you do not run with them in the same flood of dissipation, speaking evil of you. They will give an account to Him who is ready to judge the living and the dead. For this reason the gospel was preached also to those who are dead, that they might be judged according to men in the flesh but live according to God in the spirit."

We sat back down, and I was filled with thoughts of the past year. What it was filled with and what I made my life circle around, and I found a common theme. Others. I was giving in to others. I wanted so much to become loved by someone or something that I let myself pass into a realm I never wanted to enter in the first place. I had come here trying to start a new life, and I turned to making it worse. Was there joy in that at the time? Yes, sometimes, but what had that gotten me? Suddenly I felt like I was suffocating, and I couldn't breathe. *I am going to hell! Look at me, what I have become? What I have allowed to let myself become? And for what? For what?* I heard shouting in my head and a heaviness in my heart, and I needed to run. To run far away. I looked over at Amy, whose eyes were huge upon looking at me. She grabbed my arm and excused us past the others in the pew and walked quickly outside. To my surprise we didn't stop outside. She just kept walking quickly to the car. We stepped inside the car, and she sat for a second with her head down then looked at me.

"Kate, go ahead. Scream. It is okay."

I was shocked. How did she know?

"Amy, I am sorry I just needed to get out of there. Seriously, I couldn't take it anymore. I felt like I was suffocating." I felt warmth running down my cheek, and I realized I was crying.

"Kate, it's okay. I understand, please just let go. You feel pressure in your stomach like you are going to throw up, and you feel like you want to scream. You are confused, angry, and depressed all at one time. Just let go…let it go."

"How? I can't do this. I feel like I am losing it."

"That's good, Kate, that's the first step in finding it, funny enough. We have to lose ourselves in order to find God! Deny ourselves and fill ourselves with Him."

"But what if He won't accept me? I have done terrible things. I have lived a life like he was talking about in there. That is me. I wanted to be someone. I didn't want people to talk evil of me, and I wanted so much to be liked and loved by others. Especially Paul, who said I wasn't fun enough to date. So I gave in. I wanted so much to come to school and make something of myself. To get out of my parents unloving arms and make something of myself. To get away from the evil that always seems to follow me and make a good life and now look at me. Literally broken and bruised, inside and out."

"I know, I know." Amy put her hand on my shoulder. "God knows who you are, Kate. He knows what you have been through. Listen to Him and find Him. He will give you strength. He will forgive you. All you have to do is ask. Just ask!"

"Will you help me, Amy? Will you help me ask?"

She bowed her head right there and then prayed for me. Prayed for my strength to find Him, and for Him to show me the way. For Him to protect me from the evil around me and that awaited me. For me to lean on Him and love Him for all things.

I listened and felt with every second that passed I knew what I needed to do. When she ceased her prayer, I kept my eyes closed and prayed myself. "God, I don't know you well, but I feel your presence and sense your love for me. I am so sorry. So sorry. Please forgive me. Please help my unbelief. Please help me come to you."

After a few seconds, I felt Amy's hand on mine and heard her whisper, "Amen." I looked up, and she had tears in her eyes.

"A great start!" she said.

I smiled and cried at the same time. We sat in the car in silence for some time until Amy finally broke the silence, suggesting we get something to eat.

"Actually do you mind if we go back to the dorms? I think I need to be alone for a little while."

"I totally understand." With that she started the car, and off we went back to the dorms.

At my door Amy told me if I needed anything she would be in her room. I thanked her and went inside. My mind was reeling from the morning's events. Yet being back in my room gave me a sick feeling of terror. What am I going to do now? How was I going to do this? Would Sam stick by me? Thoughts flooded my mind, and I felt myself suffocating again. So I prayed, asking for strength to figure things out. As I was about to say amen, someone knocked on my door.

"Kate? Are you in there? It's me, Sam."

I got up and opened the door. Sam walked in without looking up and sat on my bed.

"So," Sam finally said, "where were you this morning? I came to get you for breakfast, and you weren't here."

"I went to church with Amy," I said.

"Oh great…well, I am glad you have a new best friend. Hope God gives you enlightenment, Kate. But just know that running to be someone else won't help you. You can't run to a cult and think that it is going to make everything okay."

"What? What are you talking about, Sam? I am not running to a cult, and Amy is not my best friend. She is trying to help me, though, which is more than what you are doing. I mean what *are* you doing, Sam? What is this? I had something awful happen to me, and you are just sitting there condemning me. I don't get it."

"Well it seems you don't want my help. You have been running off to Amy to find who knows what. Something happens to you, and you decide you need religion? I don't get *you*! I want to help you, Kate, but how can I do that when you have decided you suddenly need God in your life to make it better? Sounds like you are going a little crazy to me. You are willing to throw away everything you have right now for what? And why? You haven't even talked to Jay to see what happened. He told me you wanted it just as bad as he did."

"What?" Throw up was pooling in my throat. "Why would I talk to him? Look at what he did to me, Sam. And I can't believe you would believe him over me. Look at me, Sam!"

"I didn't say that, Kate, I just said you haven't even talked to him. I mean you were drinking and smoking pot. No wonder you don't remember anything. I ran into Jay. I didn't seek him out, and he asked me if you made it home okay because he said you were pretty upset when he fell asleep during sex."

"*What?* Okay, first off I don't remember anything past the first drink, so I know something is up! I have a high tolerance for alcohol, if you haven't forgotten, Sam, and I wouldn't forget things after one drink. You even said that yourself. Plus I would never, I could never." I could feel my face turning red and anger boiling in every part of me. Flashes of not only the last night but also my whole freshmen year started filling my head like a weird strobe light. I fell to my knees and grabbed my trashcan and threw up.

"Kate! Oh gosh, Kate! It's okay. I am sorry. Look, I am just trying to help you here. Really!"

"Well you're not, Sam. Please leave. Just leave."

Sam stood up and stormed out of the room. I threw myself on my bed and cried till I fell asleep. When I woke up it was 1:00 a.m. My stomach was in knots, and my face was dried to the pillow. I got up and grabbed a water bottle from the mini-fridge I kept in my room and sipped it slowly, testing my stomach. I grabbed a protein bar from my cabinet and sat back on my bed thinking and praying over the last couple of days. My mind then flashed to the fact that it was now Monday and in seven short hours I would have to be in chemistry lab.

"Take it a day at a time, Kate," I said to myself. I would start with going to class. I went to my purse to grab my phone and put it on the charger when I found the little Bible Amy had given me the day before at church. I climbed back in bed after making sure my alarm was set for the right time and opened the book. I had no idea what to read or what each book contained. So I just thought I would start at the beginning of the New Testament. Who was this Christ and why and how did He die? So I opened the table of contents and found Matthew was the first book. I began to read. Before I knew it, my alarm was going off. I hadn't slept a wink. My mind was spinning with thoughts of Christ, of who He was, His miracles, His life, His death, and His resurrection. I spent the last seven hours reading Matthew and the next book, Mark, over and over again, and my mind was overfull. How could they be so different yet so much the same? Who were these men that wrote these books on Christ, and could they be trusted? If so this was amazing. I didn't understand many of the parables, but somehow I knew what a lot of it did mean. It gave me peace and hope. I got out of bed with a sense of strength that I could make it. Not knowing how I was going to but that it would somehow work. If Christ's life in these books was true, then I had nothing to fear.

I got ready for class in my own room this time just applying some makeup using the tricks I had seen Amy use. I got dressed in some jeans and a black, long-sleeved shirt, once again wanting to hide the bruises and still feeling naked somehow. As I was opening the door to leave, I ran into Amy, who was about ready to knock at my door.

"Good morning, Amy!"

"Good morning, Kate! How are you? I have been praying for you all night."

"I am okay, tired but okay. I read Matthew and Mark last night. Amazing stuff if it is true!"

"*Wow*, look at how the Lord is already working in your life! I am so excited for you, Kate, but please know that everything you are reading *is* true. You *can* trust it! Okay! Please feel free to ask me any questions."

"Thanks. I will. Are you on your way to class?"

"Yes, would you like to walk with me? Where are you off to?"

"I am headed to chem lab on the south side of campus."

"Oh, okay great I am headed that way too. Let's go."

We headed off taking a nice leisurely walk through the campus since we were both a little early. I looked around noticing for the first time some of the amazing greenery on campus. As I took in the sights like a newborn, I started thinking of this Creator I had been trying to give my life to. Did he really make all these trees and flowers, the beautiful birds singing overhead, the clouds raking the sky, the squirrel hopping from tree to tree? What a scary and amazing thought.

Amy broke the silence about halfway to our destination. "So what did you think of all the reading you did last night?"

"I'm confused and encouraged all at the same time, if that makes sense."

"Well, don't give up on what you don't understand. You're new at this. You'll get it eventually after more studying."

We passed by the library and were almost at the point where Amy and I would have to split ways when suddenly out of the corner of my eye I saw Jay, and he was running my way. My stomach lurched and vomit pooled in my throat choking me. I grabbed Amy's arm with so much fear and aggression that she let out a little yelp. She stopped abruptly and looked at me in confusion then caught sight of a guy running toward us.

"Oh, Kate, don't tell me. Is that…" She trailed off with complete understanding. "I won't leave your side. I promise."

"*Kate! Kate!*" he yelled. His voice brought flashes back to my mind and a scream to my throat, but I prayed for strength and peace. I took a deep breath and turned his way, letting go of Amy's arm. Amy stepped closer to my side slightly in front of me.

"Kate," Jay said as he stopped three feet in front of me with a weird glare in his eye. "What is going on? Why is Sam asking me about what happened between us Friday night? What are you telling people?"

"I am not telling people anything, Jay. What are you afraid I will tell people?"

"*Nothing!* There is *nothing* to tell, Kate. In fact the only thing you could tell is how wasted you were and how you embarrassed yourself. I even have pictures just in case you don't remember your evening!" He started to pull out his phone and thumb through his pictures.

I sat there fuming with anger but paralyzed by fear.

"Kate, let's go." Amy was pulling on my arm now. "Seriously there is no good that can come from this. Let's go."

I turned and looked at Amy but couldn't say anything. I looked back at Jay and was suddenly struck with a sickening feeling. I looked into Jay's eyes, and for the first time I could see it. Literally see it. Evil. Pure evil. There was nothing good about his eyes. They seemed to give him away, his character, his passions. Why didn't I see it before? Of course I had learned early on in our relationship he was a jerk, but what guy wasn't, really? We are always told they are after only one thing. But this seemed different somehow. As I stood there contemplating him, he stopped scrolling through his phone and a Grinch-like smile crossed his face.

"Oh, here is a great one of you with the bong, Kate, wanna see?" He started to turn the phone in my direction when I felt a jerk coming from my left arm.

"Kate, *now!*" Amy was pulling on my arm, dragging me away from the demon that was standing next to me.

"Oh, really, you're leaving? Too bad I have some great shots you should *really* take a look at," he said with a smirk. Then with a glare and a satisfied chuckle, he turned and headed back the way he came.

Amy dragged me around the corner of one of the campus buildings and sat me down on the concrete. I was filled with so many emotions I couldn't see or speak. Pictures? What were they of? What was I doing? This only proved my point that I couldn't tell anyone what happened. They either wouldn't believe me or think I was asking for it. I was suddenly struck with the realization of my circumstance as a long-term decision. There was only one thing I could do. I had to leave.

A New Beginning

I was all packed-up and ready to go. The last three weeks had actually flown by. I kept to my room except for eating and taking classes and finals. I was able to get caught up on a lot of studying to do enough to pass my classes, and now the only thing I could think of was getting away from here. The day I decided I had to leave I found Sam and told her that I couldn't stay. She was livid and hadn't talked to me since. Now all I wanted to do was find her and say good-bye. My heart broke when I thought of her. Amy said that Sam wasn't a true friend if she couldn't even try to grasp what I was going through, but I wasn't sure I agreed. Sam was or had been my best friend. We had been through a lot together over the last year, and I felt like I owed her so much. She was my first true friend, and I didn't know how that fell apart. How could someone like Jay get between us? I thought we could weather any storm, and there I was trying to get up the courage to find her and say good-bye.

Amy was taking me to live with her sister in Southern California until I could figure out where I was going to go to school. My parents didn't care what I was doing—as long as I didn't come home. Amy's sister, Charlotte, was trying to convince me to go to her alma mater, saying that it was a great school and it would be just what I needed. Amy said she almost transferred there herself after what happened to her but didn't because she wanted to be a light on Santa Barbara's campus, and now with her problem having been expelled she was vindicated in a way and didn't feel bad being there. I on the other hand, would see my predator and always be tormented by him. I couldn't stay there, and I knew it. Both Amy and Charlotte said that Redeemer University would be just what I needed to learn about God and get my life back on track to the direction it needed to be. But I still had second thoughts about it.

So over the summer I had interviews set up there and tours to see if it would be what I wanted or could live with. But in the back of my mind leaving Sam and Paul were the biggest factors making me want to stay at Santa Barbara. Even though neither one of them really stood by me. I hadn't really talked to Paul since he rejected me. My suspicions were that he heard something that happened between Jay and I because he left me several messages wanting to talk to me, but I couldn't call him back. After he rejected me, and Jay with all those pictures—I just couldn't—nor did I want to face him. I wrote him a letter saying good-bye and telling him I was leaving and to take care of himself and sent it to his house so he would get it when he got home for summer break. But I needed to see Sam, to say good-bye in person.

After filling up Amy's car with all our silly little possessions, I told Amy I forgot one thing and ran back into the dorm.

As I entered the door to the second floor, anxiety took over my body. *Lord give me strength,* I thought, *please let her be there so I can say good-bye, but please give me peace if she is there and things don't go well.* I got to Sam's door and said a quiet amen and balled my hand into a fist and rapped lightly on the door. No answer. I decided to try and see if the door was unlocked. I gripped the handle and slowly turned the knob.

"Sam," I said, "are you here?"

I opened the door and there I saw Sam lying on her bed, snoring away. I smiled a little, remembering how some nights she kept me awake with that snore. A flood of memories followed, and a tear fell down my cheek as I looked at the girl who had been my first best friend. I didn't think I would have the strength to leave, but I knew I couldn't change my mind. Amy was waiting; my new life was waiting. I looked at Sam and with a sigh I left the room.

It was the first day of orientation week at Redeemer's College and with Charlotte's help I was moving into my dorm room. Amy had left to go back to UC Santa Barbara and said she would call me later to check on how I was adjusting. The final decision to transfer had been a hard one and an easy one all at the same time. My first visit here was full of anxiety, but one step onto this beautiful and calming campus I knew I would make the choice to come here. The campus was settled into a little, sleepy town community that was surrounded by the foothills of Southern California. It was away from all the hustle and bustle of LA and had all the beauty of the mountains with it—luscious green trees, rolling hills, green grass, and fields of poppies. Yet, it had all the amenities close at hand like a movie theater, mall, Target, Denny's, etc. Anything a college girl would need.

The staff was really gracious to me and accepting of my new-found faith and was generous to let me come to the school without having a real spiritual footing. Having Charlotte with me didn't hurt since they still cherished her there. It had only been three years since she graduated, and she still helped out by doing the makeup for their drama department. I hadn't heard from Sam all summer. I had tried writing to her and calling her at home, but her parents said she was always out. It was hard for me to let it go, but being on this new campus starting a new life made it a little easier. My new faith kept me occupied. I spent the last three months attending church with Amy and Charlotte at the University Praise, which was a church geared toward college students. The sermons were focused on biblical application in college student's lives. The music was great and uplifting, and the preaching kept me eager to learn more about Christ and gave me a yearning for a deeper relationship.

I still felt like I had a lot of demons to conquer. I was by no means as strong or affirmed in my faith as Charlotte and Amy, but seeing how they were and knowing what Amy went through gave me hope that one day I could be strong and reliant in the Lord as well. Charlotte was absolutely convinced that Redeemer was the best place for me to be, to stay away from the temptation of falling back into my old ways and keep growing in the Lord. I had to admit, I was starting to feel at home. I felt a peace, like I could conquer those things from my past and actually defeat that which had made me fail all these years.

My room looked a lot like my one in Santa Barbara. There must have been some sort of dorm slate everyone followed. They probably just borrowed the architectural plans from the local prison since it seemed that small. But I quickly made my new room a home by hanging up colorful bulletin boards on the wall next to the bed and putting up all my books I cherished so much on the overhead shelf. My roommate was a junior and was part of the orientation week staff, so she was really busy, and I had yet to meet her. But as I looked over to her side of the room I saw it was filled with pink and brown bedding and coordinating sheets hanging on the back side wall with pictures of her and what seemed to be either her friends or family.

There were several of her and a guy who looked gorgeous. He must have been her boyfriend. She fit the mold of someone he would like as well. She was tall from the looks of the picture, with long, perfectly straight blonde hair. Her lips were full, and her eyes were big and blue. A typical Southern California girl, I gathered. She had little precious moments all over her shelves, and her desk had a coordinating pink laptop and pink pencil holder. The girl liked pink. I could gather she was a girly girl. I peeked in her closet just to see if my hunch was right, and there I found Coach shoes and bags with tons of designer clothing. She was rich too. I was struck by the thought that this was not going to be easy for me. I didn't really have a roommate last year. I didn't remember really ever coming in much contact with her, and she was beautiful too, so I was thankful I never had to be reminded of what I wasn't. But again

I had to be here with the same such beautiful roommate, with some gorgeous boyfriend. Plus she looked to be rich with a doting family. Everything I didn't have. A little voice inside was calling out to me that jealousy would not get me where I needed to be in life. And that was true; I needed to move on. Charlotte came in telling me she set up my locker in the bathroom with all the essentials.

"Thanks so much, Charlotte, you have been a real help to me over these last few months. Seriously like a sister I have never had! I don't know how to ever thank you."

"Well, we are family, Kate. You are my sister in Christ, and I am always here to help you. But you have your first meet and greet to get to, so I better go. Remember I am just a phone call away, and I can be here in twenty minutes if you need anything. I will see you at church on Sunday for sure." She gave me a big hug and squeeze of my shoulders.

"I should be good. I am nervous but excited."

"I will call you tonight to see how your first day was, okay?"

"Great! Thanks again!"

Charlotte smiled and headed out.

I checked my welcome handbook that showed the first night festivity was a meet and greet luau out on the Quad. There were six two-story dorms that made a sort of circle, and in the middle was a big grass area along with a basketball/tennis court and a beach volleyball area. It was a perfect place for a luau, and it would only take me two minutes to get down there. Since I was with Charlotte most of the day, I hadn't really met anyone, so I would have to head down alone. I was hoping that I would meet my roommate down there. Since I knew what she looked like I was thinking I could scout around and find her. I threw on my flip-flops and brushed my hair out a little. I started heading down the hallway when I heard my name being called. I turned around and there she stood. Ms. Perfect herself—my roommate.

"Emily?" I asked.

"Yeah, Kate, right?" She was jogging toward me with her hand extended.

"Yes, that's right. How did you know it was me?" I took her hand and gave it a nice, firm shake. I wanted to make sure that I had something going for me, so fake confidence would have to be it.

"Oh, I got a picture of you from Amy, her parents and my parents are really good friends. We lived in the same town. She is a year older than me, so we didn't hang out a lot, but our parents always did."

"Oh, I didn't know that." I felt better knowing that Amy knew her for some reason. Like there was hope for this match after all.

"Yeah, well, I wasn't sure if you had a chance to make some acquaintances yet so I thought I would run up here and get you for the luau. You are a sophomore, so I thought it would be good for me to introduce you to some of the staff that are sophomores since most of the incoming students here are freshman."

"Oh, wow. Thanks! I really appreciate it. With the moving in today I hadn't really had a chance to meet anyone yet."

"Well, that is what this night is all about. Let's go!" She took my hand and led me outside and down toward the Quad that was all set up with a huge table of food with everything from pineapples with some sort of juice drink and an umbrella in it to hamburgers and hot dogs.

"What, no roasting pig?" I asked.

"No, no," she said, laughing, "although that might have been a nice touch. We are going to start the night off with a quick prayer so let's gather over there." She pointed to the middle of the grass area where there was a small stage and podium set up. Many of the students were already sitting in front of it talking and getting to know each other. I could see bonds already forming. It reminded me of Sam and I on our first day.

We made our way and sat down just in time for the school's dean of students to come to the microphone. He was a young guy. Probably thirty years old, with dark-brown hair and a goatee. He was wearing a Hawaiian shirt and khaki shorts. He seemed down to earth, and I liked him immediately.

"Hello, everyone, and welcome to orientation week," he said. "This night is all about getting you comfortable in your new surroundings and making some great new friendships. Before we begin I am going to pray for our dinner, and then you may go eat, play basketball or volleyball, or just hang out and meet some great people. Okay? Great! Let's pray."

He prayed thanks for the food and for the incoming students. He prayed that great bonds of friendship would be made and existing ones would be strengthened in and for the glory of the Lord and closed with a very excited "Amen. Let's eat!"

"Okay, I am hungry, girl, let's get some food, and then I will introduce you to some people," Emily said as she pulled me up. We made our way over to the table of food and grabbed a burger, some chips, and a pineapple drink. Since giving into my yearn for the Lord the eating was getting better. It still took everything in me to keep it down, but I had the strength lately to do it.

"Hey, Emily!" A girl came bounding up beside us.

"Lisa! Hey, did you just make it back?"

"Yep, I got the church room all decorated for Wednesday. He will never know!"

"Great! I am so excited. Thanks for helping me with this! Oh, Lisa, this is Kate. She is a sophomore transfer, so I am helping her get acquainted." She looked at me. "Kate, this is Lisa, one of my closest friends. She is helping me with a surprise party for my boyfriend. It is his birthday Wednesday. Our church is letting us use one of their rooms to have a little surprise party, and Lisa was helping me decorate today since we have so much going on the next two days."

"Hi, Lisa," I said. "It is nice to meet you."

"You as well," Lisa said with a smile. "You are going to love it here. Not only is the weather great all the time, but it is such a nice, small school with great teaching. You can't help but grow in the Lord here."

"Oh…great." What did she mean by grow in the Lord?

"You are coming to the party on Wednesday, right? It would be a great opportunity for you to meet some more students who already attend here and are not at this luau."

"Oh, yes, of course," Emily said. "She is so right, Kate. I meant to ask you later, but please do come Wednesday. We would love it."

"Oh, thanks for the invite that could be fun." A party? Well it couldn't be what I was thinking—especially here. I hadn't been to a party since that night with Jay, and I didn't intend to relive that. But it was in a church so I was thinking their idea of a party was a lot different, and I couldn't have been more relieved.

With that Lisa and Emily struck up a conversation about the decorations and how they planned on pulling off the surprise. I looked around and took in the scenery of all the new faces mingling and eating, getting to know one another. Suddenly out of nowhere, I spotted him. Walking toward me like out of one of those movies where everything is moving in slow motion. He was tall with a medium build, and dark, dark, black hair and chiseled features. As he got closer I could see he had piercing, light-blue eyes. Gorgeous was an understatement.

Then it dawned on me, he looked familiar. Why did he look familiar? I *knew* I would have remembered someone like him. He kept coming closer with this sly grin on his face. But his eyes are what had me stuck. I never thought I would ever see anyone that would make me think Paul was dog meat, but there he was. I was getting more and more nervous the closer he got. I still couldn't figure out how he looked familiar, until when he finally reached us he put his finger up to his mouth making a *shhh* motion with his beautiful lips. He winked and then grabbed Emily from behind. She let a little squeal then turned around laughing and hitting the gorgeous man behind her.

And it hit me—this was the guy from Emily's pictures on her wall. This was her boyfriend! Of course! Of course he was! Why would he have been looking at me? He was coming over to us because of Emily. My heart sank, and I felt nervous and embarrassed. I hoped he didn't notice how much I was staring at him. The pictures definitely didn't do him any justice. I was immediately convicted of my jealousy of Emily. This girl seemed to have everything and didn't even know it. Or who knows? Maybe she did. I hoped she didn't take it for granted.

"Evan! If you scare me like that again I swear!" She screamed at him while Lisa laughed at her side.

"It's good to see you, Emily," he said.

"It's good to see you too! How was your group of boys today? Did you have fun being the stud you are to all the incoming freshman?" She stretched up to hug him quickly around his neck.

"Yeah, we have some great incoming talent this year too. I think coaching the freshmen this year is going to be great!"

"Terrific!" Emily turned to me. "Kate, this is my boyfriend, Evan. He is a senior so he tends to be a little snooty and a Mr. Know-It-All, but once you get to know him he is a nice guy." Emily was smiling up at Evan now.

"Ha, very funny," Evan said. He reached out to shake my hand.

I took his hand trying not to look at him in the eyes for fear he would see right through me.

"Nice to meet you, Kate," he said.

"Yeah, uh, you too," I stammered. Then I realized I hadn't let go of his hand yet. I instantly released it and nervously cleared my throat. "So you coach? What sport? Isn't that weird to have an existing student coaching?"

"He coaches baseball, and he is amazing," Emily said. "He was an even better player. Evan played baseball his whole life and should have gone pro as a pitcher but ended up injuring his arm last year in a fall while rock climbing. Now he helps to coach the team here. They all look up to him even though some of them are the same age. He only coached for half a year last year after the fall, so this will be his first full year coaching. Should be fun! Right, babe?" She attached herself to his arm. I could tell she was insecure about their relationship just by looking at how she hung on him, like he was going to bolt at any minute.

"Sure, Emily," Evan said, "I loved playing, but coaching gives me some of that back that I am missing since injuring my arm. Going pro was of course something I really wanted but never expected, so I am okay with where I am at."

"Well, I am sorry to hear about your accident. I am sure the team is lucky to have you." I could feel my cheeks getting red just from that small sentence. I needed to get away from him. He was taken, and I couldn't consume myself like that again. This was supposed to be about new beginnings, not old habits.

"Well, I really still have a lot to do to organize my room, so I think I am going to head back, okay?" I said.

"Already?" Emily grabbed both my hands. "Listen, Kate, I know from Amy that you might be a little shy and reserved, so that is why I am the perfect roommate for you. I will help you to get to know people. Stay, and let me introduce you around."

"Um, yeah, well, shyness and hermit-hood is my specialty, so I think I should stick to that for right now. Seriously I have a lot to do, and I have all week to meet people. But thank you so much, Emily."

"Okay, well, I will see you later then."

"Okay, nice to meet you, Lisa and Evan." With that I turned around and fast-walked back to my room.

I dropped on the bed and decided maybe I should try to ask God to help me. So I prayed that the Lord would give me strength to handle this Evan situation. He was my roommate's boyfriend, so it was inevitable I would have contact with him. I needed strength to not fall for him—to keep my eye on my relationship with God, as shaky as that was. I needed this time to grow, as Lisa had said, which I was starting to understand.

I spent the next two days getting supplies for school and organizing my room. I went to most of the orientation week meals and sporting events and met some nice people, none that were like Sam, though. She occupied many of my thoughts lately. Even though things ended badly, I couldn't help remembering how good of a friend she was and how much I had depended on her. She was the best friend I had, and I was still perplexed by how things fell apart. Part of me knew that was why I was standoffish with most people here. I was tired of getting hurt. My guard was up. Unfortunately I had no plans to let it down.

"Kate, there you are!" Emily said as she burst into our room. "I have been looking for you everywhere. I should have known you would be in here. It is time to get you ready. I need your help!"

"Ready for what? What am I helping you with?"

"It is Wednesday, silly. Remember Evan's surprise party? I need your help getting him there because I need to finish decorating, and he is down with the team coaching. My original plan to get him to the church is failing miserably, so I need you to do something for me."

"Oh, Emily, I don't think I am the right person to help you, and parties really aren't my thing. I really appreciate you inviting me, but seriously I am perfectly happy right here."

"I know you are, and that is why you *need* to come. Plus I am your roommate, and I am asking for your help! Come on, Kate, please!" She must have been desperate. I wasn't sure if she really wanted me at the party or just really needed my help.

"All right all right, Emily, stop begging. I will help you. You always get your way don't you?"

"Pretty much," she said, laughing her girly laugh. "Okay, so this is what I need you to do. I am going to run to the church and help finish decorating. In an hour I need you to run down to the baseball field and tell Evan that there has been an accident and I hurt myself at the church and you need his help. He will come running for sure."

I couldn't do that. I hadn't seen Evan since the luau, and I was supposed to go act all dramatic about her hurting herself? "Okay, I am not sure I follow. Why would I be at your church in the first place, and why would I come driving back here to get Evan to go to the church?"

"Oh, no, no, Kate, our church is right here on campus. You know that little church you pass on your way in here? That is our church. It is like a hundred steps from here, so it would make perfect sense for you to go get him. And he won't ask you why you were there so don't worry about that." She went to her closet and pulled out a sleeveless black dress and the key to her bathroom locker. "I have to go get ready right now, and so should you."

"Okay, that is another problem. Why would I be at the church all dressed up?"

"Man, you are a details girl, aren't you?" Emily said. Her eyes tilted up and I could see she was trying really hard to think about what to say.

"Okay, here is the deal. You are coming to the church for a little dinner the girls and I are throwing for you to get to know you better—thus you are dressed up. It's something I would do, so Evan won't suspect anything from that. Then say I tripped and fell, and that is why you need him. Okay?"

"Okay," I said, "sounds like a plan, I guess."

"Now come with me to the bathroom, and let's get ready."

I opened my closet and picked out the only dress I owned. It was a black dress, which seemed appropriate since that was what she was wearing. It had spaghetti straps and a long, sheer overcoat. Not the coolest dress but all I had for this type of thing. I was never into fashion; that was why Sam always picked out my clothes. I never really knew how to dress myself. I hated shopping. It was hard for us gals with curves to find anything flattering. Even after losing weight since the Jay incident, I was still hard-pressed to find anything to fit my bigger chest.

"All right I am ready to go!" And she looked great. Thirty minutes and Emily looked like a movie star, her blonde hair she had curled was now hanging to the middle of her back, and her makeup was done with a slight smoky eye. I, however, after thirty minutes just managed to get the knots out of my shoulder-length brown hair. I had thrown on a little sheer eye shadow and some mascara with some nude lip-gloss and peach blush. It was as good as it was going to get.

"Okay, then I guess I am ready for action in what, an hour, you said?"

"Yes, you finish getting ready, maybe add a little more color to those cheeks and eyes and then, let's see…it is four now, and everyone is supposed to come at four forty-five for his five o'clock arrival, so go a little before that and put on your best acting, okay?"

"I will do my best to not let you down," I said.

"Great, I will see you soon! Thanks, Kate!"

She left the bathroom, and I took another look at myself in the mirror. I guess I could use a little more color. I was often told how pale I looked. I added a little brown to the creases of my eyes and some more peach to my cheeks then went to sit in my room till it was time to go. As I sat there, I was going over how exactly I was going to do my acting job, and with Evan nonetheless. I didn't even want to run into him, let alone have to go to him and be a dramatic dope. I loved my drama class in high school, but it was in a play, not real life. I wasn't dramatic in real life. I liked things plain and normal, not crazy and chaotic, and now somehow I had to figure out how to pull this off. How was I going to do this? I went over and over scenarios in my head, trying to think of something to say. But I didn't know Evan that well, so who knew what he was going to say.

Before I knew it the clock was ticking at 4:50 p.m.—show time! It would take me five minutes to walk to the field, so I needed to get going. I didn't want to disappoint Emily by being late. I headed out the door and down to the field. I was getting a few looks from people considering my attire; I didn't blame them. So I walked briskly with my head down. I saw the field and took one last deep breath to calm my nerves, and I started to run. If she were really hurt then I would be running to get him, right? As I got closer, I could see him on the pitcher's mound talking to another guy. Lucky for me as I reached the fence behind the catcher's area, Evan looked up and spotted me. I waved at him as I kept running to the right to get into the little gate that led into the field.

"Kate, right? Is everything okay?"

"Oh, um, yeah." Suddenly I was stuck like a stammering idiot trying to figure out what to say. Evan was standing in front of me looking even better in his baseball cap and uniform that fit nice and snug like they all do. I was looking into his crystal eyes again feeling lost. I shook my head remembering that I had a mission to accomplish and realized that the baseball team was staring at me knowingly. Were they in on it? Of course they would be since they were probably all invited to the party. Out of the corner of my eye I caught one of the players in the dugout making a circling motion with his hand as if to say "get on with it." Right, okay, drama.

"Oh, yeah, uh, sorry, Evan. Something bad has happened to Emily, and you need to come to the church with me quickly!" Even I had to admit I wasn't buying it.

"Oh wow, something bad huh? At the church you say. What is she doing at the church?"

"Yeah, she was throwing me a welcome dinner party with some of her gal pals and tripped over herself in her high heels, and I think she broke her arm." Now I was pushing it!

"Wow that sounds serious, you're right! I better call nine-one-one for her right away!" He smiled.

"No, nine-one-one is not necessary but your presence is, so why don't you just come with me please, Evan!"

"Dude, Evan, it sounds serious you better go!" The pitcher guy was trying to save my attempt at acting. He would probably laugh if he knew I had actually got the lead in *Our Town*.

"Hmm. I don't know. I am not sure I could be of much assistance here. I think I should just call nine-one-one and let them handle it."

"Okay, Evan, seriously? I am about ready to take this stupid heel off and smack you with it so please just come with me! Emily really needs you."

"Okay, wow smack me with your heel? I am shaking now, but I still don't think I should come this is far too much fun. What else you got?" His smile got even bigger as he let out a chuckle.

"Dude, stop making the girl sweat. She is trying to do Emily a favor, and you are obviously making it hard for her," the pitcher said.

I looked up at Evan, pleading. It was obvious he enjoyed watching me squirm, and squirming I was.

"Okay, okay, let's go help Emily."

"Thank you!" I started to lead the way out of the field and up the street toward the church. Evan was walking right beside me, and I realized that one by one cars filled with baseball players were screeching by us. Subtle!

"Hmm," Evan muttered, "maybe since this was such a tragic and utter dramatic accident we should have driven to get there sooner."

"Uh, yeah, well…" I stopped, tired of this game. I looked up at Evan's face, and he was smiling down at me waiting for my witty response. "Oh, stop it seriously! I told Emily not to ask me to do this. But do me a favor, will you, and not let Emily know I failed miserably?"

"I have no idea what you are talking about," he said with a wink.

"Thanks!" Then I once again turned my head toward the street and walked in silence.

The church was coming into view. "Should we make a run for it, then?" he asked. "Since you were supposed to be coming to get me for such a tragedy, I guess we should act it out."

"Oh, right, well, then let's get our run on."

"Can you run in those shoes?" he said, pointing at my black, three-inch heels.

"Yeah, no problem. I ran down to get you, didn't I? Even though I hate heels I have had far too much experience with them, so let's go." With that we were off running. I directed him to the correct room, and he went charging in. He was great at his part. Acting like something was really wrong. When he entered the room with me trailing everyone shouted, "*Surprise!*" I shrank off to the side to be unseen. He was instantly surrounded by friends congratulating him on turning the old and decrepit twenty-three.

I mingled a little, getting a few bites here and there, and saying hello to the faces Emily had introduced me to earlier in the week. It had been about an hour before I really started to feel like an outsider. Conversations were going on between people who really knew and cared about each other, and I didn't really feel like I had much to add to the conversation, so I slipped out the side door onto a little courtyard. There was a gazebo in the courtyard, probably used for weddings, so I made my way over to it and sat down to enjoy the pink and purple visions the sunset was creating in the sky. I had an urge to pray then. Pray that I would gain courage to know God more, to really let Him inside to heal the still present wounds in my heart. Pray that I would have courage to meet people and not be afraid of heartbreak. Pray that one day I would meet someone like Evan who could fulfill that dream I always had of having love in my life.

"Hey, not much for parties, huh?"

I looked up to see Evan standing there at the entrance to the gazebo, and my stomach dropped, and I could feel my face already getting hot.

"Uh, yeah I have had bad experiences with parties, so I don't tend to like them much."

"Hmm, guess we have similar thoughts on the subject, then."

"Really? I wouldn't have suspected you as one who wasn't much for a party in your honor."

"Oh…ouch!" He winced and acted like he was hurt as he moved closer to the bench to my right and took a seat. "I guess I deserve that after giving you such a hard time on the field."

"Yeah, thanks for that by the way, but my comment was not meant to hurt you just now. I just perceived you as someone who never had any issue with being the center of attention. You must always get what you want."

"Is that what you think of me? What have I done to give you that impression?"

"I'm just saying someone who looks like you and is talented like you are, people are going to fall all over themselves to be near you and with your choice of girlfriends it seems to just fit the mold." I looked at my feet, wishing I hadn't said anything.

"Well, my looks are overrated, and so is my talent, which obviously God didn't think was enough for me to do anything with. And my girlfriend, well…she is your roommate. I would think you would like her. Emily has been nothing but nice to you, right?" Now he seemed to be getting defensive.

"No, don't take me the wrong way. Emily is very nice, and I appreciate her trying to get me involved. She and I are just very different people. I am ugly and reserved, and she is gorgeous and outgoing. A little too much for me to compete with."

"First off, you must have some whacked-up mind to think of yourself as ugly, and secondly, what do you have to compete with her on? We are all here for one thing, and that is to get a good education to be something in life and grow in the Lord while doing it."

"Never mind, this conversation is not going anywhere I would like it to. I don't mean any disrespect to anyone. Seriously. What are you doing out here anyway? Can't a girl pray in private anymore?"

"Oh, gosh, Kate. I am so sorry. You were praying? I had no idea. I just came out to get some air. Like I said, we share common feelings on parties. Don't get me wrong, it was great of Emily to throw me this party, but it is what she wanted. Not me. In fact we even talked about this a while ago, and I told her I had no interest in anything like this. But what Emily wants, Emily gets. So I guess the surprise party was under way. Which reminds me, I am glad I caught you out here. I wanted to tell you not to feel bad about your poor acting performance. I actually already had several clues that this was going on."

"Really? That actually does help me to feel a little better knowing I didn't ruin the surprise. I know I am not the greatest of actresses. I am not offended by that at all. I don't pride myself on being some-one else in real life."

"I am gathering that. If you were priding yourself on that, then I would assume you would be inside pretending to have a good time."

"Apparently the way you were doing then, huh? Actually I was quite impressed at your acting ability when you went inside the room. I truly think Emily thinks she tricked you. And here you knew even before I flubbed it up." I hesitated, coming to a realiza-tion. "Hey, wait a minute. If you already knew what I was up to when I got down to the field, why did you give me such a hard time?"

"Aw, I couldn't resist having a little fun with you. You were too cute trying to squirm your way into your acting job." He was try-ing hard not to break out laughing, while I was stunned by the fact he called me cute. At first I was excited by that comment, then I thought of Paul. Cute? Probably just another sisterly affection.

"Well, thanks for having fun at my expense."

"You make it too easy, really."

"Once again, happy to oblige. Don't you think it is time you get back to Emily and your party?"

"Oh, are you trying to get rid of me? I know I interrupted you, and I am sorry about that, but do you mind if I just hang here for a few more minutes? I really am not ready to get back in there yet."

"Don't you think they are going to notice you are gone? I don't want someone to come looking for you and get the wrong idea out here." I quickly regretted what I said. "Not that they would get that idea. I mean there is nothing and not that you would do that…or I would even or that you would even think—"

"Seriously you are too much fun. Look at you squirm again. I am not thinking anything, Kate. Just enjoying some real company for a change."

I let myself relax at that and tried to calm my racing heart. "Okay, you keep talking about this. So tell me what is going on here. Why do you feel you can't be yourself?"

"No, I am myself to some extent. I think, like you, some people get the wrong idea of me, and then I just kind of follow suit. I have always grown up just following what everyone else wanted me to be. I have never really looked at who I want to be or who God is directing me to be. Sometimes I get so caught up in this idea of who I am that I totally forget who I am in God's eyes. Does that sound ridiculous?"

"No, not at all. I don't know much about what God sees or what He would want us to be. I have only been seeking God, so to speak, for a few months. Yes, gasp, I am not a long-time Christian, so I am probably not the person you want to be talking to about this.

"You enlighten me, Kate. Seriously I don't know why I am opening up to you. I haven't opened up to anyone. Maybe because you are a newbie here who knows nothing about me, and it would be nice to have one person know the true me. Or it could be just because you are really easy to talk to. It is actually refreshing to know you are a new Christian. Even though I grew up in a Christian home, sometimes I still feel new at it because I have always just gone with the flow instead of really finding out for myself who He is. You are lucky."

"I wouldn't really call my circumstances lucky. But I would say that I am lucky, or I guess I should say blessed, to find myself here. Although hearing you makes me think twice about that."

"Oh, no, don't get me wrong. These people are great. But like all kids our age we are still figuring things out. Take Emily for instance. I love that girl to death, but she really has no idea who she is. She loves spending money and getting her way. She is sweet and bright with a lot of friends because she really is loving, but she has a long way to go till she can find out her place in the world."

"So is it your love that keeps you with her, then? Hearing you talk makes me think the two of you are not a match made in heaven like I had originally thought." Right away I wish I could've taken it back. Who was I to tell him what to do or who to see?

"You are an honest little spitfire aren't you?"

"Sorry!" I said, shrugging my shoulders.

"Actually, you aren't saying anything I haven't thought for the last year. Emily and I got together halfway through her freshman year, my sophomore year. We have been together for a year and a half. When I went rock climbing last year, I had plans to break up with her when I got back. Then I got hurt. She was by my side every day. I loved her for that. She helped me to recoup and get back on my feet. I couldn't let her go then. But now that we are back and I feel like things are falling into the same pattern, I am getting the feeling that I should let her go. There are so many guys here lucky enough to take my place who would be a better match. Yet, I know Emily and I will always be friends because we really do love each other and have been through a lot together. I pray about it every day hoping I will have the strength to let her go."

"You are selfless to think only of her. But you need to think of yourself too. What if there is someone out there for you that you are meant to be with? If you know the two of you are not meant for each other, then maybe it is better to break it rather than hang on because it is too painful to let go."

"You are wise for a young Padawan."

"Oh, thank you, Master Jedi Evan. You are such a dork."

"No, seriously you are right. I just need to do it."

"Okay, but not tonight please! And please don't bring me into the conversation! She is my roommate, and I don't want to make enemies my first week here. I mean, gosh, I am already breaking people up, and I haven't even started classes yet."

"There you go again thinking you are the reason for failure. Don't give yourself so much credit."

"Oh, gosh, no that is not what I meant…" I stopped, realizing he was playing me again. So like a little sister I shoved him so hard he fell off the bench seat. He was so shocked at first he just looked up at me, and then we both started laughing.

"So you are a strong little freak as well huh?"

"Oh, yeah, I have been pumping the weights lately!"

The night was turning unusually cold for August, and I was beginning to wish I had brought a sweater since my sheer overcoat was doing nothing for me.

"All right I guess it's time to get back to the party," Evan said.

"Actually, I think I am going to go home. It has been a long day for me, and I am looking to hit the hay. Plus it isn't tempting in the least to go play dumb with Emily right now."

"Look, Kate, I am sorry to put you in that position. I should have never confided in you like that."

"No worries. Really. I'm glad I could be here for you. You seem like a great guy who could actually use a little reality in his life. You know how good of an actress I am. I think staying away from Emily right now is a good idea."

"You gonna be okay getting back to the dorms?"

"Oh, yeah, no problem. Have a great night."

"You too, Kate. It really was a pleasure talking to you. I hope it isn't the last time."

I could feel my cheeks flushing again, so I quickly turned to leave. I waved a quick good-bye and headed up the hill back to my dorm room. The campus was fairly quiet. Only a few kids mulling about. I looked up and enjoyed the seeing the stars light up against the black sky. I got back to the dorm and got ready for the night, said a quick prayer of thanksgiving for my talk with Evan, and fell into bed. Immediately I knew I wouldn't sleep right yet, but I had to get my mind off of my conversation with Evan. I didn't want hope to creep into my mind that Evan could find me appealing. It was impossible. I was sure he saw me only as a friend.

I just helped him decide to dump my roommate, and I couldn't help that give me a little hope. But would Emily find out? How would she, unless Evan told her? Would he say something? Did someone see us talking? I began to panic, so I decided grabbing a book to get my mind off it would be the best thing. I reached up and grabbed the first book that my hand came to. It was the first book in the *Mark of the Lion* series. Charlotte had given it to me and said it was a must-read, so I opened the first page and began reading. Before I knew it, I was awakened by a slamming door and screaming.

Just Friends

Emily came screaming into the room. I looked at the clock—1:00 a.m.

"Emily? Are you all right?"

"Do I sound all right? No, I can't believe him! I threw him a party, and he breaks up with me! Who does he think he is?"

"What do you mean? Evan?"

"*Yes*, Evan, who else? Breaking up with me because I threw him a party?"

"Okay, wait I am totally confused. I thought everything was fine."

"So did I! Well, I mean not always great. But great enough! It just made sense. He always seems like a dud when it comes to going out, but I was willing to overlook that. What is he thinking? I understand he said he didn't want a party, but who doesn't want a party? Who doesn't want to be the center of attention for a time? Obviously Evan. *No, no,* I will not cry any more over him. He cannot treat me this way. I have a million men lined up to take his place. God obviously has someone better for me."

"Gosh, Emily, I am so, so sorry! But it sounds like this isn't an all-bad thing. It sounds like you guys are very different and that maybe God does have someone better suited out there for you."

"But he broke up with me. It should have been me breaking up with him. I was going to, you know, right around the time of his accident, but then he needed me, and I couldn't leave him, not like that." She was wiping her eyes with a tissue and daintily blowing her nose. She turned to her wall and started ripping off the pictures of her and Evan.

I was laughing a little in my head. How ironic that they both were going to break up with each other around the time of the accident, but the accident kept them together. What was the purpose of that? Amy said there are reasons for everything, but I didn't understand that in this situation. Evan would never play baseball again, and he and Emily have wasted, or what seemed like wasted, the last eight months of their lives in a relationship neither one of them wanted. What good could come of that?

"Well, that was remarkably selfless of you, Emily, to think of him in his time of need and to stay with him even though you weren't sure that was what you wanted. Although I have to say when I first met him Sunday the two of you seemed very much lovey-dovey."

"All an act, really. I guess these last eight months have been all about acting for both of us. Did you know he knew about the party tonight?"

"Um…well, to be honest I gathered that when he wouldn't come right away. I really had to almost tell him just to get him to come to the church."

"See? What a jerk to do that to you. He already knew about the party and yet he makes a sensitive new girl go through the wringer to get him to come."

"Well, I am not that sensitive, but thanks for the sympathy."

"I didn't mean it that way, Kate. Let's not talk about you right now, okay? I need to think about me right now."

I rolled my eyes, letting what Evan had told me about Emily soak into reality. It was true Emily was a little high-maintenance and had a lot of growing up to do. I knew she loved the Lord. I could tell earlier in her devotions that morning when she was crying over reading the crucifixion of Christ again, but she still put herself before anything else. Christ was always quickly forgotten next to all the daily things in her life.

"You are right, Emily. You need to grieve. I am going to try to get some sleep and let you have some time to think."

"Thanks, Kate. I am sorry I woke you up. Good night."

The rest of the week before school started was filled with trying to avoid Evan and listening to Emily tell everyone, and I mean everyone, about the break-up and how unfair of Evan to do it the night of the party. Yet by the following Sunday she already had another date with a guy from the soccer team. That cheered her up. I enjoyed my Sunday with Charlotte going to University Praise and out to lunch telling her of all the things that happened that week. It was good to be with Charlotte for a day and get my mind back on track. She always knew what to say and how to encourage me.

I was all set with my classes for Monday, and the nerves were sinking in by the time I went to bed that night. I came into the school as undecided, which really described my life in more ways than one, but knew I would have to pick a major by the end of the year. Being a doctor became just a dream to me—not a reality. Knowing my luck I would only cause harm and no good.

Classes started with a breeze, and I found myself excited to dive into my studies once again. Like I had purpose to my life again. I continued to hang out with Emily and her posse knowing that was probably the best way to avoid Evan at the time. I didn't need to be reminded of his friendliness, yet I was wishing I could talk to him again. The girls were great, but I never truly felt myself. I didn't have much to add in the way of makeup talk or hairstyles. Nor did I care what handbags were recently released. We occasionally had a great talk about the sermons at chapel through the week, but for the most part, the conversation left a lot to be desired.

By Friday night I was longing to get off campus and to get away from the pressure to fit in, so I headed to the local Denny's. It was always a favorite for me and Sam at 3:00 a.m. after a party, and for some reason, I was longing for Sam at the moment. I pulled up and walked inside. Immediately memories of Sam came to mind, and I regretted coming. Did I really need the torture of remembering Sam and my old school? My memories took the natural hike from Sam and school to Jay and Paul, when the hostess came up with a kind smile. "Table for one?"

"Yes, thank you," I replied.

As the waitress grabbed the menu and started to turn to lead me to a table, I heard my name being called out. I turned to my right to see Evan sitting alone three tables away waving at me. My heart began to race. I looked over at the waitress who looked back at me.

"Would you like to join him? I know I would."

I looked at her with an odd smirk, "Uh, yeah, I guess I will. You don't have to show me the way though." I grabbed the menu from her and headed over to Evan's table.

"Hey, I didn't expect to see you here." My tone was slightly disgusted, revealing my feelings that I had wanted to get away from people I knew.

"Oh, sorry to disappoint. I know you have been avoiding me, but since we are both here, I take it as a sign we are meant to have dinner together."

"A sign, huh? Was my avoiding you that obvious?"

"Well, it wasn't hard to gather since I am sure you were the first to know of Emily's and my demise, being her roommate and all. I thought you would be slightly aggravated with me for doing it the night of the party. But once I made up my mind, I needed to tell her. I couldn't pretend anymore…uh, are you going to sit or stand there all night?"

"I am still debating that," I said as I looked back toward the door.

"Oh, well, please let me know when you decide if you are going to continue to grace me with your presence."

I looked back at his perfect face and smiled, deciding to sit down. "Oh, all right, I guess I can give you a few minutes of my gloriousness."

"Nice! But hopefully more than a few minutes. I was thinking of ordering dinner, do you want to get something?"

"Well, normally my friend Sam and I always shared the Moons over My Hammy, so I was thinking of getting that for old-times' sake."

"Okay, well, I will share it with you then, if you don't mind. My name isn't Sam, but I wouldn't mind taking her place as your friend."

I knew he could see my cheeks blushing.

"Well, I am not sure anyone can take her place, but you are more than welcome to try."

The waitress came over, and Evan ordered us one Moons over My Hammy and two coffees.

"So who is this Sam girl anyway? I feel it's only fair this time together be about you since I spilled my guts last time we talked."

"Well, my guts may be more than you can handle, my sheltered little friend."

"I take it then that you are not sheltered! Do tell!"

"Actually it is really hard for me to talk about. Everything is still so fresh."

"I am not trying to pry. I'm curious about you and would love to get to know you but only what you are comfortable telling me."

"Why in the world would you be curious about me?"

"You don't give yourself enough credit. You are a mysterious little lady for sure. In fact you have the whole baseball team wondering about you."

"About me? Why?"

"Well, you are the only transfer to this small school of ours this year. All other newbies are freshmen. We hear you are from UC Santa Barbara, which actually was named the number two party school in the United States, and you are not shy to tell people you are new to the faith. You seem to shy away from people, which leads some to think that there is a story there, not to mention that no one seems to know that story. That makes you mysterious."

"So we get down to the real reason you are befriending me. You have been chosen as the one who could get the new girl to talk and satisfy the curiosity of the masses."

"No, it's not like that. The curiosity happened after the party with you when people were asking about you, and Emily could only give answers that Amy gave her. They were just curious. You are attractive and intriguing, that brings people in. I was just lucky enough to get to know you before that curiosity with everyone else began. You can trust that I will not say anything to anyone. Believe me, you know more about me than anyone else at this point, and I wouldn't do anything to jeopardize that trust with you."

"Attractive? No. Intriguing? Maybe, and only because no one really knows much about me. But I don't think I want to change that. If people knew the real me, I would have less friends than I do now, and since that isn't much, I would rather not tell."

"You think people are going to judge you?"

"Why not?"

"Judge not, lest ye be judged! Let those who have not sinned cast the first stone."

"Aw, the wise words of Christ with the beloved Mary Magdalene."

"Yes, and she was a prostitute! Yet Christ stilled loved her and offered her the forgiveness and peace she didn't deserve. In return she served him like no other woman at that time. There is no reason for you to think we would judge you. Actually forget the 'we.' Me! I would have no reason to judge you. We are all new creatures in Christ. That person you were is dead now."

"She doesn't feel dead. She feels sometimes like she is fighting to come back. I pray I'm strong enough to not give in. Plus you say no one will judge me yet you yourself are afraid to be who you are for what I assume is fear of being judged."

"It is not I who is strong but Christ who strengthens us. Take it from me. Don't try to be someone you are not. I'm not in fear of being judged. I think I just don't know who I really am inside. I have been pretending to be someone for so long I am not really sure how to act. Except for some reason when I am around you, I feel more like I am figuring it out. Maybe that is because I don't have any pretenses with you. I was able to be what I want to be. Around others, it's too late. I don't really think I would be judged for being different. I think I would just confuse people. You, on the other hand, no one knows, you can start fresh and be the perfect person God made you. You can take ownership of it."

"Okay, well, if you are so convinced I will not be judged, then it is not too late for you as you say it is. You can be yourself as well! I'll tell you what, I will be myself if you will."

"Hmm…okay! Deal!" The waitress came back then and put down our coffees announcing our meal would be out in just a few minutes. Evan picked up his coffee and held it toward me. "Cheers, to being ourselves."

I smiled at the kind gesture and raised my mug. "Cheers." We clinked mugs, and I sat mine back down as Evan took a sip of his.

"You know when you drink to something you are actually supposed to drink, or it doesn't count."

"Oh, well, you did it too fast. I haven't had time to fix mine up yet. I can't drink black coffee! Yuck!"

Evan laughed and handed me the cream and sugar.

"What? What are you laughing at?"

"I just never know what you are going to do or say. That is different for me."

"Oh, well, good. I am glad I can keep you on your toes. There, now my coffee is ready. Should we try again?" I picked up my mug and held it toward him. He nodded and picked up his mug and clanked mine, yelling cheers so loud some heads in the restaurant turned to look at him.

"Wow, with gusto!"

"Well, I mean it!"

"I gathered that," I said, putting my cup back on the table and adding a bit more sugar.

"Okay, since you gather it so well now, will you tell me your story, Kate?"

I had just started feeling at ease with Evan, and now the pain of my past was coming back. To say it out loud—how could I have done that? It would've been like living it all over again. I said a silent and quick prayer and hoped the Lord would help me to know what to say.

"Are you sure you want to know?"

"Yes!"

"You have to understand this is hard for me. No one but Amy and Charlotte knows my whole story. Actually I don't really feel like my story is over, funny enough. I guess I should say the beginning of my story."

"I have all the time in the world right now for you, and I promise you it will not leave my lips whatever you tell me. You *can* trust me. Just as much as I can tell I can trust you. It might help to let someone in. Let me be that person. You have already helped me. Let me help you!" He grabbed my hand from across the table. I looked up from my cup and into his eyes. We held the stare for some time, as I felt the warmth of his hand over mine. Tingles went up my spine, and my cheeks went hot again. A lock of his black hair fell and was hanging on his eyebrow. I never noticed how dark and full his eyebrows were or how black and long his eyelashes. They only showed off his crystal eyes more.

Could I let him in? I hardly knew him, yet he said I knew him better than anyone because I knew his secret. I could tell I could trust him and there was no one else I wanted to let in, but would he hurt me in the end? Like Paul? The waitress came then, and we quickly looked away from each other and let go of our hands. She set the plate in front of Evan and an empty plate in front of me. She asked if we needed anything else, and Evan looked up kindly and said, "No thank you," so she turned and left. Still without words he gave me half the sandwich and some French fries. He looked up at me with anticipation.

"Okay, if I am going to confide in you, my newfound friend, then I think we should properly introduce ourselves. I mean I can't tell you these intimate details of my life without knowing your whole name and a little bit about yourself, like do you have any brothers or sisters? A favorite color?"

"You are just stalling, you little nerd, but I will oblige if it makes you feel more comfortable. But don't laugh when I tell you my whole name."

"Why?" I asked, already chuckling, "Is it that bad?"

"Well, to me it is."

"Okay, I will try not to laugh. Let me have it."

"Okay, well, my name is Evanmen Sebastian Castlebrook the third." He tugged on his shirt like pulling on a jacket lapel and stuck his head up in the air, mimicking some royal from London.

"Evanmen?" I slightly spit out my coffee from laughter. "What kind of a name is that?"

"Hey, you promised not to laugh!"

"I said I would try, but I don't have that much restraint!"

"Yes, I know it is terrible, but it was my grandfather's name, and my father's name, and now mine. I am sure you can already sense the pressure to name my son…"

"Do you all go by Evan?"

"No, actually my grandfather went by EV, and my dad goes by Sebastian. So I am the only Evan."

"Well, I really like the name Evan, so I guess that saves you a little bit."

"Thanks!"

"Okay, give me the rest of the resume now."

"Okay, well, there really isn't much to tell. I am a business major with an emphasis in international public relations. I have one sister who is older than me by two years. She got married five years ago and has two kids already. They're pretty young for marriage and kids, but she has a terrific husband and things have just fallen into place really well for her. I do love my little niece and nephew for sure. They live in Idaho, though, so I don't get to see them very often. I am originally from Texas, and my parents still live there. My dad is a football coach, and my mom is a full-time volunteer. She volunteers everywhere whenever she can. Although I am not sure it is because she really wants to help people or because she is still eighteen at heart and just wants everyone to know her, like they do my dad. My favorite color is green. My favorite candy bar is Butterfinger. I can play the piano but not really well. I love all sports not just baseball, and I secretly like to read the classics."

"What? The classics? No way, are you serious?"

"Yes, but no one knows that, so I am trusting you once again. Giving you more ammo! Okay, so now it is your turn."

"Okay, let's start with the basics then. My name is Katerine Isabella McDermott. I am nineteen. I am an only child. I like the color red, love to read the classics myself. Don't know anything about sports and am not sure I want to—sorry!" I said with a shrug. "I grew up in a small town up in Northern California where, like *Cheers*, everyone knows your name. My parents still live there, and they hate my guts. That is about the plain of it."

"Your parents hate your guts? I can hardly believe that. Why would they hate you?"

"You have to understand something about my parents to understand anything about me. I was unwanted from the moment I was conceived. I mean they used every form of birth control, and I am still here. So you can imagine what it meant to them having a daughter they didn't want. I was ridiculed and abused from the day I was born. I was used and then thrown out with the trash. But that is the way it has always been, and I am used to that really. I left for college wanting a new life, to prove my parents wrong about me. So far I haven't done a good job at that."

"I take it they are not believers."

"Far from it, my friend, far from it. In fact they think I am stupid for coming to this school, but what else is new? As long as I am out of their hair, though, they don't really care where I am or what happens to me."

"Oh, that can't be true!"

"I know it is true. From what happened to me at my last school, I know firsthand that is true."

"I am sorry, Kate, truly." He reached over and grabbed my hand again, giving it a light squeeze.

"It's fine, really, I have moved on from the pain of that." I took a bite of my sandwich and likewise Evan took that as his sign to go ahead and eat.

"So what brought you to the Lord then?" he asked with his mouth full.

I looked up at him and immediately was lost in his eyes again. I could not only see but also feel his trust. I could trust him—I knew I could. Just sitting with him there looking into his eyes, I knew this was meant for us this time. I didn't know why or what would come of it, but I knew I could tell him anything, and he wouldn't think differently of me. He wouldn't be scared away. At least I hoped. So I began with a sigh telling him of my first semester at school and how dedicated I was to my studies. About Sam and how easy it was to be her friend. I even told him about Paul. I told him more about Paul than I wanted to or should have, but he was part of the story. I told him of the partying and about Jay and our first relationship and how that ended. Then I explained how that wasn't the last time there was something between Jay and me. I skipped quickly over that part. Explaining how I didn't know what happened and how I had woken up in the bathroom. I told him how my decision to leave was based on Jay and his pictures on his cell phone. I told him about how God had put Amy and Charlotte in my life to save me and how that led me to Redeemer College.

Then we sat there in silence for what seemed like forever. He had stopped eating somewhere along the lines of talking about Jay, and I hadn't looked up from my plate since then. I didn't want to see in his eyes what he was thinking. After a few minutes I felt his hand on mine again, and I looked up. I could feel my cheeks were warm and wet, and I realized I was crying. How long had I been doing that?

He squeezed my hand. "Kate," he said, and that was all he could say. Feeling like things were getting too heavy, and I was about to lose it, I decided I needed to lighten the conversation.

"I come with a lot of baggage, eh?" I fake chuckled and wiped my tears off my face.

"You don't have to do that you know."

"Do what?"

"Try to lighten the mood. It is a horrible thing what you went through, and there is no reason to act like it didn't hurt you. But I have to think on it as a terrific thing to some degree because it brought you here. I mean if you wouldn't have gone through that, where would you be right now? You wouldn't be here sitting with me. So selfishly I have to thank God for bringing you to Himself in whatever way He could."

"Yeah, well, terrific thing is a complete overstatement, but I do understand what you mean. I wouldn't trade where I am right now at this moment for anything." I knew I was blushing, and somehow I didn't care. I was happy at that moment for the first time. But I couldn't get carried away. There was no way Evan truly liked me in that way. I knew he saw me as a friend and nothing more, so I couldn't fall for him—I just couldn't.

"I am thankful for you, Kate. Really I am. I haven't known you long, but I can already tell you are going to be a great friend."

Friend! Yep, I was right. My smile fell at that remark, but it was not like I didn't know that. I did. He had just broken up with Emily, and I couldn't expect anything more from him. I could be a friend. I could be a terrific friend.

"If it makes you feel any better, I am no angel myself."

"Aside from the faking people out in the whole center of attention thing, you seem like you have it all together. I think in part that is why people are drawn to you."

"Yeah, well, acting one way and being one way are two separate things. But I think I am getting things figured out. Now that I have let Emily go and am dedicated to really being myself. But in high school I was so caught up with trying to be the perfect kid and actually at some point really thinking I *was* the perfect kid that I thought I was entitled to things. I took advantage of my parents and friends. I dabbled in things I shouldn't have and used people to degrees I am really ashamed of. But I have learned my lesson. My lesson was taught in a hard way kind of like yours. You see, one thing I left out when I told you I have a sister is that I had a younger brother as well. He died, and it was at my hands that he died. That is a lesson I will never forget."

My heart swelled for him at that moment. Seeing his grief made me want to reach out and comfort him. "Oh, Evan. What happened?"

"It was five years ago. I was a junior in high school, and my parents just bought me a brand new Corvette. I drove to a party at my buddy Mark's house to show off my new wheels. I intended to only stay for a little bit because I promised my brother, Derek, that I would pick him up from basketball practice and take him home. Then I could go back out later, but the night got away from me. Before I knew it Derek was calling me and yelling at me about forgetting to pick him up. I felt awful, really I did. So I ran out to get him. When I got to the school gym he was furious, and we got in a fight in the car. I was going too fast around a corner and…I don't really know what happened. The next thing I knew I was in the hospital recovering from some minor cuts and a broken rib.

"But I guess the airbag on the passenger side didn't work, and Derek ended up with severe head trauma and in a coma. Soon we learned he was brain-dead, and my parents decided to turn off the machines. It was the hardest thing we as a family had ever had to do. My parents never blamed me. But I blame me. I always will. But I really did turn to God in more ways after that. I realized I was living for myself, but as you can tell I still don't have it together yet. Even after five years, I am still trying to battle the demons inside me wanting me to live for myself and not for God or what is true. It is amazing what pride and selfish ambition can do to a person."

I was silent for a few moments, unsure of what to say. Then I said, "Thank you, Evan. Thank you for telling me that. It means a lot to me. It changes my whole mindset on you that is for sure. Although you have been chipping away my preconceived ideas of you since the surprise party."

"Well, that's a good thing, I guess. You know Derek would have really liked you! Actually you are the same age he would be now. Funny! Maybe you are to be my surrogate brother...but a sister." He laughed.

I fake snickered at that, thinking of Paul all over again. But I wouldn't fall into that trap again.

"Maybe we should talk about lighter things now and eat while our meal is not yet spoiled," I said.

We spent the rest of our time there talking about classes we were taking, and how it felt for Evan to be a senior. It was good conversation, and we continued to learn a lot about each other. By the time the conversation took a pause it was 11:00 p.m.

"Wow, not to sound cliché but look at the time. Can you believe we have been here for five hours? Luckily it has been slow here tonight, or I would have felt sorry for our waitress occupying her table so long." I grabbed my purse and pulled out my wallet.

"Yeah, how quickly time flies when good company is involved. No, no, don't worry about paying. This one's on me."

"Oh, no, I couldn't really. I can pay my own way."

"No, think of it as a thank you for helping me get out of a serious rut," he said.

I put away my wallet. "Okay, but if we ever do this again, it is my treat."

"You're on! And I hope we can make this a weekly habit. It is a great way to end the week."

"That would be great, but I won't hold you to it."

"You have real trust issues don't you? I plan on changing that."

We left Denny's in our separate cars back to campus. We parked next to each other and walked to the Quad where we were to go our separate ways.

"Well, thanks for talking to me, Evan, it was great to get to know you better. And thank you for not judging me or looking down on me because of my past. I am not looking for sympathy just a new start."

"I know. Me too. Thanks for being so great! Have a great week this week. I'll talk to you later. And remember same time same place next Friday."

He gave me a quick hug, and I watched him leave.

The Twist

Emily was not as mad as I thought she would be when she found out that Evan and I had become friends and were having weekly date nights at Denny's. She knew it was only a friendly thing and nothing more. Plus, Emily, in the last four months, had managed to date and dump two other boys. It surprised me a bit, however, because she and Evan had dated for a year and half, even if the last eight months had only been out of pity for each other.

She was fine until the next Friday night crept up and she didn't have anything to do. I was starting to realize that she got her purpose out of taking care of people, men especially. If she didn't have a man to take care of, then she was lost. Yet if that man didn't match up with her wish list of what she wanted in a man, then she was quick to let them go. Maybe that was why she stayed with Evan even though he didn't meet her exact standards. He was someone that she thought needed taking care of. Just like me, until recently. I had hung around with Emily because she did take care of me in certain ways. Always making sure I was dressed properly for a function, church, class, etc. Always there to get me to eat at the appropriate times, since I did need help in that area. I found her numerous times organizing my closet or desk area. At first it bothered me, until I realized it wasn't because she was bothered by the untidiness, but she just wanted to help me out. She was a hard nut to crack. She could seem so selfish and ridiculous sometimes and so caring and thoughtful at others.

I had managed to get to know some other girls in my classes whom I had really grown to enjoy my time with. Denise by far was my favorite out of all the girls. She was always so encouraging and loving. No matter what I was going through she was always the first one to give me great advice, and I cherished her. However, it was Evan that had become my best friend. We didn't do the whole hanging out at school, or meeting up for dinner in the cafeteria, or walk each other to class because then people would get the wrong idea about us. Instead we sent each other funny texts throughout the day and looked forward to our Friday night "Hammy nights," as we grew to call them.

Every Friday at 6:00 p.m. we would meet at the same table at the same Denny's and order the same Moons over My Hammy and just let out everything that was going on in our lives for the week. We became each other's accountability, confidant, and greatest friend. I could tell Evan anything, and he could confide anything in me. He knew all about my past and demons in the closet, and I knew all about his. It was great to have someone that I knew loved me for me. I had grown to love Evan, but I made sure it was in friendly rather than romantic way. At least I tried to. I couldn't let myself feel that way for Evan because I knew there was no way he could ever feel that way for me. I knew he loved me as well, because he told me on several occasions, but it was never a romantic "I love you" like I still daydreamed about, but a best friend "I love you and care for you" type. But I would take any type from him I could get. I often thought I was falling into the same pit I did with Paul, but I knew that as long as I could keep that guard up I would be okay. Some days it was harder than others. But I would rather have had him in my life than not at all. That is until he met someone. We had never talked about other people. Conversations about dating or whom we liked never came up. In fact he never had a date in the last four months. I didn't have any either. I didn't do much as even look at another guy, let alone go on any dates. It was the farthest thing from my mind. Denise often told me she thought I needed to be careful that I wasn't overlooking someone I was meant to be with because of my friendship with Evan. Charlotte and Amy shared the same concern but didn't vocalize as often. Mostly because Charlotte always said that I was still trying to find out who I was and should really focus more on that than on a relationship with some guy.

Finals went by in a blur, and I was all packed up to go back to Charlotte's for the break. Amy was coming home too for Christmas, and Amy's mom and dad were going to come down to celebrate with us since Charlotte had to work through the holiday at her new gig doing makeup for *Les Miserables*, which was in LA for a short time. It would be nice for me to have a real Christmas for a change. My parents were taking a cruise to the Mediterranean, and I wasn't invited—not that I would want to go anyway—so it was nice to have somewhere to go.

I arrived at Denny's for our last "Hammy Night" for four weeks. I was about ten minutes early and could see Evan already sitting in our booth. I quickly got out of my car and went inside. It was good to see him. I never tired of our Friday nights together. Yet this one was a little bittersweet since it would be a while until we could do it again. He was going home to Texas, and his sister and her family were all flying in to celebrate the holidays together. He was excited to see his sister and his niece and nephew, so I was surprised when his finals were over on Thursday that he was waiting till Friday night to take a flight home because he wanted to have our last time together.

I walked over to the table and noticed he had a little box sitting atop my empty plate. He had already ordered our Moons over my Hammy and was patiently waiting for me.

"Hey, you already ordered?" I threw my bag into the seat and crossed over to his side to give him a quick peck on the cheek before sitting down. I plopped down and picked up the little red box. It had a satin white bow neatly tied atop it. "Okay, I know you didn't wrap this. I don't think you could tie a bow this nicely!"

"Hey, wait a minute, no 'oh, you got me a gift you are so sweet, Evan,'?" he said.

"No way, man. You better get me a gift for all I have to put up with you on a weekly basis." I grinned reached into my bag. "Plus I got one for you too!" I quickly put his yellow, neatly wrapped present aside his plate.

"Nice! Can I open it now?"

"No, not yet. Let's eat first. And why did you order already? I am ten minutes early. What if I had been on time?"

"Well, I was hungry, and I needed something to set the present on. I didn't just want it sitting there on an empty table. That would look stupid."

"Oh, of course!" I picked up half of the sandwich off his plate and put it on to mine after setting the red box aside.

"So how was your last final today?" Evan took a giant bite. The cheese was so gooey it hung from his lips to the sandwich. He played with the cheese trying to get it to release from the bread. When it finally released he tilted his head upward and shoved the rest of the cheese into his mouth.

"We have become way too comfortable with each other I think," I said with a disgusted look on my face.

"What?" Evan looked bewildered. "You mean because of my poor eating habits? You don't like them?" He then took a handful of French fries, dipped them in ketchup, and shoved them in his mouth, getting ketchup all over his cheeks. I tried to keep a stern and disgusted face but couldn't keep it in and ended up laughing out the water I had just sipped all over the table. Evan busted out laughing halfway choking on the food left in his mouth.

"Nice. And you said I need table manners?" he said.

"Well, I guess we can take them together."

"So, finals, girl! You didn't answer my question."

"Oh, fine. I think I did well. It didn't seem overly hard, so I guess that is a good sign, right? Are you still feeling confident about yours? You said yesterday that you felt like you aced your ethics exam. That's great!"

"Yeah, I think I did well, which will bode well for me getting that internship I want."

"Right, when do you turn in your application for that? It is for the one in Italy, right?"

"I actually have two I think I decided to apply for. One is in Italy, yes, and the other is in Germany."

"Wow, so far away. What am I going to do without you?"

"Oh, you will get by! You will have all those new friends you are making to keep you busy. Plus next year you start your major classes, so that will keep you from thinking of me," he said.

"I think you underestimate the importance you have in my life, Evan. I *will* miss you!"

"I will miss you too, but that is what e-mail is for!"

"Right, so promise me we will still do our weekly 'Hammy nights' over e-mail or something? I will still want to know what's going on with you." I suddenly realized that sounded ridiculous and became embarrassed at sounding so young and naïve.

"You're blushing! Why?"

"Well, I was just thinking I have no right to ask you that. I mean you will have this whole new life over there. You are not going to have time for some young, dumb girl over here."

"You are not just some young, dumb girl, Kate," he said. He took my hand that was lingering by my plate. "You are my best friend! That is not going to change." He let go of my hand and sat back. "Plus things for you could change just as much for me you know. You could meet someone and not want to be telling me everything anymore."

"I don't foresee that happening. Even if I did meet someone, why would that make our friendship stop?"

"Because, Kate, you can't have me as a best friend and fall in love with someone. I just don't think that would be fair to the other person. Think of it from their point of view, if you told all your secrets to me and then went home to them. That doesn't make sense."

"No, what doesn't make sense is this conversation. It has no bearing on our lives at this present moment, so let's not ruin our last "Hammy night" by talking about such things."

I picked up my sandwich and started eating. I wanted the conversation to be over. Me find someone else? Why would I do that? Did he find someone else? Was he prepping me for something?

"Okay, I will let it go for now, Kate, but you have to see that in some way we are filling the purpose of a significant other in each other's lives to maybe even an unhealthy degree. I want you to feel free to be with who you want and not be worrying that about me or what I need."

I looked up then. What was he doing? It felt like he was trying to let me go.

"Evan, you're scaring me a little. I don't want to talk about this."

"Okay, okay. I am just wanting you to feel free to do what you want."

"And what gives you any idea that I have something else I want? I love what we are together. Our friendship means everything to me. And if, and I mean *if*, either of us ever finds someone that makes us happy we will talk about this then, but to be honest I really don't know why we would talk about it then either. I disagree that we can't be friends if we are dating other people. I just don't see why things would ever have to change with us."

"You are right we shouldn't be talking about this. It doesn't matter right now anyway."

"Thank you! Now let's just enjoy our time together," I said.

The meal passed in a hurry, and before we knew it, it was 8:30 p.m. Evan was catching a 10:00 p.m. plane, and it was thirty minutes to the airport. He was already pushing it, and I didn't want him to miss his plane and the time he was looking so forward to with his family. I tapped my watch as to indicate the late hour and started to gather my things.

"Should I open my present before I go?" he asked.

"No, save it till Christmas." I put my present into my bag and stood up, dragging the bag to the edge of the booth seat.

"Okay, well, then you do the same."

"It's a deal! I hope you like it, though!"

"I know I will." He put the present in his backpack and threw it over his shoulder then grabbed me in for a hug. It was a tight and comforting hug as it always was. I loved Evan's hugs because like two puzzle pieces we just fit together. He was always so warm and smelled like Old Spice or musk. I wrapped tighter to him this time knowing I wouldn't see him again for a month. He responded by tugging a little more as well.

"Text me when you land, will you? So I know you got there okay."

"Will do, Mom! You drive careful too. I know it is not far, but people could be out doing some early celebrating."

"At eight thirty?"

"Well, you know how I am a little paranoid about car accidents."

I pulled away at that. I knew he was kidding, but I hate when he joked about the thing that hurt him the most.

He kissed my forehead and gave me a wink. "I will miss you! Be good while I am gone!"

"You too!"

He let go and grabbed my bag from the seat. "Walk me out?"

"Of course."

He walked me to my car and waited for me to pull out my keys.

"I thought I was walking you out," I said.

"Well this is more gentlemanly. Plus I need to watch you leave not the other way around."

"Oh, I see." I unlocked the car and let him open it for me.

"Okay, squirt, talk to you in a few hours."

"Bye, Evan, be safe!"

"You too!"

He closed my door. As I drove away I could see him still standing there in my rearview mirror.

I got to Charlotte's about twenty minutes later with the smell of Evan still on my red sweatshirt. I knew I wouldn't wash it the whole time he was gone.

I jumped out and grabbed my suitcase and backpack and headed inside. It was a quaint three-bedroom condo. She had just bought it a year ago brand new. It was in a nice, quiet tract in an uppity neighborhood. She didn't really know the neighbors well, but she was glad that it was a safe place for a single gal to be. Her dad always worried about her living alone. Both her and Amy were pretty girls, but Charlotte was unique in her beauty. There was something unusual about her that made her stand out above the rest. Maybe it was the fact that she had gorgeous red hair when the rest of her family had brunette. I got to the door with excitement swelling in my stomach at that thought that Amy might be there already. I hadn't seen her since the one night we got to spend together on Thanksgiving evening before I headed back to school.

Before I could even knock, the door flew open, and Amy grabbed me into a hug.

"Kate! You made it! So good to see you! Now we get to spend some quality time catching up!"

"Amy! So good to see you too! How was the drive?"

"It was good, uneventful!" Amy released her embrace and grabbed my suitcase and closed the door behind me. She turned around and started heading to the bedroom we would be sharing for the next couple of weeks. "Charlotte is at the store getting a few things. She will be home in about ten minutes. So how are you? How was Hammy night with Evan?"

"Good! Weird at first, but good."

"Weird at first? Why?"

"He was going off on some tangent about our relationship not being a good idea if we were ever to find significant others. I was getting the idea he had had a talk with you, Charlotte, and Denise."

"Huh." Her lack of response got me thinking she was hiding something from me.

"How were your finals?" she asked.

"Good, I think I did well. How about you?" I replied, letting her change the subject.

"I think I did well." She said as we entered the bedroom. Amy flung my suitcase on my bed and opened it up ready and able to help me unpack. She never liked to put off what could be done right then. The room was as cozy as ever. It was small but bigger than my dorm room. Charlotte had put two twin beds with matching white and blue bedding. There was one black six-drawer dresser to the right of the beds and a nice-sized closet on the front wall. From the center of the room hung a petite, crystal chandelier, which reflected beautifully off the barrage of black-and-white family photos hanging on the left wall. I felt at home at once. Over the summer Amy and I had spent three months sharing the room together, and now in only a few minutes I felt like I had never left.

"Anything crazy going on at Santa Barbara?" I asked.

"You know I won't answer any questions about Sam or Jay or Paul, but I can honestly tell you I haven't seen any of them. Different circles you know. So I couldn't even tell you anything if I wanted to."

"That is not what I was getting at. I just wanted to know how it was, that's all." Although now that she mentioned it, I was curious about how Sam was.

"Sure you did. Off-limits topic, okay? Unless a piano so happens to fall on Jay's head, and the Lord has graciously granted my prayers for revenge—"

"Amy!" I said.

"Oh, I am just kidding! You know that! I pray for his salvation every day, not his demise."

"Right. I don't believe that either."

"Love those who hate you has to be one of the hardest commandments to follow!" she said.

"Tell me about it! Luckily I am not there anymore because God knew I couldn't handle that!"

"Yes, he does only give us what we can handle, and I find that to be true every day. Speaking of that, how are things with the accountability group you have been going to? You started one with Denise right?"

"Yeah, her and two other girls. We are working through Romans right now. It is really nice." I grabbed my clothes and steadily threw them into drawers while Amy put my shoes in the closet.

"Glad to hear it!"

"So what are our plans for these next few weeks? Charlotte said your parents are coming into town on Christmas Eve? Which isn't for three days, so what shall we do till then?"

"Well, tomorrow we are having a Christmas party. Charlotte thought it would be nice to have a little get-together for her friends that don't have plans for Christmas."

"Sounds like fun. Are they people from church? Do I know them?" I threw my now empty suitcase in the closet and went to sit on my bed.

Amy tossed off her slippers and sat on her bed with crisscrossed legs. "I think you may know a few of them from church, but some of these people are from the singles group she attends as well and a couple of people from the *Les Miserables* cast."

"Cool! I will get to meet some of the cast. That's exciting!"

"Yeah, Charlotte says they are all nice. We are going to make an authentic German meal of Roladen and potato balls. My mom was born and raised in Germany, so she raised us on German food, and Charlotte loves to serve it for others."

"Sounds great! I can honestly say I have never eaten German food before."

"Well, then you are in for a treat! Charlotte sees this as a great opportunity just to be a light for Christ amongst her coworkers since she will have others from church here, so hopefully it goes well."

"I will pray that all works out the way she is intending."

We heard the garage door slam. "Hello!" Charlotte shouted. Amy and I raced to the kitchen like little kids who were trying to see what treats mom had brought us from the store.

I ran up and gave Charlotte a hug and helped to unload the groceries from the bags while she finished unloading the rest from the car. We spent the rest of the night drinking hot cocoa in front of her quaint, white-trimmed fireplace and talking about school, finals, friends, and our growth in the Lord. We all woke up early in the morning still lying in front of the fireplace realizing we all must have fallen asleep while talking. I suddenly realized that I didn't pay attention to Evan's "got here" text and ran to my room to check my phone. There waiting for me was his text that said, "Got here safe Mom." My heart flipped just by reading his silly text. Keeping a cap on my emotions was always harder than I intended.

Amy walked in. "Text from Evan?"

"Yeah, he was just letting me know he got there okay."

"Kate, do you mind if I talk to you seriously for a minute?"

"Yeah, of course. But if this is another lecture about Evan, then I really don't want to hear it right now."

"Well, no and yes. I think I am just a little confused." Amy grabbed my hands and led me over to my bed sitting us both down. "I know how much you care for Evan, and I really have no problem with him whatsoever. He seems like a really nice guy from what you have told me and from what I know of him from Emily. I know you have told me how much you help each other through times of rockiness in your spiritual lives. Having someone who you can be totally yourself with is so important. But I have to say that Evan is right to talk to you about changing your relationship when significant others come into play *if* you aren't going to choose each other for that. I really can't understand why you aren't choosing each other for that, but if you both have decided not to, then I can understand Evan's point. Which has always been my point as well."

I sat there playing with the edge of a blanket trying to decide how to respond. "It's not that we haven't chosen each other to be that person. I think for me I just know that is not how he sees me. It's like my old relationship with Paul. I think he sees me as a sister and best friend and not someone he could fall in love with. It is that old saying, 'I love you, but I am not *in* love with you.'"

"I am not so sure you are right, but I am not going to play Sam's part in this. I think you are wise to protect yourself to some degree, but have you guys ever talked about it? How do you really feel about Evan? If he asked you to be with him as his girlfriend, would you want that?"

"Well, no, we have never talked about our relationship in that way. I would think that if that's what Evan wanted he would let me know somehow. Plus he just got out of a year-and-a-half relationship with Emily, so I don't think he is even thinking of it that way. I mean he hasn't even dated anyone as far as I know. And if he came to me and said he wanted us to take our relationship to a dating level I don't know what I would say. I love Evan, and I don't want what we have to change. I wouldn't want to ruin our relationship for anything. That is why when he talks about us not being able to be the same in each others lives when or if we ever have other relationships that just makes me not want to find anyone else."

"So you would be willing to be Evan's best friend the rest of your life and never find love of your own?"

"Yes...well, no, I don't know, Amy. Seriously I don't even want to think about it. I don't know why this is coming up so much right now. Why can't I just enjoy my friendship with Evan?"

"Okay, do you want me to be completely honest?"

"Of course I want you to be honest! I could tell you are hiding something from me. What is it?"

"Okay, so you are going to think maybe this is weird or what not, since Charlotte and I have been telling you that you need to take time for you and grow and not date right now anyway, but Charlotte has found this great guy who we think would be terrific for you. Sometimes when God opens a door we have to explore it, and I think this is something you should explore."

"A guy? For me? What are you talking about? Does Evan know about this? Is that why he was talking to me like that?"

"Don't get mad now, Kate. Charlotte is just thinking about you and your happiness. There is this guy Demetri from the cast of *Les Miserables* who also has started going to her singles group. He is a Christian and is cute with an amazing voice. Charlotte has spent a lot of time with him because of her doing his makeup and him attending her group and thinks you two would make a perfect match."

"You still aren't answering me, Amy. How does Evan know, and why would he know before me?"

"Charlotte knows how much Evan means to you, and she wanted to introduce Demetri to you at the party, so she wanted to make sure it was okay with Evan first. So she called him."

"She called Evan?" I couldn't help but raise my voice. "And said what? What did he say?"

"I guess he said that he was happy for you, that you two are just great friends and that if Charlotte thought this guy could make you happy, then she should definitely introduce you. But that's when the discussion of your relationship came up. Charlotte thought it might scare away potential significant others for both of you if they felt they had to compete with your friendship."

"She had no right to talk to Evan. What my relationship is with him is my business, and she has not right to intervene in any way."

"I wasn't trying to intervene in your relationship with Evan. I promise." Charlotte walked through the door with a melancholy expression. "I was actually trying to be respectful of him and his potential feelings for you. Which I now know to be very caring. He does love you, Kate, but he loves you enough to know that you are both headed in different directions, and he wants you to be happy."

"You still had no right. I understand everybody just wants me to be happy, but does anyone think that maybe I'm happy right now?"

"No, we know you are happy, Kate, and happiness doesn't rely on any relationship except the one with the Lord," Amy said.

"But," Charlotte said, "I truly feel like Demetri might be that special guy meant for you. If Evan isn't the one, then maybe you can make room to see if Demetri is."

"That is a lot of pressure on some guy I haven't even met yet, and I think it might be too early to blow off what Evan and I have."

"Now you are confusing me more, because you have always said that Evan and you are just meant to be friends. Now you're saying that there hasn't been enough time to develop something else. You said you didn't want something else." Amy was exasperated. I could tell I was aggravating her, and I didn't want to do that, but I couldn't let them dictate my life either.

"I don't know what I want really. I love having Evan in my life, and I have made myself not feel more for him because I'm scared of what happened with Paul. I don't want to go down that road again." Tears started to well in my eyes, and I was on the verge of losing it again.

Amy scooted closer and put her arm over my shoulder. Charlotte came and sat on the other side of me with her hand on my knee.

"We totally get that, Kate, and that's why I think it might be better to distance yourself a little from Evan and explore something new. Something and someone that might really be a good thing in your life. Not that Evan is not, but if you are constantly tormented in your relationship with him because it reminds you of Paul and because you constantly have to deny feelings for him because he doesn't feel the same, then maybe it is time to start letting go and find something else." Charlotte said.

I had to admit that part of what they were saying hit home. I knew I was tormenting myself to some degree with Evan, but how could I let go of him even just a little? I couldn't. I wouldn't. Not even if I did meet this Demetri. "I understand what you are saying, I really do. Just understand how much Evan means to me. Please."

"We do understand." Charlotte squeezed my knee. "But that doesn't mean that there isn't something better. Please just be opened minded. He is coming to the party tonight. So just see what you think okay?"

"Okay." I looked up at them. "I will meet this Demetri, but I won't promise anything."

"Good enough," Amy said.

We spent the rest of the day getting ready for the party. Cooking, cleaning, and decorating. Charlotte was excited to have her first real social gathering at her new home.

At 5:00 p.m. we started getting ourselves all dolled up. I put on one of Charlotte's black, knee-length, twirly skirts; a ruffled, white button-up shirt, which she made me tuck in; and I adorned it with a black-and-white pearly belt that hung low on my hips. She then did my makeup in what she called "holiday fare," which consisted of a smoky shimmery eye, pink shimmery cheeks, and a nude lip. I had to say it looked quite good as only Charlotte could do and was longing for Evan to see me like that. We hadn't talked since his text. I had texted him later in the day just to say thanks for the "got here" text and to tell him to have a great time at home. He didn't text me back. Maybe he knew I was meeting Demetri tonight. Would he be jealous? Or was he giving me space to get to know someone else?

At 6:00 p.m. people started to arrive. I knew them from the church. Charlotte had put on some smooth jazz holiday music and lit candles all throughout the house. It looked like a winter wonderland.

I went into the kitchen to help with getting the last of the meal together and to help get the dishes ready for serving.

"Kate," I heard Charlotte's chipper voice behind me. Somehow I knew this was the point where I would turn around and meet Demetri. I had a sudden pit in my stomach, and my thoughts turned to Evan. I took a deep breath and turned around.

"Kate, these are my friends from *Les Mis*. This is Claudia, Ashely, Killian, and this is Demetri."

I shook each hand as she said their names and hesitated at Demetri. I looked up and with a shy smile said, "Hi, it's nice to meet some of the talented people Charlotte gets to work with." I took Demetri's hand and shook it lightly. His hand was tender to the touch and warm, and his long fingers overtook my hand. As I looked up, he had a curious look in his eye, one that caught me off guard. He then smiled a gorgeous smile, and I let the look pass. He was quite tall, with a thin but muscular build. He had light-brown hair that was cropped short. He wasn't striking like Evan, but he was cute, definitely nice to look at.

"It is a pleasure to finally meet you, Kate." His voice was surprising low. It pulled me in at once.

"Can I help you out in here?" he said as the others grabbed a drink and headed back into the living room.

I glanced at Charlotte who gave me a quick wink and came into the kitchen. "Why don't you guys go relax? This is my dinner party after all, and I need to finish up the last-minute details. Dinner should be ready in just a few minutes." She pushed us out of the kitchen, and I took that as my cue to go and get to know Demetri.

I moved out of the kitchen and took a seat at one of the bar stools at the breakfast bar. Demetri followed my lead.

"So, Demetri, what part do you have in *Les Mis*?"

"Actually I play Marius. Do you know the story of *Les Mis*? Have you ever seen it?"

"Yes, actually when I was in junior high my drama club took a trip to see it. It quickly became a favorite of mine. It's impressive at a young age to have an integral part in such a beloved musical."

"I am blessed for sure. My parents noticed my singing ability when I was quite young and exploited it well. When I was only eight I was singing national anthems at stadiums and went for my first Broadway audition as Oliver in *Oliver Twist*. I actually got the part, and we moved to New York. It was the best six months of my life up to that point, and I got addicted to the theater. I was born here in LA, and my passion was to always come back here and work locally. Now here I am twenty-six and living the dream."

"Wow, seems like you have your life right where you want it." I wondered why in the heck Charlotte would think this guy was perfect for me when he seemed like he didn't need anything else in his life.

"Yes, I do, but now that I have it all, I have realized it doesn't mean anything unless I have someone to share it with. It makes me a little lonely."

Ahh, now it made sense.

"I can understand that, but I would imagine, as talented as you are, you probably have many dates, maybe even with some of these beautiful women from your cast."

"Yes, you would think that would be the case, but alas it isn't. I am a little picky about the women I date. So far nothing has really caught my eye. Until now, I would say you are beautiful in an unassuming way, Kate. Tell me more about yourself." He picked up his soda and took a sip.

I felt like he was a little cheesy, but he was a theater guy. Maybe that came with the territory. "Well, I am a sophomore at Redeemer University, although this is my first semester here. I transferred in from UC Santa Barbara. I have yet to decide a major, but I pride myself on being a good student. I had once thought of being a doctor, but now I think that might be out of reach for me, but I am sure I will come up with something soon." I could tell I was rambling and hoped he didn't think I was an idiot.

"I applaud you taking time to decide what you want to do. Sometimes I wish I had had that luxury of having a real childhood and being able to explore who I was before being thrust into what I was going to do the rest of my life. Don't get me wrong, like I said, I love what I do, but I was never given a choice. Don't take that for granted. You are young and have plenty of time to figure it out. Plus maybe you aren't meant for a career in the sense you are thinking. Maybe the Lord has something else planned for you, like being a homemaker."

I sat there a little bewildered. He seemed like a nice guy, but he seemed to have a problem phrasing his words, either that or he had no idea how to talk to a woman.

"A homemaker would be great one day when I decide I want that as my job and decide to have children. But I am only three months shy of turning twenty, so I am not even thinking of that yet. I would like to do something before having children and going that route."

"So you don't see yourself settling down soon and starting a family?" He sounded a little defeated.

"Well, not yet. I mean, I haven't really thought about that. I guess if the right person came along, but like I said I am young and feel like I have time for that later."

"I get that. I guess because I am a little older and have lived a full life already I know that doesn't give me as much pleasure as finding someone to share it all with."

I lifted my glass. "Well, here's to you finding your perfect someone to share your perfect life with."

"I will drink to that!"

He clearly didn't pick up on my tone.

I looked over at Charlotte who had a goofy grin on her face and gave me a thumbs up. She had to be kidding. He wasn't bad, but I didn't think I got him yet.

"Okay, everyone dinner is served!" Charlotte brought out the main platter filled with rolled meat and gravy. I got up and went over to the table with Demetri following close behind. I took my seat next to Amy who was at the head of the elongated table that was stretching halfway into the living room. There were ten people there, so we had to make due with sitting unusually close to each other. Demetri took his place to my right, but not before helping me push my chair in. At least he was a gentleman. Dinner was lovely and delicious. Charlotte outdid herself.

After dinner I excused myself to do the dishes with Demetri volunteering to help. I was irritated at first just wanting to use the time to think and be alone. I was not a people-person *per se* and was getting tired of being flanked by this guy. However, I was completely surprised when it turned out to be a nice time. He was polite and caring. He asked me about my family and when I told him how dysfunctional it was he said, "Well, you could have parents who use you for fame and fortune."

"Is that what's happening to you?"

"Yes, or at least I believe it to be. My father lost his job when I was six. He struggled for months trying to find something to provide for us. After getting compliments about my singing and acting ability from my teacher at school during a school play, my parents quickly realized they could be raising a potential goldmine. Only a few short months later, a star was born."

"Oh wow, Dememtri, I'm sorry."

"It turned out to be a good thing. I liked performing, but it is difficult knowing my parents were supportive just because I could splash some spotlight on them and shower them with lavish things."

"Why do you then?" I asked.

"Good question. What won't we do for the love of our parents?"

I felt sorry for him then. I started seeing him like me. A tortured soul trying to figure out the ins and outs of life. Were we all this way? Seemed like it. Not once did he mention his finding the Lord, though, so after dinner while we were all playing charades, I took the opportunity to ask Demetri about his testimony. We were sitting at the dining table toward the back of the living room, not really partaking in the game.

"So, Demetri, you go to Charlotte's singles group at church, is that right? When did you come to know the Lord?"

"Well, I was brought up in the church. My parents always seemed to find some new church for us to try if we were traveling with a musical. He has always just been part of my life."

"Oh," I said. It was simpler than I had expected. Not that everyone needed to have some sort of life-altering time where they came to know the Lord. I looked at Charlotte knowing how her and Amy had grown up with her father being a terrific pastor and Charlotte never gone through a rebellious time, and she was a terrific daughter of the Lord. "Well, from what you had said about your parents,

I didn't think they were Christians. I am sorry I assumed you were not from a Christian home."

"They try, as we all do. I do admit they should put more faith in the Lord and less on these worldly things, but at the same time we are here for now and have to live the way we can, so for what they have gone through I think they are doing pretty well."

"I am sorry if I offended you. I didn't mean anything by it. We all have our sins that we need to work through. None of us will reach perfection like Christ while here of course! We are all a sanctification in process."

"Yes, well said. Having grown up the way I did makes me a little edgy about people's judgments. I admit that my family is not the best at their relationship with God, but they do what they are supposed to do, and I think they will be rewarded for that. I feel like there are many other people out there, like yourself, who are worse off than I am or my family is. Yes, they use me for money, but maybe that is why God gave me gifts, so I can support them."

"Uh, right." It wasn't quite what I meant, but I let it go.

It was suddenly my turn to do charades, yet I had no interest in getting up there and making a fool of myself. Seeing my hesitation, Demetri grabbed the clue from my hand and said he would go for me.

He got up and blew it out of the water. People guessed what it was by the time he reached the first word's first syllable. As he was coming to sit back down Charlotte asked him if he and the other cast members would sing some Christmas carols. They quickly obliged. We spent the next hour singing carols and listening to the beautiful voices of the four talented cast members.

Soon it was time for everyone to say good-bye. Demetri asked me if I would walk him out. I looked over at Amy who quickly handed me my coat. We walked outside, and he led me to his dark-blue BMW that was parked only three spots down from mine. He unlocked his door then turned to me as I stood on the sidewalk.

"It was a real pleasure to get to know you tonight, Kate. I would love to be able to see you again, maybe without so many people around. Would you do me the honor of accompanying me to dinner tomorrow night?"

"Oh, tomorrow, um. I'm not sure what we are doing tomorrow. I have yet to ask the girls what our plans are. What if we plan for next Friday the twenty-eighth? Will you be in town for the holidays?"

"Oh, sure. Yes, the twenty-eighth would work. I am staying in town of course because of the play."

"Oh, right." Of course he was staying in town; that was why Charlotte and Amy's parents were coming. "Okay, great. Well, then I guess I will see you next Friday. Why don't you call me the night before to confirm and make plans on where we should meet?" I was hoping maybe I could make an excuse that night as to why I wouldn't go out with him.

"Why don't I come and get you around noon and where we go will be a surprise. Okay?"

"Noon?"

"Yeah, I have a performance that night at eight, so I have to be at the theater at four, but noon will give us enough time."

"Oh, right. Sorry, I keep forgetting. Noon it is then." I was slightly discouraged that he wouldn't be calling me to confirm so I could cancel. But I was glad that it would be over before four that evening.

I went back inside suddenly feeling guilty. Evan's gorgeous face came to mind. I missed him, and there I was making a date. I didn't want to go, but maybe Amy was right, and I should just try. Yet I could already feel what they were saying about my relationship with Evan needing to change because I felt like I was cheating on him by going on this date with Demetri.

"So! What did you think? Did he ask you out?" Amy asked as soon as I stepped foot into the house.

"You guys are not very sly you know, and yes, he asked me out. We are going to go out at noon next Friday, but he won't tell me what we're doing."

"A surprise! How romantic!" Charlotte was picking up the last of the glasses and putting them in the dishwasher.

"Yeah, I guess. We'll see."

"Try not to sound so excited," Amy said. She blew out the candles around the living room.

"To be honest I am not really excited. I would rather not go out at all. I feel like I am cheating on Evan somehow."

"See, Kate, I told you," Amy said.

"Yes, you told me, and all it makes me want to do is not go on the date with Demetri. I'm not sure why you think we're meant to be, Charlotte. I don't really see it."

"You aren't allowing yourself to see it because you're so worried about Evan. Just give it a chance, okay?"

"Okay! I will give it a chance, but I am not promising anything. And I'm not sure it's just because of Evan. I don't think I would be into Demetri anyway. He seems a little…I don't know. I just can't put my finger on it."

"That's just because you don't know him well yet. I have spent a lot of time with him, and he warms up more once you get to know him. He may seem a little conceited at this point to you, am I right? But that will change you will see." Charlotte came over and sat on the couch satisfied with her clean up attempt.

"I don't know if it's conceited or what, but I said I would give it a shot and I will, but please no talking to Evan about this okay. I know you already mentioned this, but no more! Okay!"

"Okay, we promise!" Amy said as she looked at her sister. "Right, Charlotte?"

"Right! Okay, now let's go get some sleep. I am exhausted." Charlotte turned off the lamp in the living room as she left the kitchen, heading to go upstairs to her room. Amy and I turned off the hall light and went to get ready for bed. We didn't say much else but good night and fell quickly asleep.

Christmas came and went and so did Amy and Charlotte's mom and dad. It was great to have them around. They felt like real parents to me. So caring and loving. They were always looking out for what was best for their daughters and continually praying for everything in their lives. They had started praying for me too, they had mentioned, and I was deeply touched.

Soon it was time for my date with Demetri. I hadn't mentioned him to Evan nor did Evan ask about him when we talked on Christmas. He was having a great time with his family, as we both knew he would. He was thoroughly enjoying his time away from school, but not from me he said. Even though it had only been a few days we both admitted it seemed like weeks. I could sense a change in his voice however. A hesitancy like he wanted to ask me something but didn't. I suspected it was about Demetri, but I was relieved when he didn't bring anything up. Maybe because I acted like everything was normal, and he was waiting for me to say something but knew I wouldn't.

We opened our gifts to each other over the phone. He loved the 1901 copy of *Romeo and Juliet* that I had found in an old estate sale. It was his favorite "classic" that he loved to read. I wrote in the front of the book, "May this book bring you as much happiness as you have brought to me. Your forever friend, Kate." He had gotten me a silver Celtic-style cross with a white gold chain. I was in awe and swore I wouldn't wear anything else. I missed him so much then my heart ached, but it was good to hear his voice. We hung up after two hours, and I wore his sweatshirt that night to bed to feel like he was there with me. How would Demetri ever have a chance when I was so attached to Evan? The girls' point was being made in a severe way. I could tell they were more excited about my date than I was. They had been talking about my wardrobe choices and choosing coordinating makeup, handbags, and shoes. I didn't know anything about that stuff anyway, and I was not liking having to worry about it now. Evan saw the fact that I didn't care about such nonsense as a redeeming quality, since that was something that he always fought about with Emily.

Soon the girls had me dressed in what they called "fancy jeans"— they had jewels on the bottom pockets—an off-the-shoulder grey sweater with a coordinating grey tank top underneath, and black boots that came up over my jeans. My hair was a mess that day, so they decided a braid and a cute hat would be a great idea. I looked nothing like myself, but it all looked good, so I went with it.

Demetri came promptly at noon, and butterflies filled my stomach. They weren't excited butterflies, but nervous butterflies.

"Wow, Kate, you look great! Are you ready for a good day?" he asked. "Yeah, ready to go!" I may have tried too hard to sound excited. I grabbed my black pea coat and was out the door.

He was dressed casually as well in jeans with brown loafers and a white button-down dress shirt with a leather jacket over. He looked nice for sure, and in the daylight he was much more handsome than I had thought before in the candlelight at the Christmas party. Or maybe it was because I was truly trying to be open minded about him.

"So where are we off to?" I asked as Demetri came around to open my door for me. First the seat at dinner and now my door—at least he was putting on the appearance of being a gentleman.

"Do you mind if I don't tell you? I love surprises, so thought I would surprise you."

"Oh, sure." I was a little anxious at this. I hardly knew the guy, and there I was in his car headed to an undisclosed location. But I could trust Charlotte, and I felt as if I could trust Demetri, so I went with it.

We drove for about forty-five minutes, which gave us more time to get to know each other. He liked classical music. Everything from Mozart to Vivaldi. I loved the classics, so it was fine, but somehow I found myself wondering if this was all a front. Could this guy be for real?

He asked a lot of questions about my likes and dislikes, trying to get to know me better. It was a nice and cordial ride and the conversation flowed well.

We pulled up into a parking garage, and Demetri jumped out. He ran around and helped me out of the car.

"Where are we?" I asked, scanning the garage for a sign.

"You will see. I hope you like it!"

We walked up two flights of stairs out onto the main street where we walked down for about one-fourth mile. We turned into a little quad that was sparkling with a water fountain when I saw a poster for *Les Mis*. Were we at the theater? I looked up at him as he continued walking toward the theater. I hesitated a little.

"Come on!" he said coming back for me and taking my hand.

"What are we doing here? Is this your theater?"

"Yes. You will see."

His hand was warm and tender, and I felt suddenly comfortable and excited to see what he had planned. We walked into the theater through a side door and out onto the stage. There sitting in the middle of the stage was a small table set with two silver domed trays and a small bouquet of roses in the middle. To the side of the table was a champagne chiller with a bottle of what I was assuming was champagne sitting in it. I was immediately thrilled and taken aback that he would go through this much trouble for me. But then turned to the thought of the champagne in the bucket. I couldn't drink! It wasn't just because I was underage. I didn't want to revisit old memories and feelings.

He drew me over to the table and pulled out my chair. I took off my coat and handed it to him as I took my seat.

"What do you think?" he said as he pulled out the bottle from the bucket.

"This is amazing, Demetri! I don't know what to say."

"Thank you would be a start! Would you like some sparkling cider?"

"Yes, I would love some cider." I was completely relieved that it wasn't champagne. "Sparkling cider was a good choice."

"Thank you. I don't drink, so it seemed like an appropriate alternate."

Part of me wondered why he didn't drink. Was it from religious conviction or from just not liking the stuff? But I decided to leave it since it wasn't important anyway.

He lifted the dome lids to reveal a beautiful red lobster sitting under each. He went all-out, I could see.

"This is wonderful, Demetri! Looks delicious, thank you!"

"You are more than welcome."

"I guess we will really get to know each other now, since eating lobster can be somewhat messy."

"Oh, no worries, Kate, I can teach you how to eat it politely," he said as he motioned for me to pick up my napkin and lay it in my lap.

Politely? I thought of Evan and his cheesy face from eating Moons Over My Hammy and longed to be back at our Denny's booth. But I had to shake off the thought. I promised the girls I would give Demetri a true shot.

We ate dinner with Demetri every now and then showing me how to "attend to the lobster," as he put it. The conversation was good, normal. Nothing that I thought was earth shaking, but enough to get me thinking that Demetri's perception of being a little cocky was not going to go away easily. Charlotte's thought that the more I spent with him the less cocky I would think him to be was getting me thinking I would have to spend *a lot* of time with him. You could tell he was very proud of his "craft" and himself and was willing to share it with whomever he deemed appropriate company. I was starting to get the idea that this date was more about him showing off than doing something nice for me when he announced at the end of dinner that Charlotte was bringing Amy here with a change of clothes for me, and Amy and I were staying to watch the show from the front and center seats. I was happy at the thought, however, because I loved *Les Mis*, and I hadn't seen it in so long. It was a memory I didn't mind revisiting.

We spent two hours after lunch with Demetri giving me a tour of the theater and showing me his dressing room and where he spent most of his time backstage. We then took a seat in the theater and talked about his dreams of becoming a playwright one day or moving to London and getting his masters at the University of the Arts. It sounded glorious for sure.

"I would love to share it with you truly, Kate. You seem like the kind of girl who would appreciate the arts."

"Oh, for sure. European history was always a passion of mine as was drama. I envy that you are able to smother yourself in both."

"Well, maybe you could come with me? I am even thinking of starting the fall semester there this coming August. Maybe by then we will be at the point that you will want to come with me."

"Moving a little fast aren't we, Demetri? I mean this is our first date. Plus I have school to think about. I have two more years till I am free to wander the world."

"You wouldn't need to finish school here, you could go anywhere. Plus what would you really need the education for?"

"Why wouldn't I need to finish school?"

"Well, you don't really need a college education to be a wife."

"Who says that is what I plan on being? Not all women just strive to be a wife. I am not thinking in those terms yet. I want to get an education and then find something I love to do that might even help the world in some way." I said.

"I am doing it again aren't I? Sorry! I don't mean to be putting my thoughts out there to anger you! You can do whatever you want, Kate. Whatever would make you happy."

"I really do plan on finding something that would do just that."

Charlotte came on stage with her hand in front of her eyes sheltering her from the spotlight streaming down.

"Kate? You out there?"

"Yeah. Hey, Charlotte, we are right here…front balcony. We will be right there.

"I truly am excited to see the play tonight, Demetri. I am looking forward to you playing Marius."

"I am going to do my best tonight just for you!" He picked up my hand and kissed it. I had to admit there were some things about Demetri that were very intriguing, while there were some others that absolutely enraged me.

The curtain went up right at 8:00 p.m. Amy and I had spent the three hours downtime in the greenroom drinking too much coffee and watching Charlotte do everyone's makeup. When Demetri had come in to get his done all he did was stare at me with a kind and loving eye. It freaked me out and was endearing all at the same time. When we left to take our seats he once again kissed my hand. Amy chuckled and whispered to me as we left, "I think someone has a crush on you!"

"Yeah, well, don't they all?" I said dramatically as I brushed my hair back with the back of my hand. Amy sensed my sarcasm and shoved me a little with her hand while saying, "Oh, please!"

The performance was great. Demetri was amazing, and it wasn't hard for me to fall a little more for him as I watched him on stage and listened to his magical voice. He had an amazing tone, and his range was unbelievable. Every time he was on stage, Amy would nudge me. I told her to stop it or I would end up with a bruise there. Yet I couldn't stop getting Evan into my head when I thought of Marius's character. In a way I felt like I was Eponine. I could understand her and connect with her. I was Evan's Eponine. I was the best friend who secretly loved him. But who would be Evan's Cossette? Was Demetri to be my Marius? I could see it in some ways, but the thought threw me a little. Could I be watching my Marius…or did I even have one?

When the performance concluded, we went backstage to find Demetri and Charlotte. I had to admit coming backstage to look for Demetri was exciting. It was crazy that this man whom thousands of people watch every night was interested in me. And there I was coming backstage at this beautiful theater to find him. And when I did find him he was waiting for me.

"Well? What did you think?"

"Demetri, you were amazing! It was just wonderful! I was crying! It was just breathtaking. You all did such a great job!"

He came closer and drew me into a hug. "It meant so much to me that you were there watching. I gave it my all tonight just for you."

"I could tell! Thank you!"

Demetri turned to Charlotte and Amy. "Girls, do you mind if I bring Kate home?"

"Oh, no, no, not at all take your time," Charlotte said already pushing Amy out of the green room. "We will see you at home, Kate! Don't be too late."

"Oh, but, Demetri, it is so out of your way. Seriously I can go with the girls."

"No, I am not ready to let you go yet. Please, just let me drive you home." Demetri gently caressed the back of my elbow and looked at me with innocent eyes. He knew how to play the part.

"Okay," I said turning to Charlotte, "but we won't be long behind you. Wait up for me will you?" They could sense my nervousness and quickly nodded in agreement, and with a gentle smile they left.

"Are you that adverse to spending time with me?" Demetri asked.

"No, no, that's not it. There is a lot you don't know about me, and one thing is I don't like getting home late. It makes me nervous. Especially when I am with someone I don't know very well."

"You can trust me, Kate, I promise."

"Well, we will find that out, I guess."

"Wait here, and I will go get changed and be back." He gave my arm a quick squeeze and disappeared into his dressing room. People were milling about filling their bags with their belongings and getting ready to leave for the night. I spotted Killian and Claudia and waved hello. Claudia gave me a huge smile hello and walked my way. She was still in her stage makeup and hair but was wearing her normal street clothes of jeans and a sweatshirt. I hadn't had much time to talk with her at the party, so I had no idea what part she played, but tonight I found out as I watched that she actually played the part of Cosette. This totally fit her, for she was blonde, beautiful, and petite.

"Hello, Kate, did you like the show tonight?"

"Oh my goodness, Claudia, it was terrific! You were terrific!"

"Thank you! Are you here with Demetri?"

"Um, yeah, he is going to give me a lift home."

"Nice catch you have there. He would make you very rich and happy. I have known Demetri for a long time. Actually we attempted dating for a little while, but we weren't right for each other."

"I am not really in the market for rich, but happy would be nice. Why did things not work out with the two of you?"

"I don't want to say anything against Demetri because I wouldn't want it to get back to him and ruin our chemistry for the show, but let's just say there is a particular girl he is looking for, and I wasn't it. But maybe you are."

"A particular girl? What kind would that be?" Now I was intrigued. Was this a good thing in that maybe because he was a Christian and I knew for a fact that Claudia wasn't?

"I will let you see for yourself because maybe you will fit the mold he has cut for himself. I gotta go. It was great to see you again. Take care." She waved good-bye and headed down the hall to the front of the theater.

I wasn't going to deny that her words made me slightly nervous, as did many things about Demetri. Yet somehow tonight I was definitely softening toward him. I had even begun to think I might just be a lucky girl to end up with someone like him. He definitely could take care of me in ways that would be nice. But considering I was not much into those types of things that take money, maybe that wouldn't matter. My mind still flashed back to Evan every time Demetri touched me, and my heart ached for him every time I found myself making a joke that Demetri didn't get. They definitely were different from every angle. Maybe I was just too young for Demetri, although that didn't seem to bother him.

"Ready to go?" Demetri came out of his dressing room with a fresh face and the same clothes he had on for our date.

"Yep, I am ready to go."

We walked back to his car, and he once again opened the door for me. We had a nice drive home. His car was quite luxurious, and it made it easy for me to enjoy the smooth ride. A lot nicer than the white beat up 1994 Toyota Celica I drove.

He parked two spots down from Charlotte's condo, and I could see the lights were still on in the living room. I was glad they waited up.

I looked over at Demetri, who was taking off his seatbelt so that he could get out of the car. He came around and opened my car door and helped me out. What was he doing? Did he want to come in?

"Well, I had a terrific time, Demetri. The lunch was amazing, and the show was spectacular, as were you!"

"Thank you! You were terrific company, and I really enjoyed our time together today. I was glad you got the chance to see me do what I love."

"We should do this again sometime," I said not really thinking of what I was saying. I started to walk up toward the sidewalk when Demetri grabbed my hand and pulled me back toward him. He spun me around and grabbed my other hand.

"Kate, you are beautiful. You have a lot of the qualities I am looking for in someone to share my life with. I see so much potential in you, and I have so much I could give you."

It felt like he was going to kiss me, but did I want him to kiss me? No, I didn't think that would be appropriate. I understood he was older and maybe that was how he operated, but not on a first date. Although for him it sounded like he was already planning our wedding. Which to some extent flattered me, but I just couldn't get myself to want that, not yet anyway.

"Thank you, Demetri, you have already given me a terrific day. I will say good night to you now and hope to talk to you soon." He backed away enough to give us space yet still held my hands.

"All right, I will talk to you soon." He brought both of my hands up and kissed them softly. I felt my cheeks flush as he dropped my hands and turned to walk back to the driver's side door.

I turned and began walking to the condo turning to wave goodbye as I unlocked the door and go in, but he was already pulling away.

I didn't take two steps into the door when Charlotte and Amy accosted me with questions about what I thought and how the evening went overall.

"I have to admit ladies that he was amazing tonight in the show for sure. That is enough to get any girl!" I said as I walked passed them and plopped down on the couch.

Amy sat on the couch with me, and Charlotte sat in front of the fireplace directly in front of me.

"So you like him then? I knew the two of you would hit it off." Charlotte was gleaming with pride.

"Hold it now, Charlotte, even though it seems like you and Demetri already have us married off, I need more time. I am just getting to know him and even though most of what I find is great, there is something about him…something about some of the things he says that gets me thinking I am not sure he is all he seems."

"Like what?"

"I saw Claudia tonight, and she said something that got me thinking."

"Oh, don't take anything Claudia says seriously. Because her and Demetri used to date, and she is still bitter because he dumped her, and no one dumps Claudia. I think that hurt her in more ways than one."

"Well, maybe, but she said that it takes a particular girl for Demetri. I kind of gathered that tonight as well. I almost felt like he was trying to be fatherly instead of someone who was trying to woo me."

"Fatherly? Well maybe that is because he is seven years older than you, and maybe because you are looking too hard for flaws in him so you don't have to leave Evan."

"Okay, let's not bring Evan into this because I won't leave Evan regardless."

"So are you going to see him again?" Amy asked.

"Uh, I don't know. We didn't really settle that. It was just a talk-to-you-soon type of good-bye."

"Did he kiss you?" Charlotte asked.

"No, thank goodness. No matter who it is, I am not ready for that yet."

"I agree," Amy said. "I am still not sure I am ready for that, and it has been just about three years now."

I touched Amy's feet that were propped up on the couch next to me and gave her a knowing look. She had a worse experience than me and could understand the physical aspects of relationships the way I saw them. I could always count on her for that.

"I am going to go to bed, you two. Thanks for waiting up," I said.

"Of course." Amy put her hand atop mine gave it a squeeze.

I got up and went to my room.

I pulled out my phone from my purse and saw what I expected. A text from Evan. I had felt it vibrating during the ride home and so wanted to see if it was him but knew that would be rude. I had been dying to check it since Demetri left but didn't want the girls to know.

The text read, "Hey beautiful. Happy Hammy Friday. I was thinking of you. Are you there? Miss you! How is LA? Are you enjoying the warm sunny holiday? I am drowning in the flood over here and missing the sun."

My heart sunk. It was our Hammy Friday, and I didn't even think about that or the fact that this was the first one we had missed since my first week at school. We knew we would be missing them these four weeks, but I guess I figured we would still have them over the phone. And there I was out on a date while he was texting me. I was riddled with guilt. The text was only a half an hour old, so I decided to try my luck and text him back.

"What's up shaggy?" My nickname for him because of his hair that was always hanging in his face. I went on, "Miss you too! Sunny California is just that. Sunny. I think it was 80 today. Crazy!"

I hit send and waited. No reply. So I decided to go to the bathroom and get ready for bed. I took the phone to the bathroom, but still after the ten minutes it took me to wash up there was nothing. I climbed into bed wishing I could have talked to Evan before I went to sleep and feeling as though I let him down.

The next day Demetri called bright and early and wanted to have an early picnic before his show. I was hesitant after feeling so guilty for missing Evan the previous night, but the girls convinced me to go and that I would be home in plenty of time to give Evan a call.

Once again Demetri outdid himself and took us to the Descanso Gardens where he had a picnic waiting for us on the floor inside a gazebo. A girl could get used to this.

We had a great time talking and laughing about some of the mishaps that went on in the show as well as some stories about some of the other shows he was in when he was younger. He didn't try to kiss me this time when he dropped me back off at Charlotte's. He did come and open my door again and walked me up to Charlotte's door this time, then with an old renaissance bow he was off. I entered the condo with a grin on my face to find the girls not at home. There was a note on the door to the bedroom that had stated they went shopping and I could either meet them at the mall or meet Amy at four for dinner at Islands. I actually didn't feel like either, so I texted Amy and asked her if she would just pick up sandwiches on her way home and we could have a carpet picnic in front of the fire watching *Pride and Prejudice* for the fiftieth time. She texted back that she loved the idea and would see me soon.

I had the sudden urge to call Evan but resisted. I didn't want to interrupt him. He never responded to my text, and I didn't want to be the one to call. Just then, like he was reading my mind the phone rang, and Evan's handsome face lit up the screen. My heart skipped a beat, and I answered immediately.

"Evan! Hey, sorry I missed you last night."

"Hey, there she is! Yeah, you must have had a hot date or something huh?" Was he joking, or did he know?

"Yeah, or something like that," I said. "So how are you? Are you enjoying your time with your family?"

"Oh, it is the best, Kate. It is so good to see Kaylie and Kyle. They are getting so big. They don't even look like the picture I have in my wallet anymore. I am taking more pics though, so I will show you when I get back. You will be amazed."

"It's good to hear your voice and hear you so happy!"

Suddenly I felt a weight on my shoulders. A pain deep in my heart. He was happy. Happy without me. He was planning his life. He had his family, his talent, his potential internship. Life would go on well without me. I choked up and began to ask him questions that would require great detail so I wouldn't have to talk and have him hear the tension in my voice.

"Oh, man I do miss you, Kate. Wish you were here enjoying this with me. But wait you haven't even told me. How things are with you ladies?"

"Oh, good, good, you know just hanging out. We went and saw *Les Mis* the other night."

"Oh really? How was it?

"So good! It is one of my favorites."

"It sounds like you are having as good a time as me."

"Yeah." I cleared my throat to disguise my thoughts. "So how is your dad treating you while you're there?"

He went into a long story about the complications of having a father that expected too much out of his son, and I sat patiently listening glad to have changed the subject.

"Well, I gotta get going. I promised Kyle I would play some Xbox with him. He got the new Lego Batman game for Christmas, and I have to admit I am just as addicted as he is, but let's talk soon okay!"

"Okay, have fun pretending you are five."

"Oh, you know I will!"

What was I doing? I had no idea. I had about another twenty minutes before Amy would be home, so I decided to spend it reading the Bible. I really needed some wisdom. I decided to read James again for the fortieth time and hope and pray for new insight. None came, but maybe that was because I wasn't really looking for it. I was afraid of the real answer.

Amy came home, and it was relaxing to just spend time with her watching our favorite movie and hanging out. I didn't think of Evan or Demetri, and it was great to not be burdened for a change.

During the next three weeks I divided my time like I was dividing my actual being. I was one person with Amy and Charlotte, I was another person with Demetri, and another person with Evan. When it was time to go back to school I was relieved. It meant I didn't have Charlotte and Amy's constant talks about how great Demetri was and no more having to hide Evan from them. It meant not seeing Demetri every day, which wasn't all bad. I really enjoyed most of my time with him, but to some degree it felt forced. School also meant that I could go back to my Hammy Fridays with Evan. Not to mention the added benefit of seeing Denise again and having my accountability group back that I really missed. Demetri and I said we would try to talk on the phone when we could and maybe meet somewhere the following weekend. We had seen each other after church the Sunday I was to go back to school, and we decided to have a late lunch on my way out. When we were saying good-bye, he had grabbed my hands as I leaned against my open car door and he asked, "Kate, I want to leave you knowing we have a committed relationship. This might sound high schoolish, but will you consider leaving knowing you are my girlfriend?" I was a little shocked but knew from Charlotte this was coming. I knew I needed to say no. Everything told me I wasn't ready for this yet.

"I don't think I am ready for that yet, Demetri. I am so sorry. I love spending time with you, and you are terrific, but I just think that I need more time to get to know you before I commit to you that way."

"More time? It's been four weeks. How could you need more time?"

"Well, that is the kind of gal I am I guess. I don't make commitments lightly." Truthfully, I didn't really mind commitments. I just wasn't sure I wanted to be committed to him.

"Listen, Kate, I really like you. I think we could be good together, but I won't wait around forever," he said with frustration.

"I am not asking you to, Demetri. You don't have to wait at all if you don't want. It's your life."

"You will see, Kate. You will see that you would be lucky to have me. Just wait." I could see in his eyes he took it as a challenge, as a chase, and he relished in it. He turned around and went to his car and, without looking back, drove away. I should have felt disturbed by his departure, but it left me intrigued, which was probably what he wanted.

The ride back to the dorm seemed so long, probably because I was eager to get there. To get back to my little cell. To even see Emily.

When I got back to my room, Emily was already there unpacking. I opened the door and with her girly, little scream she ran over and gave me a huge hug.

"It is good to see you, too, Emily." I laughed.

"Oh, Kate, I had the best holiday! You wouldn't believe all of the stuff I got for Christmas..." She went on for about thirty minutes about all the designer clothes and handbags she got, showing me each individual piece and how to pair it with stuff she already had. She was nice enough, however, to offer to let me borrow anything I wanted. I really had missed Emily; even though we were so different she really was a caring person. We went to the cafeteria to eat that night, and the rest of the girls caught up with us there. I saw Denise that night as well and told her how I missed her and was looking forward to our group meeting this week. We headed back to our room and finished our unpacking and getting our supplies ready for school the next day. I went to bed wishing I had heard from Evan.

The next day on my way to my English literature class, which I loved, I heard a whistling from one of the big oak trees that flanked the side of one of the school buildings. I looked toward the tree but didn't see anything and kept walking.

"Kate!" I heard someone whispering. "Kaaaate, come to the wise willow!"

I knew then it was Evan. My stomach filled with excitement, and I slowly walked to the tree with a huge smile on my face. As I peered around the tree I saw no one. Confused, I started looking around the tree like a little puppy dog trying to find its bone. Suddenly Evan dropped down from the tree directly in front of me. I screamed and fell back, landing on my tailbone. Evan stood there laughing his head off.

"You should have seen your face! Classic! You didn't think to look up?"

"Oh, seriously, Evan, if I wasn't so glad to see you I would smack you." He held out his hand and helped me up pulling me into his arms for a bear hug.

"It is really good to see you! It seems like forever since I got to see your face! Even if it was twisted up like some scared baby," he said "I think you have been hanging out with your nephew too long!" I said, while reaching to pick up my backpack off the ground. Evan reached down at the same time, and we bumped heads. We both started laughing this time.

"Oh, I really missed you!" he said, while rubbing his head.

"So are we on to reconvene for our Hammy night on Friday?"

"Definitely! Are you off to class?"

"Yes, I have English lit right now. We are actually studying *Hamlet*. I am really excited."

"Sounds like it. Well, I won't hold you up. I will see you Friday, okay?"

"Okay!" I watched him walk off toward the dorms. I couldn't move. I just stood there watching him. The sun was hitting his dark hair as it bounced and moved in the wind. He had cut his hair over the break. Not much, but the back was nice and groomed, and the top was a little shorter to where it would probably just hang above his eyebrow now when the pieces would fall out of place. I imagined him sitting across from me in our booth with his hair falling the way it does from time to time and thought I would miss how I always had the thought to brush it away from his eyes. But the difference did mature him slightly. He didn't look so boyish, which wasn't a bad thing. I shook my head and realized I needed to get to class, but knew I would be thinking of Evan the whole time, which was too bad since I really liked *Hamlet*.

After class I ran back to my room to get some things before meeting Emily for dinner at the campus deli. I stepped inside the door and felt for one second I had the wrong room. On my bed was a huge white box with a red bow on top. It looked like one of those flowers boxes I always saw on TV. I did a double-take, realizing it was my room and my bed the box lay upon. I went closer to the box and dropped my bag. I sat there for a few minutes just staring at the box, not certain I wanted to open it. What if it was from Demetri? I wanted it to be from Evan, but knowing it wouldn't be, I couldn't get myself to open the box.

Emily stormed in then. "Hey! Good you're here. I was afraid I was going to miss you. Some of the girls decided they wanted to order from that new pizza place and have it delivered to the quad for dinner. Are you up for it? It is such a beautiful night. What is up with the weather? But I have to say I like it…"

I didn't answer as Emily rambled on getting a change of clothes appropriate for a quad pizza picnic. Emily finally realized I was just standing staring at my bed and came over.

"What is the matter?"

"What is this, Kate? Do you have an admirer? Why haven't you opened it yet?"

"Um…I don't know. I guess I am just stunned to see something on my bed."

"Oh, I can't stand it, can I open it for you?"

Knowing it was most likely from Demetri, I didn't mind. "Sure, go ahead," I said as I moved a little to the side and Emily slid the box closer to her. She tore off the red bow and opened the box. Inside were two-dozen gorgeous red roses with a crystal vase wrapped up in tissue underneath.

"Oh, gosh, Kate these are magnificent! Oh, here is the card, let's read it." She grabbed the card and read it aloud. "'Here is hoping your first day back at classes was terrific. Can't wait to see you this weekend. With my love, Demetri.'

"Ah! Kate! You have so much to spill. Who is Demetri? Why is he sending his love?" She was squealing now and was overjoyed. Was she happy to see there was someone in my life that wasn't Evan, or would she even care about that now? Then realizing what this meant, if Emily knew about Demetri, then Evan wouldn't be far behind. She would probably make it a point to tell him. I would have to mention him on Friday after all even though I didn't want to.

I proceeded to fill Emily in on some of the details about Demetri. She about fainted when she found out who he was and said I was the luckiest girl in the world. I should have felt the same way. She was so excited for me she took the roses into the bathroom for me and arranged them. They were beautiful and breathtaking for sure.

"Okay, I am going to head down to the quad and wait for the pizza guy. Meet us down there when you call your man and say thank you." And with that she left me alone with my flowers.

She was right; I should've called him and thanked him, but it was a call I didn't really want to make. Why didn't I feel lucky? Why couldn't I make myself fall for him as he was falling for me? Maybe with time I would. I picked up my cell and dialed Demetri's number. I felt a relief when he didn't pick up. I left him a very polite message thanking him profusely for the gorgeous flowers. I realized after I hung up that I was getting better at this acting thing in real life! My drama teacher would have been proud.

I went down to dinner where the girls all kept asking me questions about Demetri. Obviously Emily wasted no time in telling them. I think she was more proud of who I was seeing than I was. I kept telling them that we were just seeing where things would go for right now and we were not anything serious or in anything committed.

"You better snatch that up quick, Kate. That doesn't come around every day!" Lisa said. I had to admit they were talking me into it a little bit. They were right about him taking care of me. That was one thing he definitely could do, but did I need or want that? Maybe it was just that that was turning me off. Maybe I didn't want someone to take care of me, but someone to live a life equally with. Someone who would help me grow in my relationship with the Lord and share in life's loves and trials. Could I see Demetri doing that? When I got back to my room that night there was a message from Demetri saying he was going to pick me up Saturday for another special date. I texted him quickly saying I was looking forward to it, when I really wasn't sure if I was.

Friday came quickly, and I couldn't have been more excited. It was Evan's and mine first Hammy date since coming back from break. I grabbed my purse and went to my car almost skipping due to happiness. When I got into the driver's seat and started the car I realized there was a piece of bright yellow paper flapping in my windshield. My heart dropped at the thought it might have been from Demetri, but when I opened the note it was from Evan:

> Hey! I thought since this is our first Hammy date back we would switch it up a little bit. I am grabbing us some food, meet me at the Hilltop picnic area.

I immediately loved the idea and was off. I had heard Hilltop was a beautiful place. It was set atop the hill behind our school. I could take a little trail and walk up to it, but since it was getting late, and I was still averse to being anywhere off campus alone, I decided to drive. I was excited to be going there with Evan. It would be a lovely change to our norm and a great way to relax at the end of a long week back at school.

As I parked the car next to Evan's I was at ease knowing he was already there and I wouldn't have to be there waiting alone. I was not as excited to see that there were two other cars in the parking lot, knowing that meant we'd have to be sharing our space with other people. I got out of the car and headed up the tree-lined path. The smell of the roses and lilies that flanked the trees filled my nostrils, and the twinkling of the lights above the trees captured my sight. I felt like I was walking into heaven. It was beautiful even at dusk of night. Why hadn't I come here before? I had known and heard about it since moving here, yet this was my first time coming here. But being here now I knew it wouldn't be my last, but was excited my first was here with Evan.

I continued to follow the tree and rose-lined, 100-foot trail up to the small park. It had beautiful rose bushes, plants of all kinds, and trees that opened up to a gorgeous view of the city. It had five picnic tables and two grills and a gorgeous fountain in the middle of it all.

I saw Evan sitting at a table across the area on the other side of the fountain away from the other two groups. They all looked blissfully happy, and I couldn't help smiling, not minding their presence after all. I passed by the fountain giving it a second look. It was a small replica of the Trevi fountain, and it made me think of how I longed to go to Italy and just wander looking at the beautiful history, art, and architecture. My mind flashed to Demetri and how he told me with him I would have this, my dreams fulfilled. But would they be fulfilled in more than a worldly way? I glanced up at Evan who was looking at me bewilderingly and got up to come meet me at the fountain.

"Hey! Fountain more appealing than me, huh? I just remembered you haven't been here before. For a second I was wondering why you were looking like Alice just stepping into Wonderland."

"This is amazing, Evan. Thank you for thinking of doing this. I love it here! I really can't believe I haven't made it up here before. Especially since I could just walk up here."

"Well, if you like it here that much maybe we should make this our new meeting place. Hammy's are starting to get a little old, to be honest, especially since you *never* finish your half, and I am stuck eating most of it every week. I have to admit the last four weeks of no Denny's has been pleasant."

"I have to agree. I was excited to know we were going to someplace new, and I can't say I will ever get tired of this place. So what did you bring us to eat?" I peered around him to our table seeing only paper bags from Trader Joes.

"Well, let's go see," he said, taking my hand and leading me over to the table. "Okay, it is nothing outrageous, but my sister loves this stuff, and I ship it off to her every chance I get." He pulled out pitas and humus, mangoes, and some generic Oreos called Joe Joes. It all looked much more appetizing than the eggs, ham, and cheese from Denny's.

"This looks delicious," I said.

Evan laid everything out, handing me a napkin and a water bottle and some pitas. He then ripped his pita up and started dipping it in the humus, and I quickly followed suit.

"So how was your week?" he asked with his mouth full of humus. His manners never filled me with more joy than they did now. For most people they would be a turn off, but I loved that he felt so comfortable to be himself with me, like we promised we would be. And now, having had so many opportunities to dine with Demetri, it was slightly refreshing not to have to watch my manners either.

"It was good, you know, school. Nice to be back, though, I do have to say that. I missed being in the comfort of my own room, even missed Emily."

"Your break must have been a doozy then!"

Was he wanting me to make reference to Demetri? No, I didn't feel like bringing those two worlds together yet.

"Yeah, well, let's just say I am fighting even more demons now than when I left."

"What is going on? From what I heard I thought you would have a fabulous holiday." I could tell he was curious, and he wanted to ask me right out about Demetri.

"I know what you are referring to, Evan, and I really don't want to talk about it. Not right now anyway."

"Look, Kate, I know from our last conversation before break I made things a little awkward, but Charlotte had just called me a couple hours before, and I was...I don't know, a little taken aback. I didn't know what to say about it. I mean of course there is nothing going on between us. I love you too much to have something ruin that. And now having time to think over break I have come to realize that your friendship means too much to me to let it go because you start dating. I mean who says I can't be great friends with whoever this is? It would be great if we could find people who we could all get along and hang out with."

"Of course that would be great, Evan, and I would love that, but over the break I started to kind of see what Charlotte was getting at. I mean to be honest I think I would be somewhat jealous of whomever you dated…not of course because of anything romantic," I said, "but because they would be taking the time I have with you away from me. They would become the one you are yourself with, and there would be no place for me left in your life."

"I can't see that happening, Kate. But maybe you have different insight. I mean now that you are dating Demetri, maybe you are seeing that he is the one you want to confide in."

"Dating is a strong word. Demetri and I hung out a little over the break, but that was it. We aren't anything serious for sure."

"Okay, no reason to get huffy about it. I get it!"

"No, I don't mean it that way really. I just don't want you to get the wrong idea."

"Why not? Don't you like him?"

"Sure…I mean he is nice…I am just not sure he is right for me."

"That's not what Charlotte thinks."

"Yeah, well I don't live my life by what Charlotte thinks. Plus I think she wishes he were perfect for her. I mean why doesn't she go for him if he is so perfect? Right? Why is she pawning him off on me?"

"From what I can tell, Charlotte is just trying to do what she thinks is best for you. She and Amy love you like their own sister, and they think that this guy would be great for you. There is nothing wrong with that from Charlotte's end. But if you don't think he is right for you, then there is nothing making you date him."

"I know, of course there is nothing making me date him. This is where I am having my troubles, to be honest."

"And that is all I want you to be with me! Still!" he interrupted.

"Evan, you are the only person right now I feel that I can be truly myself with. To some extent that is the problem…I don't feel like I can be myself with Demetri. I feel like he is fathering me, and it just turns me off. Yet, on the outside he seems like the perfect catch. He's rich, up-and-coming, a Christian, seems to be a nice guy."

"Hmm." Evan looked down and picked at his plate of food.

"But I feel like I am forcing it."

"Well…it hasn't been that long, maybe you just need to give it some time."

"Now you do sound like Charlotte."

"Sorry, I guess I just don't know what to say. I want to see you happy. You really deserve to be happy, and I hope you find everything you are looking for."

I wanted to take his hand then and tell him *he* was what I was looking for, but I couldn't. I just kept having flashbacks of Paul. And why would Evan want me when I obviously wasn't what he was looking for in a significant other?

"Thanks, Evan, and I hope the same thing for you. But to be honest I am happy, right where I am. In fact sometimes I think right now it is better to be on my own. I mean some days it is just plain hard to make it through the day. I am still trying to work on my relationship with a God, who I am not sure even is calling me."

"Why would you say that, Kate? Of course He is. I mean look at where you are now compared to a year ago."

I contemplated that for a minute and then shook it off not wanting to relive it.

"No, I know, I know. I just feel like some days it is so much work to be dedicated to Him. I feel like some days it is one sided. I mean I don't feel Him. I don't…" I put my head down on the table. "I don't know."

"Believe me, I know exactly what you are going through. You just need to grow. You are right. Maybe this isn't the time for romance in your life…unless it is with someone who can spur you on with your relationship with God. Help you with it."

"Yeah, well I am not really sure if that is where Demetri's head is at. I can't really pinpoint what his relationship with God is. I feel like he is more about looking a certain way than really being true to what he believes. Like the saying goes, talking the talk but not walking the walk."

"Well, unfortunately that is more common than you think. It is hard to dedicate your life to the Lord. But once you know that it is truth, it gets easier. Once you really learn who God is, it gets easier. Of course I am still trying to figure it out. I still have my own things to deal with."

"We all do, Evan."

"Yes, we do. Don't be so hard on yourself."

"Sorry, I don't mean for this to be all somber. It is our first time back. Let's not talk about Demetri or anything anymore. I want to focus on you...tell me how your break was. I want to see those pictures of your niece and nephew."

He pulled out the pictures from his wallet, and with utter devotion and pride he talked for almost over an hour about his treasured family. It was great to see him smile and be so excited. It made me slightly jealous that I didn't have a family to really feel that way about or who felt that way about me. The conversation then turned more toward his plans after graduation while we played our Friday night game of Gin Rummy and Spite and Malice. We even showed off some of our individual silly dancing while we listened to Lecrae. He was hilarious pretending he had groove when he really didn't. We were both on the ground laughing. It turned out to be a great evening, and I was sad when the night turned cold, and we had to leave.

"Thanks again, Evan, for this. This is my new favorite place!"

"Of course, no problem. I just can't believe you haven't been up here yet."

We walked down the lit tree-lined pathway to our cars taking in one last time the sweet smell of the lilies. We hugged briefly at my car saying we would look forward to next Friday. On my drive home I was even more confused and plagued with decisions that I knew would only get worse. For tomorrow I would see Demetri.

The Return

The next six weeks went exactly the same. I had my now renamed Hilltop nights with Evan on Friday night and my Demetri dates on Saturdays. It was awkward at first, but once I told Demetri about my good friend Evan and he knew that Fridays were reserved for him, I felt better about it. At first he was not pleasant about the idea, but quickly came to the realization that he felt Evan was no threat to him. They had never met each other, and I liked it that way. I felt like if they were to meet that the two halves of the person I was would collide. I felt guilty about it, though. I had promised Evan to be myself with Demetri and to really see if this was a good fit, but I was breaking that promise. I felt like I was myself with Demetri but a different version of myself. One who was more refined and mature. While with Evan I was more laid back and carefree.

Denise told me to think about the person I wanted to be. Who was that? And which one helped me to grow in the Lord? I knew Evan helped me grow in many ways. But could two tormented souls really help each other grow? Amy told me I had to stop thinking of it as two options. I didn't have Evan as an option, and she was right. He was my friend and nothing more, and I needed to let it go. But something in me was afraid to let it go. I knew in time I would and that he, too, would find someone to be with. I dreaded that day. Mine and Demetri's relationship had grown. I still hadn't let him kiss me, but he could hold my hand. Which he was patient about. In fact, he always seemed the gentleman. I started not minding the little manner reminders; I thought I could use some growing up, and he definitely helped me in that area. Now here it was my birthday, and Demetri was taking me to dinner and a concert. I couldn't help but be excited. I loved concerts, and I had come to like the spoilings Demetri gave me. I had never had anyone spoil me, and it was easy to get used to. Needless to say he was growing on me. Charlotte and Amy couldn't have been happier.

It was 5:00 p.m., and Demetri would be there any minute. He sent me a text to wait outside for him. I gave myself one more look in the mirror. Emily, who adored Demetri, let me borrow her dark-blue beaded off-the-shoulder gown. Demetri said we were VIPs, and I needed to dress up. Of course Emily knew all I had was that silly black dress I wore to Evan's surprise party and wasn't going to let me go in that. I did my now longer hair in soft curls, and Charlotte advised me to do natural makeup to show off the dress. I agreed, and so now there I was looking just like I was feeling—like someone else.

I grabbed the matching clutch Emily loaned me as well, threw my phone and some lip gloss, my wallet, and keys into it. I headed out to the quad to wait for Demetri. As I was heading out the door into the quad, I looked up and saw Evan.

"Wow, Kate!" He stammered. "You…you look beautiful!"

"Uh, thanks! I don't really feel like me, but it will work," I said with heat rushing to my cheeks, remembering how he used to make me blush all the time when we first met.

"Well, you look beautiful nonetheless. You must be excited about tonight."

"Yeah, I think it will be fun. I am being spoiled for sure…but… what are you doing here? I thought you had a big night with the guys planned?"

"Yeah, I do, but I just wanted to come and wish you a happy birthday before you left."

"You wished me a happy birthday last night, and you texted me this morning. I think you are fully covered!"

"Yeah, well I realized this morning that at our hilltop I forgot to give you your present."

"You got me a present? You didn't have to do that, plus you bought the food last night, and it was my night so that was present enough."

"Oh, whatever. That is not a present! Plus I had already bought it and forgot to bring it, so here it is." He handed me a book-sized box. "It's nothing big but something that comes from the heart."

I opened the box and inside was a burgundy, leather-bound Bible with my name in gold lettering in the bottom. "I thought it was time you had your own. I know that one Amy gave you means a lot to you, but I thought it would be nice for you to have your own full-sized Bible with your name on it."

Tears welled up in my eyes. This was most definitely a gift from the heart, and I couldn't have been more astonished that he would even think to give me a gift like this.

"Evan, thank you!"

"Okay, well don't get all emotional over it. I don't want you to ruin that great job you did on your makeup and look all haggard for your big date."

"You really know how to ruin a moment," I said, laughing, knowing what he was doing. "But seriously, nicest gift I have ever gotten." He stepped closer pulling me into a hug, when I saw Demetri come down the trail from the parking lot. I didn't think he recognized me in Evan's arms, and I was glad for that because I didn't really want to break loose. I was happy there. As he came closer, though, he noticed me and saw I was looking at him, so I pulled away from Evan and waved at Demetri. Evan looked at me with confused eyes and turned to see the man he had yet to meet coming toward us.

I quickly walked about five steps in front of Evan to meet Demetri. "Hey!"

"Hello! Happy birthday!" he said. I thought with his first look at me hugging Evan he would be angry, but his face had softened by the time he reached me and seemed to not be bothered by what he saw.

"Thank you," I said as he drew me into a hug. I pulled out of the embrace and took Demetri's hand to guide him to meet Evan. Something I never wanted to do.

Evan's face was smiling as he stepped forward.

"Demetri, I would like for you to meet my good friend Evan."

Evan put out his hand. "Demetri, I have heard so much about you. It is great to finally put a face with the name."

"I wish I could say the same about you, Evan. But it is nice to meet you nonetheless."

I could feel my face getting hot as Demetri spoke.

Evan didn't say anything in return just gave me a puzzled look as he dropped Demetri's hand. "Well, I hear you guys have a big date planned for Kate's birthday! I will let you get to it. I was just dropping by to give Kate her present," he said pointing to the Bible I was clinging to.

"Oh." Demetri looked down at my hands

"A beautiful Bible with my name on it, see?" I held out the Bible so he could see it.

"Nice, why don't you run that up to your room? We do really need to get going." He was completely disinterested in the present.

"Actually, you know I can take that for you, Kate. I will just give it to you later." Evan held out his hand to take back the Bible.

"No, I want to use it tomorrow. I will just take it with me, because Demetri is dropping me off at Charlotte's tonight so I can go to church with her tomorrow morning, so I will just bring it with me."

"I hope you brought other clothes to wear to church," Evan said with a smirk.

"No, I decided I would be formal for church tomorrow. Maybe start a new trend," I said sarcastically.

"She usually borrows Charlotte's anyway, so I think she will be fine," Demetri said, interrupting our banter. The smiles on our faces vanished, and Evan took that as his cue to go. He wished us a good night and headed back up the walkway to his dorm. Demetri grabbed my hand once again and with a quick, "Let's get going," we were walking up the pathway to the parking lot. I looked back to see Evan quickly turn away and enter his dorm.

The thirty-minute ride was quiet. Upon entering the restaurant, the hostess led us through the main dining hall and out the back to the patios. Out on a jut there was sitting a small gazebo with a table set for two. The gazebo was lit with hundreds of twinkling lights, and there were scattered rose petals all over the floor with huge floral bouquets at the entrance. The table was elegantly set with fine white china, silver settings, crystal goblets, a petite red rose, and white candle center piece. It was breathtaking. The gazebo overlooked the city, and the sun was just starting to set. The sky was tenderly filled with clouds that were just beginning to turn pink and purple from the setting sun. I was awestruck. Once again Demetri pulled out my chair and helped me arrange my seat. I was immediately excited to spend this night with him, with Evan slipping to the back of my mind—that is, until Demetri sat down, and his look became stern.

"So before we fully begin to enjoy our night, I would just like to get something off my chest."

"Uh, okay."

"I don't really think it is appropriate for you to be hugging other guys while dating me. I understand you say he is a friend of yours, but let's just not have that again. I was embarrassed and put in a very awkward position."

"I didn't intend to make you feel that way at all. But I told you before, Evan is one of my best friends, and he gave me a very nice gift, of course he deserved a hug."

"If he is truly that good of a friend to you, why haven't you fully described him to me, or talked of him more? You once told me that you spent your Fridays with a good friend, but you didn't disclose a lot about him. So either he is not as good as a friend as you say or he is someone you want hidden from me and therefore a threat to our relationship."

"You are being absurd, Demetri. I haven't really talked about him to you because…well…I don't really know. I guess maybe because of this. I didn't want you to feel threatened by Evan. I didn't really want to mesh the two of you together." It came out all wrong. I actually couldn't explain why I didn't want Demetri to know about Evan. I knew why I didn't want to really talk to Evan about Demetri, but I never really thought about it for the other way around. And now here I was stammering and not saying what I want or should say.

"'Mesh the two of us together'? What is that supposed to mean? If we are both in your life, then we are already meshed together. You say I shouldn't feel threatened, and to be honest, I'm not. I didn't see anything in him to be threatened by. I mean for goodness sakes, he gets you a Bible for your birthday? Look at what I give you, Kate. Think about what I can give you."

"It's not a competition, Demetri."

"You are right it isn't," he said, taking my hand from across the table and giving me a stern look. "Because I have already won."

I didn't know what to say to that. I could tell with that statement he was done with the conversation. It was like he was telling me instead of stating his opinion. It brought me back to my conversation with Evan, Charlotte, and Amy before Christmas. I wasn't ready for this. I could have both! I had to because I didn't want to lose Evan, and the more I spent with Demetri the more I wasn't sure I wanted lose him either.

The dinner passed without another conversation about what had happened. I let myself relax and forget it and enjoyed the beautiful five-course meal. Our talk ranged again from the nightly troubles of theater life to his trip to London that was coming up. He often used "we" when discussing it. At the end of the meal we enjoyed a cup of coffee while staring out at the twinkling lights from the city below. Soon it was time to head to the concert. Demetri spared no expense. We had front-row VIP seats. I thought I felt the singer's spit at one point. It was amazing. The ride to Charlotte's was filled with the talk of the concert and what we loved and what Demetri thought could have been done better. He was also very frustrated that we were not asked backstage as most celebrities were. I guessed Demetri was bigger in his head than in reality. I started realizing that early on in our relationship, but I honestly did think that, with his talent, reality would match his opinion of himself one day.

Demetri pulled into a space at Charlotte's as he always did. This time, however, as we walked up to the door I could sense a change in him. When we got to the door he turned and grabbed both my hands.

"Kate, I hope you had a great birthday today, and I hope I was able to make it special for you. I think you are terrific, and I love our time together. I know that I can help you grow in more ways than anyone else can." Somehow I got the idea there was someone in particular he had in mind. "We belong together, and I would love for you to be mine, only mine. Please tell me you are only mine."

I was frozen. I wouldn't put Evan out of my life. He would remain my friend, my best friend, if I could help it. But I didn't want to pull him in this. I didn't want another discussion about it.

"Demetri, I love spending time with you. I wouldn't want you to not be in my life, but I don't know what to say. I am not good with labels I guess. I mean what are you asking me?"

"I am not asking you to marry me or anything, Kate. I just want to know you aren't dating anyone else nor are you looking to."

"No, Demetri, I am not dating anyone else. I wouldn't do that to you," I said.

"So we *are* in a committed relationship?" he asked.

"Yes, we are if that is what that means."

He smiled deeply and put his hands to my cheeks. "Kate, I love you. I didn't want to tell you till I knew you were committed to me. But I love you, and you have my heart completely." With that he kissed me. It was soft and yet all I could feel was the lack of feeling. He loved me. The first man to ever love me in this way, and I stood here kissing him feeling…nothing.

He released my lips and looked into my eyes with such happiness. I loved seeing him happy. I could tell I did love him in ways that I really did feel for him. I wasn't *in* love with him, but I cared deeply for him and his happiness. I enjoyed holding his hand, or having his arm around me, it felt protective. But hugging him, or now kissing him, I didn't feel the spark or the fit I was hoping I would feel. But maybe it would come. I had come to feel for him; maybe that feeling would grow. I was always told that love was something that was grown, and infatuation was something that was immediate.

"I will see you tomorrow at church, my love. Get some sleep. Happy birthday." He kissed me quickly again, and I smiled at him not really knowing what to say or do. I unlocked the door and stepped inside as he walked away.

"Well, well, well," I heard from the darkness. A light flicked on as I jumped out of my skin.

"Charlotte!" I screamed realizing she had been sitting there the whole time.

"He loves you!" she said, laughing at my fear. I too started laughing and threw one of the throw pillows at her.

"Eavesdropper!"

"Well I *am* living vicariously through you at this point. Come sit here and tell me everything. Oh, happy birthday by the way!"

"Yeah, thanks!" I said as I flopped down on the other side of the couch hitting her again with another throw pillow. "Thanks for the MAC gift card…it came this morning."

"You are so welcome, half of it is from Amy! I will go with you tomorrow after church and help you use it."

"I am sure you will!" We both started laughing, and immediately I looked forward to it.

"Okay, so now spill!"

"Spill what?" I asked coyly.

"Ha, very funny! Tell me everything."

"It is a great feeling to have someone love you…"

"I noticed you didn't say it back, stammering girl."

"Yeah, well I don't say things I don't mean. I don't love him yet."

"Love grows," Charlotte said.

"What are you my bumper sticker?"

"Ha, no, I just mean that you should give it time. I think you guys are going to be good together. Plus it is always nice to have a hot, rich guy in love with you."

"Ah yes, the power of women," I said sarcastically.

"Just give it time. You are still trying to heal and grow yourself. Okay! Just think of it this way, this birthday will now help you to always remember this one and not your last one."

"Very true. I actually hadn't thought about it since Evan came to give me my present earlier. So sweet. I'll show you!" I went and retrieved the Bible and brought it over to her with a huge smile on my face.

"Oh...it is beautiful and very thoughtful," she said.

"Yes, very thoughtful! I love it."

"Be careful, Kate, okay? I know Evan really cares for you, but you have a man who *loves* you! Just remember that."

"I will, I will, Charlotte. I promise. Plus I feel like the only person who could really get hurt here is me."

"I don't think that is true...but I will leave it at that. We have an early morning. Let's get to bed."

The next morning after church and lunch, we headed out to the mall to spend my gift card Charlotte and Amy had given me before heading back to the dorm to study and get ready for classes. Spring break was a week away, and I needed to really take that week to prepare. Evan and I were still planning on meeting Friday night, but I told Demetri Saturday needed to be reserved for studying and that I would spend Sunday afternoon with him after church.

The week flew by as it always did with classes. I enjoyed my Bible classes and chapel, learning about the history of the Bible and the contexts of passages. So I always loved studying and really enveloping myself into the work. Not to mention it always made Friday come sooner. This Friday was no exception. It was a beautiful spring evening. I was more anxious to see Evan that week because we hadn't talked much due to such a heavy study load. Our conversations never went to Demetri outside of the first conversation and the generic "did you have a good time on your birthday" and my generic "yeah" response. I figured it would come up tonight.

It was my turn to pick up the food, so I headed out a little early to get the sandwiches I had promised him. When I got to the Hilltop parking lot there was only one car, and it was a nice black Acura, so I wasn't hesitant to get out and head up the beautiful tree-lined path to the open park. I took in the evermore-fragrant flowers as I walked up the path. I stopped at the fountain as I always did and threw in a coin over my back like I was really throwing in a coin at the Trevi. I headed over to our normal table before I realized the park was empty. Who did the car belong to then? I took a good look around hearing only the chirping of birds and the dancing of the water at the fountain. There was a little path off to the right that led down to to the college and thought maybe whoever's car that was had headed down there. I shrugged it off and started setting up. I had packed my backpack with a tablecloth, cards, drinks, and my little portable radio. I set out the tablecloth, put out paper plates with our wrapped sandwiches, put napkins out by each plate, and set up the radio with my phone attached and playing my favorite Fire Flight-inspired playlist. I was taking a step back to admire my work knowing Evan wouldn't be far behind now.

"Well, who do we have here?" My heart sank immediately as I recognized the voice. I wouldn't forget that voice in a million years, for it rang nightmares in my ears. Jay. I stepped forward and gripped the table closing my eyes, hoping I was dreaming.

"What, no hello for your ex-boyfriend? I mean you did leave without saying good-bye."

Suddenly my mind started shouting at me. Evan would be there soon. I just had to hold him off. I couldn't seem panicked or vulnerable. I needed to turn around and look him in the eye. So I obeyed, and standing straight up, I spun around.

"What are you doing here, Jay?"

"You mean how did I find you? Well, let's just say we have a mutual friend."

"Amy would never have told you where I was," I said.

"Oh, yes, you are very right, and believe you me, I tried! That girl is a hard cookie to crack for sure. Too bad I hadn't met her first. She would have put up a much bigger fight than you. Don't get me wrong. I am enjoying our little cat-and-mouse game here. You leaving made for an interesting turn. One I wasn't expecting, but I have enjoyed trying to find you."

"You are deranged, you realize that right? Again I ask you, what are you doing here?"

"I missed you, Kate." He came forward and stroked my hair. I flinched back, and I was now leaning backward over the table. "Glad to see you haven't lost your feistiness in this wretched place. I feared you had gone soft and this would be no fun, but I see I was wrong." He grabbed my wrists as I tried to push him away.

"Get away from me, Jay, I swear."

"Oh, Kate, be careful. It is a sin to swear."

I stopped struggling as he pressed my arms to my side and pulled his head closer to mine. I looked with fear into his possessed eyes and silently prayed.

He closed his eyes and took a nice long inhale through his nostrils. "Mmm, you smell exactly the same—of fear. I love it!" He opened his eyes and glared right into mine, "You know why I am here, Kate." He slowly moved his mouth to my left ear, and I closed my eyes as he whispered, "I put my time in, Kate. I will get what I want. I always do."

Fear gripped my stomach and a tear started to fall down my cheek. *No, Kate don't cry, don't cry you have to be strong.* I could feel his strong and tense body pinning mine against the table and wanted to scream, but I knew no one would hear me. I could only pray that Evan would come in time. Suddenly, there was a great force as Jay was ripped away from me, and I fell to the ground.

"Kate!" Evan was here! I opened my eyes as Evan started helping me up. I looked and saw Jay about fifteen feet away getting up off the ground.

"Jay," is all I had to whisper to Evan for him to come to full realization of what was going on. He took a protective stance in front of me pushing me even more behind him so I was peering around his broad shoulder. Jay stood up and faced the two of us wiping the dirt off his jeans and black T-shirt with a smile on his face.

"Ah, I didn't expect this. I saw you were setting up a dinner, but when I was told you were up here with your BFF I didn't picture a guy. Interesting."

"I suggest you leave, Jay. I don't know how you found Kate or why you did, but it would be in your best interest to leave." Evan was forceful and strong, and I felt safe with him protecting me, but I also felt fear for him. Jay looked psychotic, and I could tell he would do anything to get what he wanted even if that meant getting rid of Evan. Evan was a surprise to him, so whoever told Jay about where I was living now didn't know about Evan. Evan was going to make him getting what he wanted harder, but I could tell from the look on his face that he didn't care. It only increased his adrenaline from the chase even more.

"Oh, I'll leave, but only because I'm having too much fun with this to let it end here. I didn't realize how much I have really missed you, Kate. So you guys have a nice night…I will see ya real soon."

"Seriously, man, if you don't start walking I won't hesitate to rip you limb from limb."

"Yeah, yeah I got it." He winked at me and then walked away.

"I don't trust him, Evan, please let's go," I begged.

"Wait till he leaves then we will get out of here."

"But what if he has something in his car or something?"

"Okay, don't panic or get paranoid, he is leaving."

"Paranoid? Who knows what he is capable of…I really can't say I do. I mean what kind of lunatic will come find me like this just to finish the job?"

"Well, I guess we just met the kind."

Feeling it was safe to turn around, Evan took me in his arms. I hid my face into his chest and started to cry.

"Kate, you're shaking! What was he saying to you when I came up?"

"That he came to finish what he started."

"Was he here when you first got here?"

"No, well, probably yes. I saw a car in the parking lot, but when I got up here I didn't see anyone, so I started setting up for our dinner and then he came up behind me and…" I couldn't talk anymore I was crying so hard.

"Kate, you promised me you wouldn't come up here alone!"

"I didn't think I was alone, in fact I was right, but it ended up being for the worse that I wasn't alone." I started hyperventilating.

"Okay, okay, shh. I am so sorry, Kate. I will never let him hurt you, I promise." Evan was stroking my hair, and I could tell he kept turning around because I could feel his body jerk to the left every few seconds. I knew he meant what he said, and I felt comforted knowing he was watching out for me. But I couldn't let this affect him. This wasn't his problem. I wouldn't let this affect his life. I wouldn't let him get hurt because of me. There had to be a solution.

"Okay, I hear a car starting up. Let's get packed up and get outta here and go to the police."

"No. No police!" I grabbed his arm.

"What? Why?"

"Evan, I never reported him in the first place. I don't want to relive that or have this he said, she said crud. Plus I know the drill. I will be lucky to get a restraining order at this point, and then they couldn't do anything anyway. Seriously I am not going to deal with this now. I will figure out some way to deal with this. I will."

"You are being stubborn. Your safety is in danger. I am not going to stand by and just let something happen to you."

"It won't help, Evan. Believe me. Let's just pack up and get back to the dorm. I need time to think. I need time to figure this out. I have to figure out how he found me!"

"So you have no idea? No idea who could have told him?"

"No, I mean the only person who knows is Amy really. I mean obviously Paul knows I left, and that I was staying with Charlotte, but he doesn't know where I am going to school. Sam wouldn't even talk to me. So I don't see how she knows. And Amy would have told me if she asked. Amy says she doesn't even see Sam anymore since she doesn't live in the dorms anymore. She is not even sure she goes to that school anymore." My heart suddenly hurt for Sam, wishing I did know where she was. I prayed for her every day and hoped that someday our paths would cross again.

"Okay, well, it doesn't matter, he knows you are here and obviously someone told him you were coming up here, so first thing we need to do is tell your gal pals, especially Emily, not to say where you are to anyone. Not even if they think it is Demetri on the other end."

I immediately felt fear for Demetri then and wanted to call him to tell him about Jay and not to talk to anyone, but then I thought better of it. He didn't know my story, and I didn't want to tell him, not this way, not after he said he loved me.

We got everything packed up and with great caution made our way to the parking lot seeing Jay's car was gone. I got in my car, locked the door, and started it waiting for Evan to get into his and lock and start his car before pulling out. He followed me down the hill and back around to the dorms with no sign of the black Acura. For some reason I felt safer being back at the dorms. Maybe because of all the people. Evan and I sat down at one of the picnic tables in the quad feeling safe that there was a men's volleyball game going on.

"I can't deal with this right now, Evan, I have midterms! I know that sounds stupid, but I finally feel on track for once in my life and now this happens. I don't want my life to mess up now."

"It won't get messed up, Kate, I promise. Between me, Charlotte, Amy, and Demetri we will figure this out."

"Not Demetri. I don't want to tell him."

"Why? He needs to know."

"No, he doesn't. He doesn't know anything really about me before I came here. He definitely knows nothing about Jay. I don't want to tell him now, not this way."

"Why haven't you told him? It's who you are, Kate! It is part of who you have become. How can you leave that out to someone you have been dating for months?"

"He wouldn't love me if I told him."

"If that were true then he doesn't deserve you."

"Thanks, but that isn't true. I don't deserve him. That is why I haven't told him. I already feel like he is fathering me, and this would surely drive him away. For me to be tainted."

"You are not tainted, and that is stupid for you to think that way. I seriously don't think you are giving him enough credit. He seems like a nice enough guy. He obviously really cares for you. I think he would want to protect you as much as the rest of us do. I don't think his thoughts are going to be of you being tainted."

"I'm not so sure."

"Kate, if you keep seeing yourself in this light no one will ever respect you the way you deserve. You will always see yourself as not worthy of anything and you will let people walk all over you. I wish you could see what I see. I wish you could see who you truly are and what you truly look like. Then you would see that you *are* worth something. You *are* worth protecting." Evan looked at me with his soft blue eyes, and I melted. I knew he would do anything to protect me then. I didn't know really why he looked at me the way he did. Maybe because I was the only one who really knew the "real" Evan. But looking at him with the moonlight glistening off his shiny black hair and sparkling off his glorious blue eyes I had to protect him, not me. I would do anything to make sure my sins and my issues never hurt him.

Slippery Slope

Fear gripped my every moment. The Sunday after Jay made his presence known I didn't tell Demetri. I told Charlotte that night after I got back to my room. She promised not to tell Demetri, understanding the reasons why. I made sure I put on a brave face when I saw Evan when he walked me to my classes I never wanted him to know I was that afraid. I had put on my ever-growing drama cape and pretended to be fine. I needed him to think I was fine so he wouldn't be so protective. I even went as far as not telling him when I got a terrifying text from Jay. How did he get my new phone number? I didn't want Evan to get hurt; therefore I had to pretend like there really wasn't any danger. I had to act like Jay was leaving me alone. But he wasn't; he was in my every dream taunting me. He was calling my cell and leaving me hideous messages about how good it would feel to finally have what he wanted.

Finals were difficult to get through. I decided passing was going to be as good as I could do, if even that. Being a doctor was out of the question for me now, and I had to come to grips with that. Evan had felt better about spring break coming, knowing I wasn't going to be alone but be with both Charlotte, Amy, and their parents at their house in Northern California. Evan didn't want me to tell anyone where I would be for spring break, but of course I told Demetri I was going to go somewhere with Charlotte and Amy to relax and have girl time. Actually we all told him that I didn't know where I was going and that it was going to be a surprise for me. Charlotte told me that he tried to get the information out of her, but she said she played it off that she wasn't telling him because he might let it slip and tell me. I had changed my phone number right before I left for break, so for the beginning of the break it was peaceful and some of the fear started to subside. I had a great time relaxing with Charlotte and Amy, and I truly felt like one of the family. My mom and dad were off on a tour of Australia, so they didn't care where I was. We spent time reading, doing each other's nails, going to the movies, and just plain relaxing. Boy topics were completely off limits, except for Amy because she had just started dating this guy named Luke that she had met while serving in the youth group at her church. He sounded terrific and perfect for her, and I couldn't have been happier to see her glowing with joy.

By the Thursday during our one-week break the happiness broke as I received my first call from Jay again. Charlotte and Amy had gone to the store to get some rocky road ice cream. I had felt secure enough with their golden retriever Ralph and the security system on. And to be honest, I was needing some time alone. When the phone rang I didn't recognize the phone number but thought it might be Demetri calling me from a different theater number.

"Hey, Kate, getting a little tricky on me, eh? Changing your phone number? I am going to start to think you don't want to talk to me."

"I don't!" I said, trying to keep it together.

"Wow, way to hurt a guy's feelings. Sad of you to take off for your break and not tell me where you were going. I would have loved to have spent it with you the way I was planning on. My break is up this week too, you know. I took the last week off from school before break because I wanted to surprise you, but now I am getting a little impatient. I might have to miss a little more school, and I don't like that. Considering it affects my business grade, and you are now not only affecting my physical life but my professional one as well."

"Whatever, Jay, you are never going to graduate anyway. You are too dumb," I blurted out.

"Hmm, you think highly of me I see, well that is what rich daddies are for, ya know. To buy their kids an education. But luckily for me you are only two hours away from me, so I can really come visit whenever I want, and once again no one will expect it was me…

wow, in class one minute and with you the next. Not even your little boy toy will be able to get in my way. I am already taking care of that."

"What are you talking about, Jay? Please don't hurt Evan! You are not that kind of guy, are you? You're not a killer!"

"No one said anything about killing anyone, Kate, but if he gets in my way I can't promise anything."

"He won't get in your way. Just don't hurt him."

"Love to hear you begging. But why are you not fighting for your beloved Demetri this way?"

Demetri? He did know about Demetri! My mind felt as though it was spinning. All these people whom I loved, who actually loved me, I was putting in danger.

"Demetri? I haven't been fighting for him as you say because I didn't think I needed to."

"Of course you didn't because you haven't told him about me have you?"

"How do you know what I have or haven't told Demetri?"

"Oh, I have my ways of knowing most things, my dearest Kate. Why haven't you told him about yourself? Ashamed of the wretched sinner you were? Ashamed of having giving yourself into the gluttony of life? Oh, how I love reliving those days! I am most excited to relive them with you. Those pictures just bring back so many memories. And this time I won't overdo it on the alcohol. Goes to show you what an amateur I was. But I have grown in so many ways—don't you worry! It won't happen again."

Vomit filled my mouth and words escaped my mind. I was stuck, and I didn't know how to get out. I couldn't let my friends get hurt, but how could I fight against this man alone? I ignored that small voice telling me to pray. What would prayer do? What had it done for me since? I was in love with someone I couldn't have—again. I had a madman after me, my parents could care less about me, and I was plagued by nightmares of my past every day whether trying to force myself to eat and keep it down or with all the drinking and drugs I did. I was haunted by the past daily and now even more so with Jay in the flesh haunting me. And on top of that it sounded as if, because of my silence, other girls had paid for it. I felt hopeless.

"What have you done, Jay? How have you grown in these ways? Please please tell me you haven't—"

"Haven't what, Kate? Can you say it? Raped other girls? Much more successfully than I did with you. I learned many lessons from that, so thank you! The pictures are the key in every one, though. Get 'em drugged and take pictures of them partying, and it is my golden ticket of silence. You will even be happy to hear that Sam and I have shared some intense moments as well."

"What? Sam? She wouldn't!"

"Wouldn't she? Now to be fair to her, she was pretty out there, so I don't think she had any idea who she was doing at that point, and that wasn't even my doing. Her little friends that she used to bring around with you all are getting her into some great stuff. I mean what they brought around with you was nothing."

"I don't believe anything you say, Jay, and I won't start now. Sam may have gotten into some stuff when I was there, but I know those guys, and they were a little crazy and brought some crazy stuff, but them seemed to really like Sam. They wouldn't drag her into something that would do what you are saying."

"What do you know, Kate? You aren't here. Have you even talked to her? You left her. You abandoned her. When you left those people were all she had, so she turned to them for that void you left there. They are witches, you know. Self-proclaiming! It's great! They wear fangs and all. In fact they did a very accurate taro reading for me that said I would find myself involved with an old friend...hmm could that be you? Sad though really because Sam is biting off more than she can chew with them. They are over the top for her, but that is all she can fit into because you left. If you would have stayed not only would I have had my fun, but you would have saved your friend. How does that make you feel, Kate? You have destroyed not only those girls I have had to test on but Sam as well."

"Stop it! What you chose to do is your fault, Jay, not mine. Don't you dare put this on me. Sam is a grown girl. She was a lot stronger than me. If she wanted to get into that kind of thing then that is her business."

"If that is the way you want to think of it. But when she dies of an overdose or from one of the rituals she performs with her witchy friends I can guarantee you will be riddled with guilt. And I look forward to it. You deserve nothing but the worst."

"Really, why? Because you didn't get what you wanted from me? Is that the only reason, because you met someone who didn't actually want you? Or someone who actually had morals for a change? You are insane. Completely insane!" I was yelling so hard my voice was getting hoarse. I was fighting to keep the tears from pouring.

"Maybe, but I am getting to you, aren't I? I am feeling satisfied knowing tonight you will fall asleep thinking of all the girls who I have raped because of you, and you will think of Sam and all the hell she is into because of you. Because you didn't stay. Because you ran like a little baby."

"I didn't run! I found the truth, and I embraced it."

"Oh, yeah, well how is that truth treating you now? Your God can't save you, Kate, just as much as he can't save your precious Sam, or soon won't be able to save your precious Evan or Amy." He said with disdain yet dramatic calmness.

"If you touch them or hurt them in anyway, Jay, I—"

"You what, Kate? You can't even protect yourself."

This comment hit me with a ton of bricks. He was right. I couldn't. I began to panic as I thought about not just myself but my friends.

"What do you want from me, Jay? What will it take for you to leave me and the people I love alone?"

"That's a dumb question," he said.

"Fine, what if you got what you wanted? Would you promise to stop what you are doing and leave my friends alone, along with this spree that you are on?"

"I can guarantee your friends, but gosh I am having too much fun getting away with whatever I want. I can't go around making promises I know I won't keep."

"No, you need to promise me, Jay. I will come after you with everything I can. Regardless, of what you say or what evidence you have, I will tarnish your name so much that not even your precious daddy will be able to save it."

"Them there is fightin' words. I like it. Okay, fine. I don't care about anyone else anyway. I just want what I can't have, and that's you. I get you, and I will try not to harm anyone else."

"Fine. Next Friday I will be walking the path from the school to the hilltop at eight p.m." I said.

"Okay, but any funny business, and I go after Amy. And, Kate, if Evan shows up I won't hesitate to do what I have to. To uh…defend myself." With that he hung up.

I took the phone down from my ear and realized my hands were shaking. Emotions took hold, and tears began spilling uncontrollably. My chest began to burn and ache before I realized I wasn't breathing. How would I go through with this? How could I get through this? And Sam. What had she done? What had she gotten herself into? I remembered those people. There were two girls and two guys, and they were gothic but nice. The drugs they brought weren't too crazy, and they never got mad at me for not doing what they were. But there was the pressure.

Maybe Sam became convinced into the power of their world. Of the simplicity of turning off reality. How could I help her? Would she let me? I was attempting to pray, but heard the garage door opening. Charlotte and Amy were home from the store. I needed to get it together. I needed to put on the best act I could. I ran into the bathroom and washed my face so it would look like I was getting ready for bed and explain the red blotches on my face. I looked at myself in the mirror not recognizing the girl that stared back. I suddenly felt as lost as I had before coming to Redeemer. The girl in the mirror looked tired and worn out; she looked confused and depressed. I shook my head and put on a smile seeing how it looked. Fake, but it would have to do.

"Hey, getting ready for bed already?" Amy said as she peeked into the bathroom.

"Yeah, I just felt like getting comfortable for our carpet picnic. What movie and ice cream did you guys pick up?"

"Um, we got *Say Anything*, a classic, and rocky road just like you asked…are you okay? You didn't answer when I was calling for you, and I got nervous."

"Oh, I probably didn't hear you over the water, sorry. Let me just finish up here and get my pajamas on, and I will be there in a minute."

"Okay…see you downstairs.".

Maybe I wasn't being as convincing as I thought. Memories of Evan and the baseball field popped in my head and a short-lived smiled crossed my face. I wouldn't tell him about this of course.

I got dressed and went downstairs where the girls already had blankets and pillows all set up on the floor in front of the big screen with the movie paused at the beginning waiting for me. There was a bowl of ice cream sitting in what was supposed to be my spot.

"Hey, took long enough, girl. Get over here. Let's get this party started," Charlotte said.

I went over and plopped down on my side of the blanket. I could see Amy looking at me curiously from the corner of my eye.

"Are you sure you are all right? Did something happen while we were gone?"

"No, I'm fine. Just tired. Excited to watch the movie, though, so let's start it!" I said with fake enthusiasm.

"Amy leave her alone, if there was anything going on, she would tell us. Wouldn't you, Kate?"

"Right! Of course."

"Okay, then let's start the movie." Charlotte pushed play. I was thankful for that and tried to melt myself into the movie thinking maybe a comedy would have been a better choice.

Two days later we were heading home. I had called Evan and told him I wouldn't be home for our Hilltop on Friday because I just didn't feel like coming back yet. He totally understood and said it probably worked out for the better because he needed more time with one of the guys who would be taking over his coaching position on the team for next year. He was almost sure he would get that internship he wanted, in fact he was due to find out that week since graduation was only a short six weeks away and he would be leaving right after that. I couldn't think of that right then. In fact I thought it might be best if he did because then he wouldn't have to be around me. Fighting for my safety. Not that he would have too much longer. But something told me that Jay wouldn't go away even if I gave into him. I felt a deep sorrow knowing I wouldn't have my hilltop with Evan the following week either. I was going to be faking sick. Demetri also understood why I had to cancel our lunch on Saturday, and I told him I would make it up to him on Sunday after church. We drove straight to Charlotte's house. I decided I would spend the night there with the girls and go to church with them in the morning; then Amy would head back to school, and I would head to lunch with Demetri.

Saturday night was filled with nightmares and haunting memories just as had the night before, and I looked even more worn out for church. Charlotte agreed to do my makeup for me as she accepted the nightmares as just part of everything going on, even though she didn't know the half of it. I could tell she wanted to bug me with questions but knew she shouldn't.

After church I couldn't get myself to really look at Demetri. I knew I was being standoffish, but I didn't feel I even deserved to be having lunch with him when I was keeping so many things from him. Did he even know the real me? No…he wouldn't like it if he did, and I didn't want to lose the person I was becoming with him. A very mature young lady, everyone said. I felt the furthest from that then. In fact in church I kept playing with my nails and several times Demetri put his hand on top of mine to silently tell me to knock it off. I couldn't concentrate on the message. I almost didn't care. I felt like a fraud being there. All these people whose faith seemed to be strong and mine was failing. My faith was not strong. I felt like the Lord had abandoned me and literally left me for dead.

"What is going on with you today, Kate? Is everything all right? You seem like you don't want to be here, like you didn't even miss me while you were gone," he said as we sat down to lunch at a nearby restaurant.

"Oh, no, sorry, I do want to be here. I missed you very much. I thought about you a lot. I am sorry. I just have a lot on my mind that's all."

"Okay, well, can you at least try to enjoy this time together? At least act like you want to spend time with me."

"Don't be so dramatic, Demetri, geez. I mean can't I ever not make you the center of attention for once? Not everything revolves around you. I have problems and things in my life too. You never ask me about them. Don't you even care about my life at all? Every time we are together we just talk about you and your stuff, and you never ask me about mine. Or if you do, then you say I am being stupid or that I need to grow up. Well I am only twenty, so sorry I am not as mature as you are."

"Seriously this is how you are going to behave, Kate? Fine you can just sit here and eat by yourself then, I'm outta here." With that Demetri threw money on the table and stormed out. The people in the restaurant were all looking at me, so I got up and ran into the bathroom crying. I couldn't get a grip. I was definitely losing it. Some of those things probably should have been said to Demetri but not that way. I was sabotaging my life. Like always I could never have anything good in my life happen. Maybe once I was rid of Jay...but the way I would have to lose Jay would stay with me for the rest of my life. Was that worth it?

I got back to the dorms earlier than I had anticipated and was glad to see Evan's car was not in the parking lot. I looked around for Emily's and was relieved to not find hers there either; I needed time alone. I went to my room unpacking my things in a daze just wishing I could wake up from this nightmare. I went back to my suitcase to grab what was left, and there staring at me was the Bible Evan had given to me. I lifted it out of the suitcase setting the suitcase on the floor and crawling into a crisscross position on the bed. I didn't want to open it but knew that I should. That maybe this would bring the answers I had been seeking. I decided to close my eyes and flip through it. As I opened my eyes I was surprised to see Psalms was lying open. I peered down and started reading Psalm 27.

> The Lord is my light and my salvation—whom shall I fear? The Lord is the stronghold of my life—of whom shall I be afraid? When evil men advance against me to devour my flesh, when my enemies and my foes attack me, my heart will not fear; though war break out against me, even then will I be confident.

I couldn't make it any further. My tears consumed me. That which should have given me comfort didn't. The Lord laid before me the perfect verse, and all I could think was, *Yeah, right.* I couldn't be confident. Confident in what? I wasn't David, or Abendigo. No light was going to save me from the peril that was ensuing. I had no strength. I had no faith. There was no protection for me. I had to go through with it or else my friends would be in danger, and I would do anything to protect them.

"Kate? Are you okay?" I heard Emily whisper. I didn't hear her come in.

"Oh, Emily," I said jumping and wiping tears from my face. "I am good. Sorry I just get emotional sometimes when I am reading."

"Please, Kate, don't shut down. What is going on? Let me help you. I know I haven't been the greatest of friends to you, but I truly do care about you. Please let me help you."

"There is nothing to help, Emily. I am fine. Really. You know sometimes life just gets a little hectic. I just need a little extra strength these days."

"Okay, I will pray for you then. But please, Kate, don't hesitate to ask me for anything at any time. I am here for you."

"Oh, thanks, Emily, really all is good!"

"Okay, well, I am running down to meet some of the girls for dinner. I was just dropping off my suitcase. You wanna join?"

"Uh, thanks for the offer. I don't think I would be much company tonight. I am just going to read and turn in early."

"Okay, suit yourself, but we will be down in the cafeteria if you change your mind."

"Thanks, Emily."

Emily put her hand on my shoulder and squeezed gently. I loved Emily this way. Not self-serving but self-sacrificing. She was growing on me every day.

I was a hermit for the next two days, except for classes, and I could tell everyone was starting to worry. I had two voicemails from Amy and Charlotte each, one from Evan, and three from Demetri. I hadn't called any of them back. I sat in my room glaring out the window wondering how to help myself and those I cared about. Unfortunately, my answer was to back away from them. To had them get so mad at me they would just walk away, and I wouldn't have to worry about them anymore. I was doing it really without noticing. It partly started because I hated lying to them, and I wasn't good at it, and the rest just followed. It was working too because the third message from Demetri was full of aggravation. His first voicemail started off with apologies for the lunch date we had Sunday. Saying he had been a jerk and that I was right about him never talking to me about my life. By the third message he was back to calling me an immature little girl who needed to grow up. Charlotte and Amy, on the other hand, were just plain worried, and Amy said if I didn't call her back she was going to come home and see me. I didn't want her to do that, so I just texted her a quick, "I'm fine, lots to do, studying hard call you this weekend." She bought it.

Charlotte's messages were more on the sisterly side offering me heartfelt sympathies of how things will get better and how great it is that Jay seemed to be leaving me alone. Then she said she wanted to make sure I was okay and to please call her. So I sent her roughly the same text I did Amy. Evan was harder. Even though he only called me once, he sounded anxious saying he had something he had to tell me, but needed my advice. He said he wanted to see if I was okay and asked if I heard from Jay telling me he knew I would tell him if I had. The last part of the message really hurt because he said he was really looking forward to our Hilltop this Friday and he missed me. I ached not only because I knew I wouldn't get to see him again for our Hilltop, but because of what would have to happen that night instead. How would I recover from it? How could I face anyone again? I shook it off and for the sixth night in a row cried myself to sleep with nightmarish dreams that awaited.

Friday arrived way too fast, and I was sitting in my room after class trying to figure out what I was going to say to Evan. I had called Demetri and apologized for not calling back saying I was really busy, but missed him and was excited to see him on Sunday. He forgave me for my lack of communication and for the things I had said on the previous weekend. He also said he was sorry for blowing up the way he did and he understood my point and would make more of an effort to ask me how I was doing. The conversation played out well even without me truly listening to what he was saying or even caring. I just wanted to smooth things over before tonight just in case something were to happen to me, and I didn't want to leave a negative thing behind with him. Now on to Evan. I needed to make sure he understood that I wasn't blowing him off, but that I was sick and needed to rest. The thought of two weeks without seeing him killed me, but I knew this was only the beginning of breaking the ties. I had to let him go, somehow, it was for the best for him. I picked up the phone and dialed his number.

"Hey, she's alive!" he yelled.

"Yeah, sorry, I have been really, really busy."

"I guess so, no time for a good friend, eh?"

"Of course I have time for you, but just not a lot of time right now. Sorry, in fact that is why I am calling. Unfortunately, I have to cancel our Hilltop again this week. I am really not feeling well. I must have overdone it this week on staying up late and whatever, so I am just not feeling up to going anywhere."

"Oh…I am sorry you are not feeling well. You need to remember to take it easy and not overwhelm yourself with things." He paused. "Kate, you are lying to me aren't you?"

"What? No, I really don't feel well."

"Did you hear from Jay?"

"No! I would tell you if I had."

"Would you? Why are you blowing me off?"

"I'm not!" I said, getting frustrated.

"Well, it sure feels like it! And I had something I really needed to talk to you about tonight, Kate!"

"What is it?"

"I don't want to talk about it over the phone. Please let's just meet in the quad."

"I can't. Really, Evan, I just want to be alone right now, okay?"

"You're pushing me away, aren't you?"

I didn't know what to say, I should've lied and said no, but he knew.

"You are being ridiculous. I just want to get some rest. I will call you later okay."

"Okay, I am not going to force you to talk to me, but I really do need to tell you something. I can't make this decision without talking to you first."

I felt like I got punched in the stomach. I had a feeling he was talking about the internship. I forgot he was supposed to find out this past week. What if he got it? That would be good right? If he got it I would have to act so happy so that he would be excited to go. This was the perfect way to get him far away from me. It would seem that God wanted the same thing.

Eight o' clock was approaching quickly. Emily would be back soon from her movie she went to with her new beau of the semester. I got up and looked at myself in the mirror remembering what I looked like now one last time. I never thought I would appreciate that reflection, but I did somehow. Who knew what I would look like the next day or if I would be alive at all. I looked at my clothes. What does one wear to their death or misery? I would make it as hard as possible. So I layered on the clothes. I put stockings on, jeans, three t-shirts and a sweatshirt. I was sweating, but at least it would take more time. Then as I pondered that I figured I didn't want it to take time I wanted it to be over with. So I changed into sweatpants and a long sleeve T-shirt. Tears rolled down my cheeks as I thought about why I was changing. I hoped in some way he would kill me, so I wouldn't have to bear the pain.

I walked out the door of the dorm; the quad was unusually quiet. It was a Friday night, and I expected people to be out having fun. I made my way up to the back part of the parking lot where the trail was that led to the Hilltop. The trail to the Hilltop was about a mile, so I was told. But I knew I wasn't going to make it that far. I looked up at the stars just starting to become fully visible and wondered if God was looking down at me. Given my circumstances I surely doubted it. The tears that began to fall back in my dorm room hadn't stopped and flowed even heavier now. They were quiet tears, though, with no deep heaves of pain from my chest. I didn't have the energy to cry that hard. I was about a quarter of the way up when I heard a branch crack behind me. I jumped briefly, but my mind knew to expect him, so it didn't take me too much by surprise. What did take me by surprise was the direction of the crack. Did I pass him in the bushes along the way? Did he want to sneak up on me? I closed my eyes trying to prepare myself and turned around. With my eyes still closed I heard him speak.

"Kate? What are you doing out here?"

"Evan?"

"I thought you were sick? Why are you walking the trail?"

"I...I...just needed some air, and I guess I wasn't even looking to where I was going."

Just then I heard a crackle coming from the hilltop behind me, the direction I figured I would hear Jay coming. Realization seized me as I stared with watery eyes at Evan. I had to get Evan out of here. Jay was coming. Who knew what he would do to Evan.

"Kate! What's wrong?" Evan asked seeing the panic in my tear-streaked face.

"Nothing, Nothing, I guess I'm just now really realizing where I am. What am I doing out here? Let's go, okay!" I was panicked to get him back to the dorms. I ran over to him taking his arm and dragging him behind me back down the trail. I began running, and I could hear Evan running right on my heels, but I heard no one else. I didn't think Jay was following us. I glanced quickly behind me seeing a flashlight swaying in the distance close to where Evan and I had been standing. Jay was there, and he could probably see us running down the hill. Evan's face was confused as he ran after me. He didn't look back as I did. He probably thought I was looking back at him.

We reached the parking lot, and I felt his hand grab my shoulder and pull me to a stop.

"No, don't stop, Evan, don't stop. Let's keep going to the quad okay."

"Kate! You are acting crazy what is going on?"

"Please, please just let's get to the quad, and we can sit and talk."

"Okay, okay," Evan said taking my hand and quickly walking with me down to the quad. "Actually let's go the gazebo at the church where we had our first real talk okay?"

"Okay, fine," I said without really knowing what I was agreeing to, just wanting to get as far away from the trail as possible.

We walked down to the church and into the gazebo in the courtyard and sat next to each other. I just looked down at the ground and said nothing.

"Okay, do you want to explain to me what is going on?"

"I don't know. I guess I just wanted to go out for a walk, and I ended up the trail."

"I thought you were sick and didn't want to go anywhere. You don't look sick to me. You look a little crazy but not sick."

"Well, maybe I am a little crazy, Evan."

"Kate, don't do that. I know you have been going through a lot lately and something tells me you are not telling me the whole truth, but it's okay to be scared and confused, you know. I think anyone would be in your position."

"How did you find me?" I asked trying to change the subject.

"I was leaving to get some air myself. I was disappointed we were not having our Hilltop and frustrated thinking you were lying to me. I saw you walking up the parking lot. I of course was mad at first wondering if you had ditched me for better plans, not that I would be angry at that, but I was mad that you would lie about it. Then I saw you heading up the trail. That just plain frightened me, Kate, so I followed you. Once I realized you had no intention of stopping I ran to catch up with you. I didn't want you going any farther up the trail."

"Oh, I see, well, good thing, I guess, right…" I sighed still looking at the floor.

"Kate, please don't shut me out. I can see you are in pain, please tell me what you are feeling. Has Jay talked to you more? Did he find your new number? Have you run into him?"

"No," I lied.

"Kate!"

"It's fine. I'm fine. I guess I just needed some space to think that is all."

"Well, if Jay isn't bugging you then what or who is?"

"Well, to be honest I'm just trying to figure out my relationship with you and Demetri. Sometimes I think you're right and I am not being fair to Demetri by hanging out with you all the time." The words just flowed without me really thinking about them. I was doing it. I was trying to lose Evan. For his own good. And this is how I would fake it. I would pretend it was because of Demetri, which to some degree was the truth.

"Oh...I see. Well, that's kind of why I wanted to talk to you tonight."

I was shocked. "Really? I thought it would be about your internship...I know you were supposed to find out this week."

"Yeah, well, that is also part of it."

"Okay, I'm confused," I said finally looking up at him. He looked strangely serious and hurt. I didn't like seeing him this way. He had a grimace on his face, and his mouth was turned down.

"Well, it all has to do with each other..." He paused, and I didn't say anything, so he turned even more toward me and took both of my hands forcing me to turn more toward him. His look in his eye made my heart beat faster.

"Kate, I got the internship in Italy..." He paused.

"Evan, that is wonderful," I said with fake enthusiasm.

"Is it?"

"Of course it is. Why wouldn't it be? You have worked so hard for this. I am so proud of you." And I truly was.

"Well, the only thing is I leave in two weeks."

My heart felt like it stopped. "What?"

"Yeah, well it came as a shock to me too. But they want me to start in two weeks. I already had a meeting with the dean here, and he said that since I did so well in midterms and had such strong grades already each class would let me write a final paper, and I could be officially done next week. I would miss graduation, but as my dad says this is an opportunity of a lifetime, not one to miss just to walk on a stage to get a piece of paper."

I remained silent.

"Well, Kate, what do you think?"

"Um…wow, I think that is amazing. Again I am so proud of you."

"Look, I agree with my dad. I won't stay to walk across a stage, but I would for something else."

"What? What could possibly make you not go Evan? This is such an amazing once in a lifetime opportunity! I mean Italy! Your dream!"

"Yes, I know, and I would be a fool not to go, but I would also be a fool if I left when there would be reasons to keep me here."

"What could possibly keep you here?"

"You!"

"Me? Why would you stay here for me?" I said.

"Well I mean…look at tonight. Who knows what would have happened if I wasn't there? Who would protect you?"

"Oh," I said coming to quick realization it had nothing to do with anything but his protective feelings of brotherly love. Feeling slightly defeated I became a little defensive, but then realized this was perfect. He needed to go, he needed to be away from me, and this was the best way for him to be gone. This was better than just me picking Demetri because this way we wouldn't see each other. I wouldn't have to be reminded every day of how I felt for him. He could be safe in Italy away from me meeting the woman of his dreams.

"I don't need your protection, Evan. I have Demetri, Amy, and Charlotte. Tonight was a fluke. I'm not concerned anymore." I was getting good at this lying thing.

Defeat and hurt filled his face, and I was struck with guilt. I wanted to take him in my arms and tell him I was lying that I needed him more than anyone, but that wouldn't do him anything but harm in more ways than I could count.

"Okay…well, that's great. I mean, yes, of course you have Demetri. He is your boyfriend, so why wouldn't he be the one to protect you? I mean what am I anyway, you know. Just the friend, and this is what I needed to know."

"No, no, Evan, that is not what I meant. I just mean that..." *Stay strong, Kate, let him go,* I thought. "I just mean that I can handle myself. I of course love having you as my friend, but that is partly why I have been so upset. I think it is better for us to maybe take a step back on our friendship. It is not fair to Demetri, just like you said before."

"Stop saying that's what I said. That was even before you met Demetri, and I was wrong. We can be friends."

"Of course we can be friends but just not best friends the way we have been. I really need to start seeing if Demetri can be my best friend. You know he wants me to go with him to London this fall, and he has even talked about us getting married before that."

"Married? What? Are you serious? You guys just started dating, and from what you have told me I didn't think he was the best match for you."

"Well, maybe that is because I have you as my best friend. Maybe I am pushing away something that is meant to be because I don't want to lose you, and that is not fair to anyone."

"Okay, well, great, I guess I have my answer then," he said.

"Yes, well good, I am glad we had this talk. I think this internship is coming at the best time, Evan, really I do."

"Great, well, so do I then." He was starting to choke up, and I knew if he lost it so would I, but luckily he didn't want me to see him this way and turned to head out of the gazebo. He stopped at the opening and without turning around said, "I am sure you and Demetri will be very happy."

"I know you are going to do so great in Italy, Evan. I truly am proud of you."

"Yeah...right...thanks." And he walked away.

I watched him walk up the hill to the quad, and I sat there. I felt like I couldn't move. What had just happened? It went exactly the way it should have, but it hurt so much. I felt like I was dying inside. Like I had just killed off a piece of myself. Snapping out of it by the sound of a cracking stick I realized I was alone in the dark, and I took off running to my dorm room. I had changed my mind about Jay. He couldn't hurt Evan now. I needed to rethink how to deal with him.

I ran into my room and lay on my bed, letting the bawling begin. I was hyperventilating into my pillow when I heard a knock at the door. Jolted into reality I sat up trying to catch my breath hoping whoever it was would go away.

"Kate? Kate, are you in there? It is me…Denise."

Oh, Denise. I had missed accountability that week on purpose, and I had forgot to even acknowledge it. I wiped my face and opened the door.

"Hey, Denise. I am sorry I missed accountability this week. Things have just been crazy."

"Hey, there! Um, can I come in for a few?"

"Yeah, of course," I said sniffling as I opened the door. There was no way to hide my red swollen face, so I didn't even try. We both took a seat on the bed, and I pulled my pillow into my lap leaning up against the back of the bed.

"I know things have been hard for you. I'm not sure in what ways. But Emily told me that you were having a hard time. And considering you didn't show up last night without even a text I knew something was wrong. I gave you a day to see if you would call, but I finally decided to come see if you were okay. I'm sorry if I'm intruding."

"No, no, it's good to see you. I feel terrible about not calling you!"

"What's going on? You know you can tell me anything. That is what I'm here for."

"I know, I'm just having a difficult time right now, everything seems to be falling apart around me. I can't seem to make the right decisions, and I feel like the decisions I am making are not only hurting me but everyone around me. To be honest Denise…" I said, choking up again, "I'm very scared."

"Oh, gosh, Kate, I'm so sorry to hear that you are dealing with some things that are causing you this much pain. Is it about Evan? I heard from Emily today that he got the internship."

"Emily knows already? I just found out. How did she know already?"

"Well, this is a small school, and news travels really fast. Plus I think she overheard part of his conversation with the dean."

"Oh, I see."

"I know him leaving is painful for you. I know you have been confused on your feelings for him and Demetri."

"No, I'm not confused with that anymore. He's going where he needs to be, and I am with who I am supposed to be with."

"Do you really feel that way?"

"Yes. I do."

"Well, that's good, Kate. Really I'm glad that you were able to come to that conclusion. But if you really feel that way, then why are you so upset?"

"There are other things that I would rather not talk about going on with me. Let's just say I am really confused more on my relationship with God right now than anything else."

"Oh, well, we have all been there."

"Really? Have we? I mean have you?"

"Sure, of course. Everyone gets confused at times, especially when we are going through trials. But it is the trials that make us stronger in Christ. Like it says in James how it produces perseverance and patience."

"Yeah, well, I think it is having the opposite effect on me, and it's scaring the crud out of me."

"What do you mean?"

"I am feeling further away from Him. Actually I am starting to feel like I never knew Him to begin with. Why, if He loves me so much, would he have me go through so much pain and confusion and suffering?"

"I know it is hard to understand, Kate, but He does love you. More than you can ever know, and if you are going through things right now it is for a good purpose."

"What good could come out of what I am going through is beyond me."

"Well, maybe that is because you are thinking in your terms. You are seeing your present circumstances instead of seeing the big picture. You are trying to take the lead with God instead of trusting Him and letting Him lead you."

"I don't know how to do that, Denise. I just don't know how. Especially when I can't even fathom Him really being there or caring about me."

"He does, believe me! Actually would you mind if I shared a passage with you?"

"I'm not sure I am in the mood for God's Word right now. Every time I read it I get a sick feeling in my stomach of disbelief."

"Well, that's the devil trying to kick you when you are down, believe that! This may not help you now, but I think it will later. Let me share it with you."

"Okay, I will listen."

"Okay, where is your Bible?"

I pointed over to the desk where my Bible from Evan was laying. Seeing it made me sick to my stomach all over again. Denise reached for it and started thumbing through the New Testament.

"Okay, here it is," she said with the Bible open to Luke. "Any time I am going through something that makes me question God's love for me or makes me think I can't handle that which I am going through I go back to this and it gives me strength and I hope it does the same for you my sweet sister in Christ. Okay, so it is Luke 22:39 through 44. Christ is just about to be betrayed by Judas, and he is in the garden of Gethsemane, so He is two days from being crucified.

Coming out, He went to the Mount of Olives, as He was accustomed, and His disciples also followed Him.

> When He came to the place, He said to them
> that you may not enter into temptation." And F
> withdrawn from them about a stone's throw, ai
> knelt down and prayed, saying, "Father if it is You
> take this cup away from Me; nevertheless not My will,
> but Yours, be done." Then an angel appeared to Him
> from heaven strengthening Him. And being in agony,
> He prayed more earnestly. Then His sweat became like
> great drops of blood falling down to the ground.

She paused and looked up at me closing the Bible with a tear in her eye. "Do you see how scared he was, Kate? How He was begging for God to take the cup He was about to drink away from Him, yet he knew it wouldn't be taken from Him, because being God He knew He had to go through with what was about to happen in order to fulfill the sacrifice for us! For us, Kate! He was so scared that He was sweating blood. He was so scared and grieved that it could have caused His death itself. But He wanted God's will. He would do nothing to change that will because He knew that was what was the perfect thing that had to happen. Do you know why he was so scared Kate?"

"Because He was going to be judged and beaten and die on a cross," I said with certainty.

"No, He was scared not because of what was going to happen to Him earthly but spiritually. He would have to pay for our sins not by his earthly death as much as His spiritual death. He would have to be forsaken by God to pay for our sins. He would have to take on the sins of the world...pay for all of them. Do you understand that? It would be bad enough if we have to pay for our own, let alone pay for the whole of the worlds, this is why He was so grieved."

I was so moved that I couldn't speak.

"See, Kate, Christ has gone through more than you ever will have to or ever will know. He grieved and was scared, but He still followed God's will and let Him lead, knowing He could trust Him because Christ had to die that death in order for us to have communion with Him. Do you see? The full picture is greater than the small puzzle piece, so you need to try to see yourself as part of the picture and let God lead, for He knows what needs to happen to strengthen you and guide you. Let him lead!" She squeezed my knee and smiled.

"Thank you, Denise. I appreciate you more than you know." I leaned forward and gave her a hug.

"Anytime, dear girl, anytime. Know I will be praying for you okay, and if there is anything you need please ask." She got up and went to the door wanting to leave me to think about the passage.

"I will. Thank you!"

After she closed the door I laid on my bed thinking about the passage. Christ was grieved? Even He asked to be saved from something, but He knew He wouldn't be. It gave me temporary relief, and I tried praying that my cup, too, would pass. That I could somehow get rid of Jay and be with Evan. That moment was short lived as I looked at my vibrating phone with Jay's number flashing at me.

Fear was my first reaction as I decided not to answer the phone, knowing that maybe with Evan now becoming more out of the picture that I didn't need to be as apt to conform to him. Then on the fourth call in three minutes I decided I should pick up.

"What no hello for your bed buddy?"

I remained silent as I felt shivers run down my spine.

"I don't think you have any right to give me the silent treatment, Kate. You are the one that broke the rules here not me."

Fear started turning to anger, and I couldn't hold my tongue any longer. "What rules, Jay? You don't play by any rules."

"Oh, come now you know what rules that I am talking about... bringing pretty boy along with you."

"I didn't bring, Evan. He followed me without me knowing."

"Well, then why leave in such a hurry? I could have taken care of that."

"Why didn't you then?"

"What?" he asked.

"You heard me, why didn't you?" I said.

"I thought I would give you a second chance to make it right. I don't want to get my hands dirty if I don't have to."

"You know what? I don't think that's it." I was suddenly feeling cocky and angry, and it was making a dangerous combination. "I think you are scared of Evan. I think you are so used to getting what you want through drugging people you wouldn't know what to do if someone actually fought you, especially a guy."

"You are on dangerous grounds, my dear. I would be careful if I were you."

"Oh, yeah what are you gonna do? Drug me? Give me a break. I am not afraid of you anymore, Jay. You can't hurt me. I have already let you get me to destroy my own life enough as it is. I'm done being afraid of you. You are all talk."

"You are getting awfully gutsy for a girl without any cards to play."

"I'm calling your bluff, you little loser."

"Really, okay, little girl, just wait till your next Hilltop and see what happens."

"There won't be another Hilltop. I got rid of Evan. He is leaving the country, you having nothing left to threaten me with."

"Wow, I'm impressed. I have to say this excites me a little to know you are slowly destroying your own life. I am getting my revenge without even trying that hard."

"I don't need Evan to make me happy."

"Coulda fooled me. Well let's see then, who do we have left? Precious Demetri?"

"I have a feeling you have no idea who he really even is. Plus Demetri would wipe the floor with you."

"Yeah, we will see about that. But actually it might be more fun to start with Amy, if you are going to be so bold."

"You can't touch her. She stays away from your type of crowd. She knows better than to be alone at any point. There's no way you could get to her without someone seeing you. Seriously, Jay, you're all talk. Have a nice life, you freak." I hung up the phone shaking. Dropping the phone on the bed, I froze. I wouldn't let him bully me anymore. I was going to take my life back. I looked down at my phone on the bed as it lit up with a text. "Game on" from Jay.

I immediately picked up the phone staring at the text. Without thinking I dialed Amy's number. It was time to tell her the truth. Who knew really what Jay was capable of? If I made him mad enough he was capable of anything. I needed to warn Amy. She picked up on the first ring.

"Kate! Hey, how are you?"

"Hey, Amy. I don't know how to start but I have to tell you something, and I need you to listen to me."

"What's going on?"

"Okay, well, first off I have to apologize because I have been kinda lying to you, but seriously it was only because I was trying to protect you."

"I knew something was up."

"Jay has been calling me, and not just recently. He first called me again during spring break. I didn't want to say because I didn't want anyone to get hurt, and I just felt like it would be better for everyone if I just stepped away. I thought it would make Jay leave you all alone."

"What do you mean leave us alone? He was been calling you even during spring break and you didn't say anything?" I could tell she was more than angry.

"He has been threatening you and Evan and Charlotte if I didn't give in to him. I had promised him tonight I would let him have what he wanted if he promised to leave you all alone, and he did. But then Evan followed me tonight, and I lied and said I was just going for a walk and got Evan out of there before Jay could hurt him. Then when Jay called I was angry at myself for giving in to him, and I called his bluff. But, Amy, now I am afraid he is coming after you. Please, Amy, be careful. I don't know what he's capable of, and I don't want to put anything past him. He said he would hurt you, and I don't know how he will do it, but please, please just surround yourself with people. Okay?"

"Oh, gosh, Kate, I don't know what to say. But how ridiculous for you to sacrifice yourself to the hands of such evil. Don't you have any trust in God at all? My dear friend, don't give up, okay? And don't worry about me or Evan or Charlotte. We are here are for you no matter what. We can all handle ourselves with Jay, okay? You just take care of yourself and be careful! Don't do anything stupid. We will figure this out. Listen I will come home tomorrow, and we can talk with Charlotte and Evan and come up with something. I think it is time to get the police involved since this is getting out of hand."

"No. Don't involve Evan or the police. Evan is living his life. I am getting what I am praying for in that instance. He got the internship in Italy he wanted, and he's actually leaving in a couple of weeks. Just let him be. I don't want anything to get in the way of his dreams. Promise me!"

"Okay, okay, I won't tell Evan if you are sure that's what you want. I'm sorry that he's leaving. I know this has to be hard on you."

"Obviously this is what God wants as well, to have Evan away from me."

"Kate, that's not how God works, and you know it."

"Do I?"

"Wow, my friend, I think we need some serious talk time this weekend."

"I know, I know. Please, Amy, just be careful, okay!"

"I will. I can handle Jay. I will see you tomorrow."

We said our good-byes, and with a heavy heart, I hung up the phone. I was so anxious about Amy, I couldn't relax. I was thankful she agreed not to tell Evan. At least I could be relieved where he was concerned. My sleep that night was anything but restful. I couldn't stop dreaming of Jay and what he would do to Amy. I couldn't wait till she was with us at Charlotte's.

I got up early and got dressed, trying not to wake Emily who looked so peaceful in her sleep. Now more than ever I wanted to be anyone but me. I stared out the window watching as life went on. The sun rising, the birds singing, flowers blooming. Life went on for everyone and everything, except for me. I felt like I would forever be stuck in some sort of nightmarish life. Never having a way out of the despair I was destined to live since I was born. The chances for me never increased.

Emily started to stir, and I realized the last thing I wanted to do was answer more questions. I was also upset with her for knowing about Evan's internship acceptance and not telling me. So I decided to leave for Charlotte's before she woke up. As I got to my car I realized that I shouldn't go to Charlotte's yet. It was too early, and she had had a show the previous night, so she got home past midnight. I needed to let her sleep. Especially since she had no idea what was going on and it was likely we would be up late again tonight. So I headed to Denny's for old times sake to grab some coffee. It felt lonely there though. Sitting in "our" old booth drinking coffee all alone. It made me think of how I have ruined everything with Evan, but I would not ruin everything *for* Evan. Letting him go was the best thing I could do for him. I couldn't help but think if things could have worked out differently for us. If chances were on my side instead of against me, could I have ended up with the man of my dreams? At least I got to be his best friend even if for a little while. Knowing Evan had been the highlight of my whole life and now I was left with nothing. Of course I had Amy and Charlotte, but that was different of course.

I had Demetri, but I still wasn't sure about that. Was I meant to be with someone who treated me like a kid? Was there even such a thing as meant to be? In church they always talked about how all things work for good and how nothing happens outside of God's will, but I was never sure of that. If that was true, how could I trust God since my whole life had never been good for anything? I was always hurting the ones I loved or getting them hurt. Even Sam, my first true friend. Look at what I had done to her. If only I hadn't left, I could have helped her. But then again, could I have? I hadn't really helped Evan, Amy, or Charlotte's lives at all.

So maybe Demetri was a good match for me. Maybe I didn't deserve anything more. At least he could take care of himself. I couldn't possibly see how I could hurt him. He was so confident in and of himself. He really only wanted me to be his caretaker—a mother, maid, wife, slave—whatever it was. Maybe I could learn to love him. He could take care of me, and I couldn't really hurt him. Unless of course I fell into that category, which I was sure to follow, of not being able to have children. Then he would be hurt because that was what he wanted. A family of his own with a wife to take care of it all. Would he even get rid of me then? Maybe I should have had that tested first. Was there a test for that? I realized I was again losing it. I would be best in some remote island away from everyone.

Suddenly my phone vibrated, and I looked down to see Charlotte's cell calling me. Amy must have told her we would be coming and maybe she wanted to know when I was coming.

"Hey, Chars! Good morning. You awake?"

"Kate, something has happened," she said in a solemn serious tone.

My heart stopped as I knew she was going to tell me something happened to Amy. But how? Between last night and this morning?

"It's Amy isn't it? Tell me, Charlotte. Where is she!!"

"She is in Santa Barbara Regional Hospital, but she is going to be okay. She had a fall this morning I guess. I got a call from her cell phone this morning from a student that had called nine-one-one when seeing her fall down the stairs in the Murdock building. He had found my phone number under her emergency contacts. He said the paramedics were on their way and were taking her to SB Regional. She was unconscious, but they said her vitals were good. It looked like she had a broken leg and maybe a broken collarbone but wouldn't know for sure till they got her to the hospital. I am driving there now, can you meet me there?"

"Of course I can. I'm on my way."

"Hurry, Kate!"

I threw some money on the table and ran to my car. She fell down the stairs? Maybe it was a freak coincidence. Thank goodness there was an eyewitness to her fall and she was able to get help right away. Horrific thoughts filled my mind the whole two hours it took to get to the hospital. I was hoping to find Amy okay and able to tell me what happened. She had promised me she wouldn't be alone, and it sounded like she was alone that morning or else why would some stranger be there calling for help? I got to the hospital and ran inside frantically looking for Charlotte. I knew that she would have beaten me there since she got a head start on the drive. I couldn't find her, however, so I asked one of the front nurses if Amy Snider was brought there. She directed me to her room and said her sister was with her. I peered in the room thankful to see Amy's eyes open. Her left leg was in a cast propped up in a sling and her neck was in a brace.

"Amy!" I entered the room with both girls turning to look at me.

"Kate!" they said in unison, but with Amy's voice a little less audible and scratchy.

"Amy, please tell me you are okay." I drew closer to her and started seeing she wasn't just broken but bruised as well. Her right upper cheek and eye were a bluish purple, and her arms had weird bruises lining them.

"I am okay," she said as she took my hand. "I have a broken leg, and they thought I had a broken collar bone, but they think it might just be pretty bruised. They are confirming with a look at my MRI I just had. They should be in soon to take this dumb neck brace off." She was remarkably good spirits. That was what I loved about Amy; nothing ever diminished her love for life and the Lord.

"How in the world did you fall down the stairs, and why were you alone? You promised me you wouldn't be alone." I looked up at

Charlotte knowing we hadn't told her any of this yet, but was surprised to see her with a knowing look and with anger in her eyes. She did know. Amy must have told her.

"Why didn't you call me last night? No, wrong question. Why were you hiding any of this from us, Kate? I am trying really hard not to be angry right now, but because you decided to hide this from us Amy is now in the hospital!" Charlotte said.

"Charlotte!" Amy yelled.

"Wait, what? Did Jay do this?" I looked at Amy for answers.

"I didn't want to tell you this, Kate. I really didn't, but Charlotte just had to open her mouth. I wanted to turn in my paper to Professor Colt this morning before heading to Charlotte's. I didn't think doing that was going to get me hurt. Plus there are always plenty of people around the English building, and I figured it wouldn't be an issue. I had just dropped off the paper and was heading back down to the car when in the corner of my eye I saw Jay right as I reached the stairs. He came out of nowhere. Before I could react he walked by me shoving me down the stairs. Those marble stairs are not so forgiving, ya know! But for that kind of fall I'm doing really well. I am thankful to the Lord for His grace at watching over me."

"Watching over you? How can you say that, Amy? How is lying in the hospital watching over you?" I asked.

"Because it could be much worse. Don't you see that? I will be up and out of here this afternoon and walking again in six to eight weeks. Without God's protection I would be dead right now. That's how!"

"Seriously, Kate, you should have come to us sooner with this. Jay is more dangerous than we thought. It is time to go to the police. We even have an eyewitness to say that he saw Jay push Amy down the stairs. This can be over," Charlotte said.

"No it won't. Not for me. It will never be over. I am so sorry, Amy! So sorry!" I cried. "It would be better if I weren't in your lives. I know this for sure now. I am so sorry for all the pain I have caused you. You have been the best sisters I could have asked for and I will always love you and keep you in my heart."

"What are you talking about, Kate? Don't be so dramatic. Amy is fine. I am sorry I got angry. This isn't your fault. I am mad at Jay and what he has done to you and now Amy. He has to be stopped, and I know with God on our side he will be." Charlotte leaned over Amy and took my free hand. I looked up at her beautiful face, and I knew I would just continue to bring harm to her if I stayed in her life as well as Amy's. I loved them too much for that. She was right before to be angry with me.

"He isn't on my side, though, Charlotte. And as long as you are on my side He won't be on yours. Amy, to know you will be okay is the greatest gift. Jay won't hurt you again, I promise. I love you! I love you both!" I let go of both their hands and ran out of the room. Charlotte came out of the room shouting my name, but I knew she wouldn't follow me and leave her sister. I ran back to my car at first not knowing where I would go. I felt so alone. I needed someone. I needed to figure all this out. There was only one person who could help me now and that was Demetri. He was mature and responsible; he would know what to do. He promised to be there more for me, and this would be the chance to figure that out. Plus if he was going to be the one I chose to spend my life with he would have to be able to handle these things with me. It was time I trusted Demetri and let myself fully commit to him.

I texted him that I was going to come over, that I needed to talk to him. He texted back saying he would be home waiting for me. I drove quickly. Thoughts of Amy crept into my mind. How could Jay have done that to Amy? How could he do what he did to anyone? Yes, he had to be stopped but how? I couldn't do it. But I couldn't let him win either. He had all those pictures of me doing things I shouldn't be doing. I wouldn't stand a chance against him. If I could find out who the other girls were maybe I could get us all to come forward. But they were in the same situation I was in, yet worse since he succeeded with them. The pain I caused those other girls. They were raped because of me. I should have turned him in when I had the chance. When I was covered in evidence. But it was my word against his. And with a powerful father, he would surely buy his way out. I didn't stand a chance—even if I wasn't cursed with bad luck.

I arrived at Demetri's at about two in the afternoon. It took a little over two hours to drive there, but I needed that time to be alone and put my thoughts together. I had only been to Demetri's twice. We usually went out for extravagant picnics or dinners or concerts, and he usually came to me. He lived in a gated community about twenty minutes from the theater, which was about forty minutes from Redeemer. He had bought the condo while still living in New York doing *Phantom of the Opera*. It was a beautiful place with gorgeous white columns and matching balconies lining the walkways. Large evergreens filled in the spaces between each condo providing privacy. Demetri's condo was at the end of a line of five with a little river/fountain that went the length of the walk across from the doorways. It was peaceful and the perfect place for him. I hurried up the door, eager to see him and hungry for a little sympathy and love. I had to only knock once and the door flew open with Demetri there to greet me with a hug. It was nice that he was just as eager to see me. I melted into his arms soaking in the affection, pushing to the back of my mind that his hugs didn't fit like Evan's. I pulled away and looked up at him smiling, truly glad to see him.

"Wow, it is nice to see you so happy to see me. I don't think I have ever seen you like this. Everything okay?" he said.

"Actually no."

"What's wrong?" He pulled away, taking my hands and putting on his I'm concerned face. Demetri had a theatrical face for everything. I didn't think he ever realized that his acting career and his real life meshed in more ways than one.

"Amy is in the hospital."

"What? Is she okay?"

I let go of his hands and walked past him, letting myself inside. His condo was a lot like Charlotte's in its set up. Directly when I entered there was a little living area with a fireplace and a tiny dining area offset with a breakfast bar that led into to the kitchen. The difference with Demetri's was first off it was a lot nicer with all the upgrades of granite and moldings, while Charlotte's was generic, and in Demetri's all the three bedrooms were upstairs. I still had no idea why Demetri needed three bedrooms. He said his old school friends who he still kept in touch with sometimes came to hang out and would end up crashing with him so it was nice to have the extra space.

I threw myself onto the couch and put my head in my hands trying to once again get a grip. The thoughts and emotions of all that was happening to me was coming on full force since being in Demetri's arms, knowing I would tell him everything.

Demetri came over and sat next to me rubbing my back, "Kate, what's going on? Is Amy okay?"

I sat up letting Demetri take my hands again as I turned my body toward him. His short hair was sticking up on it ends, and his eyes looked tired and red like he was running off of zero sleep. For a second I wondered if maybe his schedule was finally catching up with him.

"Amy will be fine. She has a broken leg and bruised collar bone from a hard fall down some marble stairs at school. She is pretty banged up on most of her body, but she will be released later this afternoon if all her tests results come back fine."

"Wow, how in the world did she fall down the stairs?"

"Well, here is where it gets tricky…she was pushed."

"What? Why would anyone push her down the stairs?"

"Because of me."

"You're not making any sense." Releasing my hands he rubbed his eyes and temples as if in confusion and distress. Always so dramatic.

"I know, and that's because I haven't told you everything about me. In order for this to make sense to you, there are some things you should know about me."

"Okay," he said hesitantly. "I'm not sure why you would hide anything from me, but I am willing to hear it."

"Look I didn't tell you things about me, because they are in my past, and I don't really like reliving it, and I didn't really feel it had any bearing on our relationship."

"I already know that you weren't a Christian before coming to Redeemer. Charlotte told me you had a sketchy past, but you're right I don't care about that. It is who you become that counts."

"Right…well unfortunately my past didn't stay there and is now back to literally haunt me."

"You are losing me."

"Okay, this is hard for me, so bear with me while I get this out. When I first went to Santa Barbara I was so excited to get away from home and make something of myself, and for a while I really stayed on track. But like most college students who are trying to find themselves I got myself involved with the wrong type of crowd. I started partying….a little too hard actually, and I started dating this guy. Well, after what I would think is a very short time of dating, he thought he would take it upon himself to declare that it was time for us to have sex. I said no, even though I wasn't a Christian. I still had morals and really did want to save myself till marriage. He backed off but got really mad at me, and we broke up. Closer to the end of the school year I saw him again at a party, and he apologized for his actions and said he was sorry and offered me a drink. I took it and accepted the apology. To make a very difficult and long story short, the drink was spiked with a date rape drug, and I woke up the next morning beaten up and lying in the bathroom at my dorm. I really don't know what happened. I don't remember fully. I only have flashes of memory from the night."

"Oh, my gosh, Kate, I'm so sorry! I can't believe how sick some guys are. I don't know what to say. I mean I was prepared for you not being a virgin, but I had no idea you lost your virginity that way."

"Well, he didn't succeed. I had thought that the morning after just because there was no evidence of him succeeding, but recently I have even greater proof that he didn't get what he wanted from me."

"Well, that's an amazing relief. But what kind of evidence do you have recently and what does this have to do with Amy?"

"Well, they coincide actually. I became a Christian because Amy is the one who found me in the bathroom that morning. She helped me in so many ways, including helping me to transfer to Redeemer and leave my old life behind. I thought truly I had left it behind. Amy was the only one there who knew where I had gone through, at least that's what I thought. The guy who assaulted me has recently found me again. I guess he has been looking for me over this past year. He found me a little before spring break and has made significant threats against me and those I love. I felt so helpless that one night I decided I was going to give him what he wanted. Due to certain circumstances I didn't go through with it, and he became angry. Even more so when I challenged him and told him his threats were empty and he would never go through with anything. Well, that is when he pushed Amy down the stairs."

"Woah, woah, woah...this is getting crazy. You were going to give this guy what he wanted? What are you insane? Sometimes I think you seek trouble, Kate. You couldn't live a normal life for ten seconds?"

"No, no, it's not like that. I was trying to protect the people I care about."

"Yeah, good job doing that. It landed Amy in the hospital. Really stupid choice!"

"No, I know, I know."

"And how did he get out of jail so soon?"

"Out of jail?"

"Yeah, I would expect he would be getting jail time for the assault."

"Oh…" Ashamed, I turned my head toward to the floor. "I didn't turn him in."

"What? You have got to be kidding me."

"Look, Demetri, I feel bad enough about my life as it is. I don't need you rubbing my bad decision in my face. I could use a little sympathy and some help figuring this out."

"What is there to figure out? It is called *turn the guy in*."

"It's not that simple. He is threatening me, Charlotte, you, and Evan. Who knows what he is capable of? Plus he has incriminating photos of me."

"Photos? What kind of photos? What have I gotten myself into?"

"Not the kind of photos you are thinking, I don't think. I mean I haven't seen them. I just know he has photos of me doing drugs and stuff like that." I was feeling sick just thinking of it.

"Great! Perfect." He stood up again rubbing his face and walking over to the fireplace putting his head down on it.

Just then I heard the sound of water running from upstairs. Like someone had just flushed a toilet.

"Is someone here?"

"What? Oh yeah, my friend Jason is here. He is staying with me over the weekend. I got home at midnight last night and then I wanted to catch up with him, so I didn't get to bed till after four this morning. I am exhausted right now. I am sure we woke him up with all this nonsense. I was going to introduce you to him after he woke up, but now I am not so sure that is a good idea. I need to think about all of this with you first."

"Why are you treating me like the plague all of a sudden?"

"Look, Kate, I saw potential in you, but to be honest, this is all a little much for me."

"Unbelievable!" I shouted, standing up. "I knew this would happen with you, but I so wanted to believe it wouldn't. You are all about yourself. I'm going through something terrible here, and I could use your support and guidance and all you can do is judge me? Great! Just great."

"Keep your voice down! Seriously, Kate!"

I heard footsteps coming down the stairs and braced myself for meeting Demetri's friend. I could tell Demetri was doing the same as we both were trying to adjust ourselves to look presentable and agreeable.

I heard him as he entered the room.

"Hey man, sorry, Kate and I were talking. You will have to excuse us." Demetri walked closer to me putting his hand on my shoulder turning me around so he could introduce me.

I turned and looked up. It was like someone had hit me square in my chest and the breath was knocked out of me. Standing in front of me, smiling, was Jay. Suddenly it all became clear. Jay found me because he knew Demetri. He knew about Demetri in my life because he was friends with Demetri. He got my cell from Demetri. It was all laid out in front of me. I almost wanted to start laughing at the whole scenario. It all was too much!

"Jason this is Kate, the girl I have been telling you about these past few months."

"You have got to be kidding me." I chuckled. "You bastard. This is how you have been playing this all along. You knew it all because of Demetri. What luck for you, huh?"

"Umm, sorry?" Jay said. "I have no idea what you are talking about."

"Don't play dumb. You're lucky I am not strangling you right now for what you did to Amy!"

"Really, Kate, I think you have me confused with someone else," he said.

"Kate, what are you talking about?" Demetri asked.

"This is him, Demetri. The guy I was just telling you about."

"What? Jason? Kate, I think you are a little delusional right now, there is *no way* that Jason did what you say."

I looked over at Jay who had a disgusting grimace on his face. How could Demetri be so blind?

"No! No! I am not going to stand for this. Not anymore. You are going to pay for this, Jay. I promise you. You can't get away with this."

"Kate! That is enough! You have no idea what you are talking about. I am sorry that bad things happened to you or are happening to you and Amy, but this is not how you act about it. Jason is not this 'Jay,' as you are calling him, and he wouldn't do the things you are talking about. Plus he has been here since yesterday afternoon, there was no way he could have hurt Amy."

"You said you went to bed at four a.m., well, it is only a two-hour drive...he could have easily got there and back without you knowing since you just woke up when I texted you."

"You are being ridiculous. I have never seen this side of you before. In fact today has been full of revelations about you. I am just not sure this relationship is best for either of us."

"You are breaking up with me now? I can't believe this. You are taking his side over mine? It all is just working out so perfectly for you isn't, Jay? You wanted to destroy my life, and now you are doing it, aren't you?"

"Again, sweetheart, I have no idea what you are talking about," he said.

"Sweetheart?" I couldn't handle it anymore. My body began shaking with fury and screaming I lunged forward at Jay toppling him to the stairs that were behind him. Before I could get a good punch in I was being slung off of him. I hit the ground hard about seven feet from where Demetri stood over Jay helping him up.

"Kate, enough!" Demetri yelled at me. "I think you better go... now!" Demetri quickly came to my side yanking me off the floor and dragging me to the door.

"What are you doing? Why are you not listening to me? You are willing to believe him over me?"

"Well, let's look at our situation today…this isn't the first time you have lied to me, Kate. I am done trying to make this work. I'm seeing you are a little on the psychotic side of life, and I am not willing to take your word on anything at the moment."

"What about Charlotte or Amy's then?"

"They are under your spell, I'm sure. They love you too much to know the difference of you deceiving them. But I am not about to let you take down my best friend just because you *think* he did something to you. And you aren't even sure if anything *did* happen to you. Jason seems to not know who you are. So yes, I am taking the side of my friend of over twenty years over yours."

I looked over my shoulder at Jay. He knew he was winning again and was taking pure pleasure out of my insignificant try of a fight. Demetri let go of my arm when he succeeded at putting me out like a dog. He then turned without a single word and closed the door. I stood there still not knowing what to do or what to think. What had just happened? Jay was being protected by the one man I thought would protect *me*. The one man who I had decided I would try to love and share my life with. Now Jay had him, too.

After about what seemed an hour, but had to be only five minutes, I started walking back to my car. Where would I go? Back to school? What would Jay do now? I had to fight back but how, I had nothing to fight back with. I was all alone without any way to fight anyone or anything. I reached my car and fumbled in my pocket for my keys.

"I told you not to mess with me, Kate."

Jay was there, but anger still gripped me instead of fear and I turned around to face him with furry once again.

"What are you doing out here, Jay? Wouldn't want to prove I am right to Demetri you know."

"Oh, he is up taking a shower. No need to worry about that. I think he wanted to wash the rest of you out of his life."

"What do you want from me, Jay?" I yelled.

"I want to destroy you, just like you said. I want to make your life a living hell. I want to prove to you that this God you thought would save you won't! There is no power but what you make for yourself. I am your god, Kate! My power exceeds anything you could ever do to me. I always get what I want, and right now I want to ravage and destroy you. But I am enjoying this slowly. For a year I thought about what a fool you made me out to be when we were dating. Paul told all my frat brothers what happened that night in your dorm room, and you have no idea what kind of grief I still get from that. The guy that couldn't close the deal. So here I am, to make a fool out of you like you did me and to finally close the deal. So don't think this is over, my dear, not by a long shot."

He stepped closer to me pinning me up against my car. His hot breath felt like spikes on my face as he loomed over me. Suddenly with force he grabbed my face and kissed me hard. I tried to knee him in the groin, but he was pressing me so hard I couldn't move. So I went with the next best thing and bit him as his lips tried to pry my mouth open. He jerked back with a yelp of pain, and his left arm swung a powerful blow to my right cheek. It swung me around to the left, and I gripped the door handle for support to not fall to the ground.

"You never learn do you, Kate? Don't worry I am not mad. You will make it up to me." He turned and started walking back toward the condo dabbing the blood of his lips with his sleeve.

I jumped into the car and drove away as fast as I could. When I reached the first stoplight the flood of emotions started to flow and tears were pouring down my cheeks. I couldn't stop shaking with both fear and anger. A honk came from behind me that temporarily popped me into reality. I started driving again, not really sure where I was driving and not really caring. I couldn't win. How could I win? Amy said she saw Jay before he pushed her, but that is probably why he spent the night at Demetri's for an alibi. It would be her and this so-called witness's word over his, just like it was with everyone else. If somehow we could get all of the girls he has assaulted to come forward and then with Amy and my story we could paint a good picture. A picture he couldn't possibly get out of. Right? I wasn't so sure.

My mind floated to Amy in the hospital, and I felt sick at the thought of her being there because of me. Sam too was in despair because of me. I had lost Evan. But he had the internship to go to. In this case at least I felt like I was saving him somehow and that made it easier to let him go. My heart ached for him now more than ever. I needed him. I needed his guidance and his love. I always had. I started crying even harder thinking of Evan leaving soon and never seeing him again. He had tried to call me that morning on my drive to the hospital but I ignored him. I felt it was best. I still hadn't listened to his message. Wanting to hear his voice I decided to listen to it. I grabbed my phone and put his message on speaker.

"Kate," he said softly. Hearing his voice made me smile and my cheeks heat up at the thought of his eyes looking deep into mine like they often did. "I am agonizing over the way we left each other last night. I hate arguing with you. You are my truest friend, and I really am happy for you and Demetri. I hope that you get everything you deserve, Kate, because you deserve so much. All I want for you is to be safe and happy and as long as you are both, I can leave you. It will be hard to leave you, Kate, it really will. I truly love you and to not see you every week is going to kill me, but I will be happy knowing you are happy. I would love to see you one last time before I go. This week is hard with all the papers I have to write, but next weekend before I go home to get things in order I need to see you. Please. Call me when you can."

Hearing his sweet voice was more than I could handle. Truly I loved him. I loved him unlike I had loved anyone else in my life. Because of that I would lie to him. I would tell him I was happy. I would let him leave thinking I was happy and he could let me go.

I was driving in deep despair and torment, so I didn't notice the rain begin. I thought it was my tears that blurred my vision. So when I was hit at fifty miles per hour on the passenger side of the car by a woman who skidded through a stoplight, I barely noticed. I came out of the blackness to the sounds of glass breaking and falling and the pressure of the air bag against my chest. I could feel the warmth of blood trickling up my face. Up my face? I took a quick look around to realize I was upside down. My head hurt with intense pain, and my legs were trapped in place losing feeling. Rain was pouring down outside the car, and it was eerily quiet. No one was coming to see if I was okay, and I had no way to get out by myself. I heard no sirens coming to my rescue or screams for help, not even my own. I tried to scream but nothing would come out. Panic started to set in as I sat there in pain just waiting. Waiting for help to come.

War Waged

As blackness started to grip me again, I heard what I had been waiting what felt like hours to hear. Footsteps. I searched the blank spaces that surrounded the car looking for feet. I searched outside the steps to hear anything else, people, sirens, still nothing. Nothing but the footsteps. As they came closer I began to get scared. Somehow I knew that I should be in fear. That what was coming was not what I wanted. Suddenly there they were, the feet that fit the steps right at the window of the passenger side. They were small feet, a woman's for sure, with black leather combat boots that glistened from the rain that was still falling. She stood there for a minute without saying anything; then I could hear a faint laughter coming from her direction.

"What have you gotten yourself into, Kate?" she said.

I had to be hearing things. It sounded exactly like Sam.

"Who's there? Please I need help!" I begged, hoping they would call for help.

"Oh, that is an understatement! I leave you for a year and look at what you get yourself into."

Now I knew for sure it was Sam.

"Sam?"

She knelt down to peer at me through the broken window. Her hair was dark black as was the rest of her clothing. I couldn't really make out her face, but it looked like she was wearing dark makeup around her eyes.

"Surprised to see me? Well, I have been waiting for this day to come."

"What? Sam, why are you just standing there? You have to get me some help." I could feel myself slipping into unconsciousness.

"Oh, I will get you some help, in more ways than you know." Sam stood up and started walking away. I couldn't believe she was leaving me. Was she getting me help? Why wasn't anyone else around? I started screaming her name begging for her to come back and help me, but there was nothing, and quickly I fell into blackness.

When I woke up, instead of blackness, there was only white. Lots of white with bright lights. As my eyes adjusted I could tell I was in a hospital room. I could hear the slow dripping of the IV that was attached to my left hand and the beeping from the monitor that was cuffed around my right bicep. As I looked around the room I realized that this was not like any hospital room I have ever seen. I was alone in a room that held only a bed with just the IV and the monitor. There were no windows, chairs, TVs—I couldn't even make out a door. Even though the room was spacious, I was starting to feel claustrophobic. Where were the nurses and doctors? Why wasn't my family there? Even though I knew my parents didn't like me all that much, I surely thought they would be there if something happened to me. I suddenly realized I didn't really feel any pain. I put my hand to my head. There was no bandage. I moved my legs and they were fine. In fact I felt great. I started to panic not knowing what was going on. I closed my eyes and tried to calm down. That's when I started to hear the voices.

"Kate! Kate! Can you hear me? We love you, Kate, everything is going to be okay."

Amy? That was Amy's voice. I threw open my eyes, but the room was still empty.

"Amy? Amy, where are you?" I screamed hoping she would answer me.

"We're here, Kate! We won't leave you. We will be here when you get out."

That was Charlotte. She was there? Get out of where? I screamed for Charlotte, but heard nothing more.

"Calm down, Kate. You are losing it," Sam said as she appeared to my left.

"Sam! Sam what is going on? Where am I?"

"You are with me, that's where. My friends and I took you from the car crash and brought you here to heal you."

"What? Where is here?"

"It doesn't matter where we are, but look at you. You have your healthy glow again. You should be ready by tomorrow." She was now looking at some chart that was at the end of the bed.

"Ready for what?"

"Your training of course."

"Training? What are you talking about? What is going on?"

"Calm down, my friend. I will explain everything, and then you will see where you belong."

She sat at the edge of my bed looking at me with a peculiar smile. Now that there was so much light I could truly look at her. She was still dressed in all black with the same combat boots now propped up on the bottom of my bed. My impressions of her from the car were correct. Her face was deathly pale, and her eyes were outlined in black, with her green eyes now looking black themselves. Jay had been right—she was far into this world she had found. I was afraid of her for the first time. This was not the Sam I knew and loved.

"Kate, I was infuriated when you left me, and I went on a search, a search to find a life for myself. And I have to thank you because I found one. I found a life that gives me both power and great peace and happiness. It is amazing to be in control of your own life. To be able to control myself and others. Just you wait Kate, you won't believe it."

"I'm truly sorry for what I did to you. For leaving you like that and not trying to bring you with me. For ditching you. Truly, I am sorry."

"Oh, please! Like I said it was the best thing that happened to me. And I won't leave you like you did me, Kate. I have been waiting for this moment to come. It's amazingly easy to manipulate things to go your way when you have so much on your side. It was a plus how all things just fell together more perfectly than I had anticipated. But here we are. Here you are!"

"Sam, you are freaking me out. Where am I? Please what are you talking about?"

"Kate, all you really have to know are these two things: One is that you are safe here, and we are taking care of you. Two, this is your true family. You have been wasting your life trying to fit yourself into a family that doesn't truly exist. But now you will see. We will show you what *does* exist and what side you should pick. The side that will change the luck you have had. Your life is what *you* make it, not what a fake god tells you to make it."

"Sam, I truly have no idea what you are talking about, but God is not fake, and His family is the one I am meant to be in. He has a plan for me. I know it."

"Do you know it? Do you feel it? Tell me, when has He been faithful to you? How has He helped you? What kind of plan would consist of you being terrorized and tortured? Of being loved and left by everyone around you. Your so-called friends' love is conditional. Not ours, Kate. You belong here! We can show you a different way. A way that puts you first and gives you more power than you can imagine. All you have to do is choose. Choose us. I promise you the world."

"How can you promise me anything? God loves me. I know He does. He has been there for me! Please stop." I started tearing at my IV and cuff to get loose. I jumped out of bed and frantically started looking for the door.

Sam came up to me and forcefully turned me around.

"Stop, Kate! You won't find it till we think you are ready. Please just trust me! I don't know why are you fighting so hard for something that has never done anything but caused you pain. Tell me what has He *ever* done for you?"

It was a question I wasn't in the mindset to answer. What had He done for me? I couldn't say. I thought of Demetri and how controlling he was and how he chose Jay over me. I thought of Jay and all the pain he caused me. I thought of Evan, how I loved him but could never be with him. Nothing good had come for my life;

that had been true since I was born. Had that really changed even since believing in God? I couldn't say it had. In fact at that point, it had gotten worse. She was right. Maybe it all wasn't real. Maybe life was what we do with it and make it for ourselves. I looked at Sam and even though she seemed slightly scary to me, she seemed at peace with her life. She seemed happy. Something I didn't think I ever really was. Maybe bits and pieces here and there, but never fully and for long. I turned and stared back at the blank white wall my soul in distress.

"I can see you are having a time of reflection, as you should. You will see in time. I will let you think about things for a minute and come back later." I turned around and she was gone. What was going on? My soul was in the greatest distress. I was torn. I couldn't figure out what was real. I could feel that Sam was wrong. There was a God and He loved me. Right? But I couldn't deny what she was saying. There was no proof that I could see that I was right. My life was worse off. What she offered me was tempting. Happiness and power. Peace and control over my life. Something I had never had. What if she was right? What if there wasn't a God, and I was wasting my life trying to live for something that wasn't true? I was going through all this pain for nothing. All I have ever wanted was meaning and happiness in my life, and I couldn't say I ever even had that when I accepted what I thought was the truth. I just looked at Amy and wanted to be her. I wanted to heal like she did, and I would do or accept anything to get it.

I realized I had stayed in the same spot since Sam left, which felt like hours ago. I suddenly became extremely tired, so I made my way over to my hospital bed. The IV was gone, but I could still hear the beeping sound of the monitor even though I wasn't hooked to it, nor could I even see it. My mind was hazy and confused. I felt like I was in a dream world. I lay down and rested my head on the pillow. My eyelids felt like bricks, and there was no fighting them any longer. I closed my eyes and let the blackness take me.

Warmth covered my hand. A softness I recognized. I couldn't open my eyes; they were still too heavy.

"Kate, can you hear me? Squeeze my hand if you can hear me, Kate."

It was Charlotte. I tried to squeeze, but I was too tired. Had she finally come to see me? Did she find me?

"Kate, we love you. Please come back to us. We are praying for you," Amy said. Amy was there too? I knew they cared for me. I knew they would fight for me and find me.

I struggled to get my eyes to open. When I managed to pry them open slightly I glanced around to an empty room. I was hearing things for sure, for there was no one there. I was still alone. No one had found me. Sam was right—no one was fighting for me. I let myself slip back into darkness with despair. As I gave in I could hear, "Fight, Kate," being whispered. Fight for what?

When I came to for real the next time, I felt it easier to open my eyes. My body ached when I woke this time, and I was surprised that it hurt a little to move.

"Well, good morning, sleepy head," Sam said. I jerked myself up realizing I wasn't in a hospital room anymore but a bedroom. I was lying in a black canopy bed that was laden with sheer black curtains. As I quickly peered around the room to the left there was a small fireplace with a concrete hearth that was flanked by demon-dragon looking statues. Two red velvet chaises sat in front of the fireplace. To the right was a black dresser with an oval mirror framed with black cherubs and a small black and red lamp set atop it. Red candles were lit throughout the room. At the base of the bed I spotted Sam. She was still looking the same as when I last saw her except this time she wore bright red lipstick as if trying to match the room. I was immediately uncomfortable with my surroundings and was longing to be back in the blank white hospital room.

"Do you like your bedroom?"

"Actually no," I said blankly.

"Is that the thanks we get for saving your life when no one else cared about you?"

"I am still not sure I believe that."

"Did you see anyone else coming to your rescue while you hung upside down dying?"

I didn't speak.

"Yeah I didn't think so."

"You know you keep telling me no one is fighting for me, yet how do I really know that? I mean how do I know if they even know where I am?"

"Well, even if they didn't, you would think they would try to find out right? But so far we haven't had any inquiries into you being missing or anything, so I can only imagine they are grateful you are out of their lives since you were ruining it."

"That's crap, Sam. What kind of friend do you think you are saying stuff like that to me?"

"The only one that will tell you the truth, like as soon as you left, Demetri left town. He gave his part to his understudy and went to Europe to join a theater company over there and study at the university."

"Who cares about Demetri? He wasn't the one for me anyway."

"Oh, that's right. You're in love with Evan…well, I don't see him here either. He is at home getting ready for his trip to Italy without you. But you already know that since you pushed him away. But you were right because he doesn't love you the way you love him, and he never will. Good save."

"Shut up, Sam!"

"Why? I am not telling you anything you don't know already. I don't know why you are torturing yourself with this. Just let it go already, and we can move on!"

"Move on to what?"

"Once you move on, then you will see. Let go of what you think you know, and you will truly be set free. I will never understand why you people who believe in gods will ever think it sets you free when all you do is follow rules." Her words stung. Yet my head was telling me she was right. It was all a set of rules. How could I truly be free if I was following someone else's rules? I was confined by something I doubted.

"Why did you save me anyway? I haven't even talked to you in a year and now somehow you show up at an accident that I happen to be in and rescue me when no one else is. Nothing makes sense."

"It doesn't make sense because you are thinking in worldly ways instead of supernatural. You will learn in time. All you have to do is choose. Choose what you are going to believe, and you will be set on that path. Choose our way, and you will have power, peace, happiness, and understanding. Choose the way you were on, and you will have nothing but pain and sorrow. It sounds like an easy choice to me."

It did sound easy, but then why wasn't it? I could feel myself holding on to what I had thought was true. I was holding on to God even though it seemed to be slipping away. I kept hearing "Fight, Kate" in my head, but I didn't know what I was to fight or whom I was fighting.

"Come on, Kate, give it up already. Look at you. You already look worse, and the pain will only get worse the longer you take. Choose us, and there will be no more pain."

"But choosing you means what? What am I choosing?"

"Power."

"But I don't understand that. What power?"

"You ask too many questions. Why can't you just trust what I am saying and just choose my way?"

"Because I don't understand your way!" I tried to get out of bed. It was more difficult though as my body and head ached.

"What is there to understand? You will get everything you want. You didn't understand Amy's way and yet you chose to follow her."

At first I thought she was right, but she wasn't. I didn't choose Amy's way. I had chosen Christ and His way. I had chosen forgiveness.

"Will your way offer forgiveness?" I asked now standing and walking to look in the mirror.

"Why would you need forgiveness when nothing you do is wrong here? You can be yourself without any regret or need of forgiveness."

My mind swirled with that idea. How would it be to never do anything wrong? That was impossible, wasn't it? I reached the mirror and looked at my reflection. I looked haggard and worn out. Dark circles under my eyes were highlighted by the paleness of my skin. I drug my hand through my lifeless, dull hair trying to comb out the ratted mess and realized my nails had grown spiky and long. My body was thin and bony, in short, I looked like death. I turned to face Sam.

"What have you done to me?"

"What do you mean?"

"I mean look at me," I said holding out my hands.

"You were in a terrible car accident, Kate, what do you expect?"

"How long ago was it?"

"A while. Look, Kate, your appearance is just a reflection of your inner turmoil. If you would just choose the right side you would look beautiful. No more having to worry about what you look like. You become the outward appearance of what you feel. Look at me for example. I feel rebellious and free...thus this is what my outward appearance is. I still look like me, just different."

Again, I was confused. What had she brought me into? I had heard things about witchcraft but this seemed different. Completely different!

"Kate, what are you waiting for? I figured with everything going on in your life you would have easily made this choice. I am a bit confused."

"You're a bit confused? I'm a bit confused. It isn't that easy to let go of what saved me."

"But that is what I am telling you, Kate! Don't you get it! You weren't saved from anything!" She was getting aggravated now and hit one of the candles sitting on the mantle of the fireplace. Immediately the candle extinguished.

"Why are you so mad?"

"Because I don't want to be wasting my time. I went through a lot to get you here, and now you are not being appreciative of any of it. There is nothing to think about!"

"But there is. When I heard that you were in trouble I felt for you, and I wanted to help you. It was all my fault. And now you're asking me to give up everything to come to the same place you are? I'm not sure I want that."

"Then tell me, what you do want?"

"I don't know. I don't know," I said grabbing my hair. "Peace, I guess. I don't know. I just want to be happy. I want to stop hurting the people around me. I want things to work out for me for once." I closed my eyes trying to find peace and imagine myself somewhere else.

Then I heard Evan's voice. "Kate, please come back to me, don't leave me, not this way. I have so much I need to tell you. I am sorry for the way I acted. I pray you can hear me. Please, God, I can't go through this again."

"Evan?" I screamed opening my eyes to find only Sam.

"What? Your precious Evan isn't here. I told you he left you for Italy. Look, you need to stop fighting this and just give in to what you know you want and need."

"I can't handle this, please can you just leave me alone right now?"

"Fine, Kate, but we won't wait forever. Either choose us, or deal with the consequences."

I looked up and again she was gone. Just like that, like she was never there to begin with.

I couldn't get a grip around what was going on. I needed to think, but I couldn't get my mind to work. I couldn't get anything to work. Why was I here? Why hadn't anyone come to rescue me but Sam? Why wasn't anyone looking for me? Yet this was what I wanted right? I wanted to have them out of my life and safe, and now they were. But Jay was still out there. Would he move on and hurt others now that I was gone? Did they think I was dead? Did they care? Did I care? All I have wanted was happiness, and I thought I had found it, until Jay came back. I was happy. Amy and Charlotte were always good to me, and Evan was the best friend I had ever had. Yes, I loved him, and he didn't love me, but I was still happy. But now everything was torn apart. Amy was hurt, and Charlotte knew it was my fault. Evan was leaving, and I was alone. Now I had the chance to not be alone. To have everything fixed again. I wanted that more than anything. But the fighting voice kept coming back. What was it telling me to fight for? What about the voices I was hearing? Was that just me dreaming or wishful thinking? I couldn't think. I was going insane. My eyes became heavy again, so I made my way to the bed and lay down.

"Kate, I love you. I always have. Trust me," came a strong, masculine voice. I couldn't pinpoint it. My eyes shot open and again the room was empty. I felt a sudden warmth and a feeling of love. I let myself soak it up and fell again into blackness.

"Dearest Lord God, please watch after our precious Kate. Bring her peace, dear Lord. If it is Your will, bring her back to us, Lord, heal her. And hold up Evan, dear Lord, as he is having such a hard time with this. He had to go through this with his brother—he can't lose Kate too. Thank you for all you have done for us, Lord. In Your Son's holy name Amen." It was Amy's voice, but again when I opened my eyes she wasn't there. What was going on? Why was I hearing things? Why could I feel the presence of love when I felt so far from it? I was losing my will to fight against Sam if that was what I was fighting. I was now in so much pain, not just physically, but emotionally and spiritually. I didn't know what to do, and I wasn't sure I could handle it.

"Today is the day, my dear friend!" Sam cheerfully laughed as she appeared near the fireplace again.

"What day?"

"The day you must choose, my dear, and I have something here I think just might convince you." She held out her hand, which contained an old tattered envelope with my name on it. I took it from her hand and examined it. There was a black wax seal that closed the envelope that had a picture of a satanic star on it. I shuddered at the touch of it. I knew this is what most people in her lifestyle used as a symbol but just the look of it sent so much evil through my veins I couldn't bear it and dropped the envelope.

"Don't be such a scaredy-cat. It doesn't mean anything."

I didn't believe her for a second. She picked up the envelope and stroked it slightly.

"This envelope holds something irresistible to you. Something that I know will help you to see who is watching out for you and who isn't."

I had to admit I was curious. I didn't even know what would be irresistible to me anymore since I had no idea what I wanted.

"Here, go ahead and open it. Don't be afraid. Believe me, it will be worth it." She came closer and handed me the envelope again. I took it with a shaky hand and stared again at the seal. Curiosity was now in control, and I carefully tore open the seal and pulled out the photograph that was inside. I turned it around and there staring back at me was a picture of Jay lying in what looked like a forest with a gunshot to his head. I screamed and dropped the photo backing away and into the dresser behind me.

"You killed Jay? What in the world, Sam?"

"No, no, silly, at least not yet anyway. But this is what we are offering you—revenge."

"Revenge?"

"Yes, what you want most. Revenge on the person who took your happiness from you. Can you imagine what your life would have been like if that night never happened? These things, this pain that you are going through and have gone through since you have met him would have never happened. Imagine it, Kate!"

And I did imagine it. It was a beautiful thought, one I had always wished was reality. But would I want him dead? Deep down, I did. I had actually prayed for that. But I never really meant it. Or did I? Maybe I wasn't good after all. Maybe I wasn't meant to be saved because I was such a sinner. What if there was no sin, no reason to be ashamed of whom I was or was to be?

"How would this happen? What would I have to do to have this happen?"

"Well, it is really simple. In order for you to become part of our family and to get everything you desire you have to pass a test. The test is very simple, in fact it should be quite enjoyable for you. You have to kill Jay."

"What? Me?"

"I will be there with you every step of the way helping you! This is what you want, Kate, and you can have everything. You just have to choose. Right now."

"Now? Why now?"

"Because we are running out of time. We only get a certain amount of time. I know you don't understand that, and I can't explain it to you, but you need to choose now."

My head was swimming. I stared down at the picture of Jay that lay on the floor. Suddenly it morphed into a different picture of him, one of him the way I remembered him that night. His evil face staring back at me mocking me and tormenting me. Telling me how pathetic I was. The look of pleasure on his face as he beat me up.

"Think about it, Kate, he never has to hurt you again. Think of what it felt like to wake up in that bathroom all broken and bruised. To have your peace ripped away from you like that. Think of how it felt when he was tormenting you and Evan and how he hurt Amy. Think of all those girls he raped because of you. You can end this, and you can end this now, and all you get in return is what you have always wanted. Not only him out of your life, but you get a new life in return. One where you won't ever feel that way again."

Anger burned inside of me, and I realized she was right. This was what I wanted. Jay out of my life. I pushed deep inside of me the thoughts of guilt, and I gave into the anger. The warmth of love gave way to the heat of revenge and I was taken with it.

"All right, Sam. All right. For Jay to never hurt me or anyone else again, I will do this."

"Good girl!" she said. "Let's get this show on the road."

Within a blink of an eye I was transformed. I could feel the strength raging in my muscles. I peered at myself in the mirror where now stared back at me a silky, black-haired girl with dark-blue eyes and beautiful yet still pale skin. I was now dressed in black like Sam, but flanked with red accents. I looked angry and frightful, reflecting what I was feeling on the inside. Sam was right. Thoughts were yelling at me in my head that this was wrong. I was choosing wrong, but I didn't care. I wanted it to end and this was the only way I could see it would end well.

"Let's go!" Sam said as she walked to a wall that now had a door.

I hesitated for a second and Sam looked back. I peered down at the picture of Jay, which was still the one of him tormenting me. I took a deep breath and followed Sam out the door strengthened by fury.

We walked outside where it was cloudy and dark. How could it still be raining? I felt like I had been inside for months. I turned around to see the building I had stayed in but found myself in the middle of a retail center right next to a little coffee shop with an outdoor patio.

"Okay, Kate, I want you to wait here for me, and I will be back in just a minute." Sam said as she pulled me over to a seat on the patio.

"Wait where are you going? Don't leave me here! I don't even know where I am."

"Well, that's a good thing, right? Then you won't run away anywhere since you would have nowhere to go. Plus even if you tried you wouldn't get far. So do me a favor and be a good girl and sit here and don't talk to *anyone*. Got it?" She turned to the left running down the road around a corner and out of sight.

I felt fear and confusion shimmy down my spine. What did she mean I wouldn't get far? Why would I run? I had nothing to run to, and as far as I could tell no one was even around for me to talk to. The place was quiet and dead, the coffee shop was dark and locked up.

As each minute passed that Sam didn't return fear took over me more and more. I pressed my hands against my temples and closed my eyes trying to focus on what I was doing here. Why I had chosen to follow Sam.

"No choice is ever final until the end, my dear." A soft and manly voice rang in my ears. I wanted to open my eyes but didn't want to see the vacancy around me again.

"Who's there? What do you mean?" I asked with my head still down wanting to talk to the darkness rather than to nothing. Even though I was directly disobeying Sam to not talk to anyone there was something about the voice that urged me to see what he had to say.

"You are given every moment to make your decision. It is not too late to fight until your time has come."

"My time?"

"Yes, the time of your death, then the choice is gone forever, and you can never take it back. But until then it is never too late. No matter what you have chosen to do, you will be forgiven. You can make the right choice!"

"But what is the right choice?"

"Deep down you know what the right choice is."

"Do I? I thought I knew what the right choice was, but that has proven to be false."

"Why do you think it is false?"

"Because if it was true then I wouldn't be in this mess, I wouldn't be so tormented. He would have proven to be true to me. He says that all things work for good to those who love Him, yet there has been nothing good for me. So if He is true He doesn't love me."

"He says all things work for good, but not that all things *are* good for those who love Him. He *does* love you. You just haven't let Him lead. You yourself have tried to take control and that is why you don't see what He *is* doing for you. You have blinded yourself to what He is trying to do for you. Remember, my sister, that you life is just a piece of an entire puzzle. Only you can see the puzzle piece, but God sees the entire picture all put together. You won't understand some things that happen, but that is where faith comes in. You can trust Him and have faith in Him because He does love you."

"But He doesn't. There is nothing I can see that says otherwise." I started to cry in aggravation.

"What of Christ? What of His torture and death? Is that not enough for you?" the voice asked. "Who will separate us from the love of Christ? Will tribulation, or distress, or persecution, or famine, or nakedness, or peril, or sword? But in all things we overwhelmingly conquer through Him who loved us. For I am convinced that neither death, nor life, nor angels, nor principalities, nor things present, nor things to come, nor powers, nor height, nor depth, nor any other created thing, will be able to separate us from the loved of God, which is in Christ Jesus our Lord." He was quoting Romans 8:35.

I could remember how many times I had read that passage, yet not really thought about it. But what did it mean to me? Because I was being overwhelmed and separated. A warm hand was placed on my back. Could there really be someone there? I quickly took my hands from my face and look toward the hand and up to the face of a man I recognized—it was Pastor Bruce from the first church I attended with Amy.

"Pastor Bruce, what are you doing here?"

"I'm here because you need me. I'm here because you are straying, and I'm a servant of our Lord trying to bring you back."

"What?"

"Kate, I'm here to remind you that God *does* love you. He sent His Son to die a terrible death for you and your sin! You can't see it because you are taking control, *you* are focusing on the wrong things. You are setting your sights on worldly things instead of godly things and trying to live your life on your own. No one can do that. We will all fail if we live that way. Every day you have to put on the armor of God and lean on Him to get you through the day. Even Jesus had to pray for strength."

"Yes, I remember."

"It is never too late to choose the right path, Kate. You can still make the right choice here. God loves you—please remember that! I know it sounds cheesy and cliché, but it is truly the most meaningful thing in your life. Hold to it. Make it your priority and you will have the true power to overcome everything."

"I just don't know how to do it. I have failed so badly, I just don't know how to accept and have faith."

"There is that word again…*I*. You will never be able to trust God completely if you keep saying *I*. Let Him be your guide. Pray and pray fervently for faith and strength and believe He will give it to you. Nothing is uncommon to man that Christ Himself has not endured. He will help you! He has helped you—you just are too hardhearted to see it, or even too hardhearted to seek it. But you have to let Him! And choose quickly my sister. You only get one life to choose, because if you are not for God then you are against Him. There is no in between. You either work for Christ or Satan and you will spend your eternity accordingly. God has taken great sacrifices for you to spend eternity with Him, don't throw it away because you think things aren't working out in this world to your advantage."

His words stung greatly. I threw my hands up to my face again agonizing over his words. What was I doing? What had I chosen?

"Kate, it's time," I heard Sam say. I looked up and Pastor Bruce was gone. Kate was standing in front of me with a gun in her hand. Suddenly I remembered what it was I was supposed to be doing.

"I don't think I can do this, Sam. I think I am choosing wrong."

"What are you talking about? Kate, don't lose it now, it has taken me a lot of work to get us where we are. You *know* you want this. You *know* you can have everything you want, just follow me. Come *on! Now!*"

She waved the gun in her right hand to follow her as she started heading out of the patio and across the street to what was now a wooded area. I could have sworn that was buildings just a few minutes ago.

I was frozen in my seat not able to move. Distress in this moment was an understatement. My stomach hurt with anxiety as I weighed what I was going to choose. How could I choose? I didn't know what was truth anymore.

"Seriously, come on, Kate! You will see this is the right choice!"

I didn't know why, but I stood up and followed her across the street. She led me into a deeply-wooded and mossy area where the day got darker. I couldn't see the sky overhead anymore for the tree-tops were too thick. I started to get cold, and I could feel the presence of evil all around me. As I looked to my left and right I swear I saw eyes glowing in the shadows. I slowed my walk to a creeping and Sam quickly noticed.

"Kate, it is truly going to be okay! I promise," she said as she came back to me and grabbed my hand to help me along.

"Sam, I felt terrible when I left. I even snuck into your room to say good-bye, did you know that? You were my best friend and to leave you like that...I just shouldn't have, I should have fought to bring you with me. But I don't think this is the way. I don't think this is what I need or want. I want love and forgiveness, not pain and suffering. I want to help people not hurt people. I want Jay to be punished, of course, but not like this. I want to have you in my life but not like this! Please, Sam, there has to be another way."

"There isn't, Kate. Don't chicken out on me now. You don't know the kind of life they can give you. We will be like sisters again. You won't have to worry about anything ever again. *Just come now!*" Her voice was forceful and domineering.

I felt for her now as I could suddenly see that she was hiding her misery behind what she thought was power. She turned and pulled me along behind her. We came to an opening in the woods that was blanketed in black rocks. As we continued into the opening I realized the black figures weren't rocks but people dressed in black-hooded robes. They parted to open to us a pathway to what seemed to be a type of wooden altar. The night got colder and darker, and Sam placed a black robe on my shoulders as we approached the altar. On the altar was another black-robed figure with a black bag draped over its head and his hands bound behind him with black rope. Sam stepped up on the altar and turned around offering me a hand up. I stepped up with her and glanced around the open space. The sea of black robes was faceless and dark with only glowing white eyes. I wanted to run. I wanted to escape, but I couldn't move my legs.

Sam could sense my fear and whispered in my ear, "It is the time we have both been waiting for. Your initiation into a new life. One that will change your life forever."

But that didn't soothe me. I didn't want to change my life forever anymore because it wasn't my life that counted. It was the eternity after. Where would I be? I didn't want to be there. It wasn't a place of love. It was the opposite of that. It was fear and evil. It was cold and darkness. Even if God wasn't true, I didn't want this.

I looked at Sam who had a worried look on her face. "Don't back out on me, Kate. I need you. I can't be here without you! You are too far into this now. They will kill you if you reject. You need to go through with this."

It was the first time since seeing Sam again that I saw actual emotion in her face. She was as scared as I was. But why?

Still holding my hand, she walked us over to the figure and aggressively threw off the bag. It was Jay.

He looked up at us and saw the gun in Sam's hand. Instead of being fearful as I thought he would be, he grimaced with his demonic grin. I suddenly realized he wasn't scared because this was his family. Unlike me, he belonged there. Even when they were going to kill him, or I guess I was going to kill him, he didn't fear. Did they tell him something to make him not fear? Did they promise him power like they did me?

"Welcome to the dark side, Kate!" He laughed.

"I will never be on your side, Jay. I just want you out of my life and away from those I love."

"I will never be out of your life. Don't you see that I will always be there to haunt you?"

Sam smacked him in the head with the gun, and I heard a sudden gasp from the black gallery that surrounded us. Why was what she did so shocking?

Anger started to fill my soul again, and I began to think I could kill Jay. Sam handed me the gun. "Go ahead, Kate, end him! End your pain and join us!"

I looked into Sam's eyes. No longer did they look black, but back to her normal green color that I remembered. She started to look more normal to me, like the Sam I had truly cared for. My first best friend. Her words weren't an order like they had been before. She was pleading with me.

I took the gun and held it up to Jay's head. He smiled at me and put his head right onto the muzzle of the gun.

"*Do it!*" His eyes turned red, and he looked more demonic than ever.

"I can't! I can't. I am so sorry, Sam, I can't do this. This isn't right. I don't want to be on your side. It is the wrong side! I love you, I do, and I'm so sorry for leaving you, but I can't do it. I can't join you."

"Don't do this to me, Kate. You don't believe in God. You can't! Please don't do this. They will kill you! Just *shoot!*"

I started to back away to the edge of the altar, when suddenly out of nowhere a tall, dark figure swiftly floated in. He came to a stop on the altar right in between Sam and me.

"You won't fulfill our request, then we won't give you the opportunity to choose the other side." He growled.

I couldn't see his face. Just his glowing eyes. His black-gloved hand came around from behind him exposing the machete-type sword he held. He raised it high in the air, and as it came soaring down toward me I felt my whole body flying backward. I hit the ground so hard it knocked the air from my lungs and blinded me. I shook my head and opened my eyes in time to see the sword being thrust through Sam.

"*No!*" I yelled, running to her. A black figure grabbed me from behind, holding me with my face only two feet from Sam's.

"Run, Kate, run! Get out of here and make the choice you know is true. *Fight, Kate, fight!* Please, for me, fight and get out of here. It's too late for me, but you can still make the right choice. I'm sorry I was so selfish to bring you here," Sam said reaching out to me.

"Sam, no, no, why did you do that? I am the one that didn't choose to do it. It should have been me. I am so sorry I left you it is all my fault," I screamed desperate to save her.

"No, Kate, it isn't your fault. I chose this! Get out of here please."

As she was talking, she floated up five feet into the air and hovered there. The black figure holding me drew me back with the rest of the sea of black as we saw a bright light open from above. A deep gasp of awe came from the crowd. Even Jay was struck with a look of trepidation. Sam was lifeless now, her eyes dark and her body limp. It hung in the air and then as if in a decision being made started floating up and then down, up and then down. A black gaping hole opened up beneath her with the sound of screaming and howling. Everyone again drew back even more, and the black figure that held me let me go. I fell to the ground looking up at Sam. Again she floated up and down and then with great aggression was dragged down into the black hole. I heard the crowd murmur, "He is true, He is real. What have we done?" I looked from the hole to the dark, tall man who killed Sam, and his eyes were on me wanting to finish the job he had started. Jay was still and silent beside him still in wonder of what had just happened.

"Kate, run!" I heard a voice shout at me from inside my head.

I got up and started to run as fast as I could through the crowd. No one tried to stop me—in fact, they parted ways to let me through. I could feel his presence behind me and panic gripped my body as I tried to find my way out of the dark woods. I looked back to see nothing behind me, but it was too dark to know for sure. I still felt the evil presence pursuing me so I kept running. When I turned back again I missed seeing the branch that stuck out in front of me, and I tumbled to the ground.

I couldn't do it. I couldn't outrun him. It was too late.

"It is never too late, Kate. I love you. Come to me," I heard a warm voice say.

"I can't," I shouted. "I don't know where you are."

"Just ask for me to be there, and I will. Call on me, and I will always be there. Trust in Me, and believe in Me, and I am there."

"I do believe, Lord. I am so sorry. Please, my gracious God, forgive me...forgive me for trying to do this on my own, forgive me for not trusting you and making you just a way of escape instead of a way of life. Forgive me for not giving you my life, my all. Forgive me for filling my life with the love of others instead of Your love. I love you Lord, and I know you are true. I know you are there. I know you sent your Son to die for me. Oh Precious Lord, I cannot believe you want to forgive me, but I know your Son is enough that you will!" I shouted now bawling into the ground.

Suddenly I felt light all around me and warmth pierce my joints. A hand was placed in mine, a hand that was so familiar and warm that exuded love.

"Kate! Kate, can you hear me? If you can hear me squeeze my hand."

I tried to open my eyes, but I couldn't—they were too heavy. In fact I could feel my whole body getting heavier, and the light that was piercing my joints felt more like pain. I tried to move, but I couldn't. I made myself calm down and just tried to squeeze the hand that held mine.

"She did it. Amy, go get the doctor—she squeezed my hand!"

"What?" I heard Amy scream.

Amy? What was Amy doing there? I struggled to open my eyes, but still couldn't.

"Kate, oh, Kate, you can hear me. I am here, Kate. We are all here. We love you, fight, Kate, and come back to us!"

It was Evan. Evan was with me. His was the hand that was holding mine, all warm and soft and strong. My heart ached for him. To look into those blue eyes I had missed so much. I really fought now. My mind was blurry and my body was heavy, but I fought and fought to open my eyes. I felt Evan's hand slip out of mine and fearing I was losing him I screamed his name.

"You better hold her hand again, Evan, she seems to respond better if you are there," I heard a deep voice say.

"Kate, can you hear me, dear? My name is Dr. Bernstein, can you open your eyes for me?"

Feeling Evan's hand grip mine again, I put all my force into opening my eyes. I could tell I was making progress because streams of light started to flood my eyes. I could feel my body more now. I could feel sheets covering my body. My head was laying on something soft and cushy. A pillow? Was I not in the forest anymore? Did God save me?

"There you go, Kate, nice and slow. Just take your time and try to open those pretty eyes," the doctor said.

I again urged my eyes to open a little more. I could now make out Evan's hand holding mine, and it sent butterflies filling my stomach.

"You got it, Kate, come on, girl!" I heard Charlotte shout.

They were all there. The people I loved the most: Amy, Charlotte, and Evan. Would they all forgive me as I could now feel God had?

My eyes opened completely now, but I couldn't make out much in the distance. It was too blurry.

"B—blurry," my tiny and shaky voice squeaked out.

"I know, sweetie, but that is to be expected. Do you know where you are?" Dr. Bernstein asked.

"N—no. The woods?"

"No, not the woods, Kate, you are safe in the hospital. You were in a terrible accident, and you have been in a coma for two weeks. We were all very worried about you. How do you feel?"

"Calm down, Amy, give her some space," I heard Evan say.

"Can you tell me how you feel? Do you feel any pain?" the doctor asked.

"Uh, yes, my h—head."

"Yes, you hit your head, and it is still healing. You also have a significant gash on your right leg from where you were trapped in the car. Can you move your feet for me?"

I kept any other thoughts out of my head but those that the doctor was asking me to do in fear I would slip back into darkness and lose my friends forever. I tried with all my might to wriggle my toes and with the "very good" from the doctor I knew I was succeeding.

"You look good, Kate. I'm going to go order some tests, and I will be right back," he said as I heard him leave the room. Something told me he was just giving my friends a moment to let loose on my being awake.

I hadn't let what he said affect me until now. But as I heard his footsteps leave and I tried to look around to see faces, only seeing blurs, I let myself react to the confusion I was feeling. I had been in a coma? Did that mean everything that happened with Sam was just a dream? It seemed too real to be a dream. I had so many thoughts going through my head. But the one that remained constant was my renewed spirit. No matter if it was real or not. I knew that the acceptance of God in its truest form was real. I had been forgiven. I had been redeemed by the blood of Christ. I would renew my life and give it to God. I would seek Him first and let Him take the lead. I knew my struggles would not leave me, but I also knew deep down I could handle it, for God was on my side! And if God is for me, who could be against me?

"Kate! Oh my gosh, don't you ever do that to us again. We thought we lost you!" I heard tears in Charlotte's voice as she came to my side. But Amy beat her to my other hand so I felt her grab my leg.

"Oh, my dearest Kate, and if you ever leave me in anger again I will kill you myself," Amy said.

"Not funny, Amy," I heard Evan say.

It was the happiest sound I had ever heard. My family. My dearest friends gathered around me. With complete forgiveness already given. But I had to say it anyway, I had to tell them how I was feeling.

"I am so sorry to all...of...you," I managed to squeak out, with my voice actually feeling a little stronger.

"Shh, there is nothing to be sorry for." Evan stroked my cheek. It felt so loving that my heart raced.

"It looks like her blushing still works too," Charlotte said.

"Charlotte, gosh, you are going to embarrass her." I heard Amy whack her sister in love as she tried to protect me from the inevitable embarrassment I always had around Evan.

"I am...so confused. Amy are...you...okay? Evan, Italy?"

"I know you must have a lot of questions, and we do have a lot to talk about, but not now okay. There will be time." Amy loving caressed my arm.

Suddenly I was so tired, and I could feel my eyes closing. I tried fighting it; I didn't want to lose this moment. "So tired."

"Then sleep, sweetie, sleep. We will be here when you wake up okay." Evan again was caressing my face. I let myself feel his love and whisk me into a dreamless sleep.

When I woke up it was dark outside. I glanced around the room, thankful my eyesight was clearer than before. Evan was asleep beside me with his head resting on the bed right next to my left hand. It looked like he hadn't moved. Amy was asleep in the chair next to my bed on the right, and Charlotte was asleep in the chair by the window. I took a moment to really take in reality. My friends were there, and I was loved. They didn't leave me. I felt guilt over Evan being there, knowing that meant that he wasn't in Italy where he should be. If I have been in a coma for two weeks then that meant he should have been in Italy for a week by then. Maybe since that I was awake he would leave. My heart ached at that realization.

I glanced to Amy's beautiful, angelic face. She would always be my angel. The one who God had originally used to bring me to a knowledge of Him. I hoped one day I would be strong enough for God to use me. Charlotte was the strongest of all of us. I looked at her beautiful, freckled face and thanked God for the best sister I could have ever asked for. Strong and protective. I looked up to her more than she knew. I needed to tell her that. My mind wafted to thoughts of Jay and Demetri. Where were they now? Had Demetri come to see me? What about my parents? As my mind switched to the memories of the apparent dream I had during my coma I thought of Sam. I couldn't help feeling that the part of Sam being in trouble was true. From what Jay told me it was true. I immediately prayed for Sam, that somehow, someway I could help to save her if God so willed it. I could feel she needed me.

I looked over to Evan again. He looked so peaceful and gorgeous. His black, thick wavy hair falling in his eyes again. I reflected on how I had made him an idol in my life. I didn't let God direct our relationship. I let fear of rejection direct our relationship and that made me think of him in a way I shouldn't have. I should have expressed my feelings for him instead of hiding them and let God direct our path. Maybe we were meant to be just friends and that was okay because I know God would have something or someone for me. I lifted my hand and gently brushed away the hair from his eyes. Without immediately realizing I was talking out loud I gently whispered, "I love you," while stroking his cheek. A huge smile came across his face, and my heart sank into my stomach as I realized he heard what I said. I was immediately embarrassed and withdrew my hand. He caught my hand with his and opened his eyes.

"Don't you dare take your hand away from me," he said.

My cheeks were burning as I looked into his opening eyes as he grabbed my hand and held it.

"Kate, you have no idea what it was like to think I wouldn't have you in my life. To think I lost you. I never want to go through that again. Do you understand me?" He whispered trying not to wake the girls.

"Evan, I am so sorry." I was pleased to hear my voice wasn't cut up this time, although still squeaky and scratchy.

"The only thing you have to be sorry about is being in the wrong place at the wrong time. You will be pleased to know though that the drunk driver of the other car is fine. She does feel terrible though and has been in a treatment facility since the night she hit you."

"Oh, that's good. I'm glad." I really was glad, but somehow that was the last thing I wanted to talk about. I had so many questions. "Why are you not in Italy?"

"You really think I would go to Italy when you were lying in a coma?"

I sighed knowing I was right and feeling guilt take over the emotions of embarrassment. "There I go ruining your life again."

"Stop, Kate, you haven't ruined anything."

"Oh, good, so you can still go? Can you leave today?" I exclaimed with quiet excitement.

"Trying to get rid of me already? I thought you loved me," he said with a smile.

I couldn't help but smile back. "I do love you, Evan, more than you know, and that's why I won't be the one to ruin your life."

"You loving me would be the greatest blessing in my life, not the greatest ruin. Because, Kate," he said, now looking down at my hand that he held in his, "I love you, and not like you think. I mean I am in love with you." He looked up into my eyes. "I was willing to let you go before because I thought being with Demetri was what you needed and what you wanted. But when Amy called me and told me that you were in an accident my whole world disappeared. Nothing mattered more than you at that moment. I realized I didn't let God lead our relationship, Kate, and I am sorry for that. I let my own fear of you not needing me keep me from telling you that I loved you. I do love you, Kate. I have loved you from the moment you came to the baseball field with that dumb story about Emily. It only grew while we were in the gazebo together and then every moment of our Denny's and Hilltops dates together.

"When Charlotte had told me about wanting to introduce you to Demetri it broke my heart. My family convinced me to fight for you, but when I got back and saw that Demetri could give you more than I ever could, I knew I couldn't fight for you, but just enjoy the time I had left with you. In fact I only really took the Italy internship to get away from the pain of not being able to be with you because I couldn't take it anymore. And then the things with Jay, I could tell you were hiding things from me, and I figured you were leaning on Demetri, and I knew then that night in the gazebo when I was going to tell you that I loved you that I already lost you. That it was too late."

I couldn't believe what I was hearing. He was saying what I had wanted to hear for so long, but never thought I would. I had had him all wrong. I thought he saw me only as a sister, but he didn't, he loved me. I let the debacle with Paul almost ruin my chances with Evan because I was afraid of being rejected again. Instead of trusting God I leaned on myself to make a dumb decision. I began laughing.

"What are you laughing at?"

"I am laughing at us. We are so dumb. Evan, I have loved you from the moment you came walking up behind Emily the first time I met you. Of course I felt guilty about that because you were with Emily, and I knew at that moment that if you were with someone like Emily you would never want anyone like me. I settled for being your friend, and it was truly the best thing that ever happened to me. But I let my fear of rejection keep me from ever telling you how I really felt. I have never wanted to be with Demetri, he is controlling and a real jerk. He chose Jay over me the day of the accident. Although part of me didn't care because I was seeking for a reason to not be with Demetri, and he gave it to me. It was always you, Evan. Always. I love you so much, and I am so sorry I never told you. God has shown me to trust Him in all things, and I didn't trust Him with you. I ask your forgiveness with that, Evan, I ask your forgiveness for not being truthful with you." Tears were falling now and Evan's hand came up to my face to wipe them away. I noticed then that he, too, was crying.

"You are asking my forgiveness?" he said now laughing. "I did the same thing you know."

"Okay, okay. Amy, wake up. Wake up. We have to get out of here. I can't get in the way of this moment anymore," I heard Charlotte yell from her chair. Evan and I looked over at her, and now Amy whose eyes were open staring at us. I had completely forgot they were even there. Charlotte came over and kissed my forehead and grabbed Amy and left the room. Evan and I looked at each other and began to laugh. He grabbed my hand with both of his and kissed it. He looked up at me and put his hand on my face.

"I promise you, Kate, that if you will let me, I will love you forever. I will guide us with the direction of our Lord, and I will try my best to take care of you and never hurt you."

"There is no letting you love me, Evan, because I am and have been helplessly in love with you. I don't think you could get rid of me even if you tried." I smiled, my heart so full of love and happiness. Evan caressed my cheek as he came closer and took my lips in his. The kiss was soft and gentle, full of love and warmth. My stomach filled with excitement, and I thought my heart would explode from so much emotion. It was like two souls becoming one. We were meant to be. He pulled away too soon, but then with a smile came back for another quick peck.

"I don't want to wear you out, your monitor might break over there."

I realized my heart racing was being broadcast for the world and a nurse came rushing in. She was about to ask if everything was okay but could see the reason for the rush of blood flow and excused herself. Again we laughed in embarrassment.

"Evan, tell me, did Demetri ever visit me? Or my parents? Has anyone seen or heard from Jay? Has he hurt anyone else?"

"Wow, down to business already, huh? Won't even let the love soak in?"

"Sorry," I said biting my lip.

"No, I understand you wanting to know. It is complicated actually, so I will give you the short version. First off, I have to be honest with you about your parents. Yes, they did come the first few days. But after not seeing improvement they left to go home. But they have called Amy and Charlotte every day for updates, and this morning were very happy to hear you were awake and are actually coming tomorrow to see you."

My heart fell at first, but I quickly realized that it was okay. I didn't rely on my parents' love or acceptance for happiness. I knew my Heavenly Father cared and loved me more than I could ever imagine.

"Demetri actually did come to the hospital the first few days, and he was instrumental in getting Jay behind bars."

"Behind bars? What?"

"I knew that would get your attention. Yes, Jay is in jail awaiting his trial date, which hasn't been set yet. Demetri said that he actually had his suspicions that you might be telling him the truth when Jay called you sweetheart in a weird way. So he said he put on a real show and threw you out, after which he caught a weird smile on Jay's face. He said he was going to go take a shower as bait to see if Jay would follow you, and he did. So Demetri followed Jay, and I guess hid behind some bush near the car where you were. He heard every word that Jay said to you. When Jay hit you it took everything in him not to go out and take care of Jay himself but knew it wouldn't help. I have to admit it, when Demetri told us what he saw and heard, I wanted to kill Jay myself." Evan said with anger in his eyes.

He shook it off then continued, "Demetri said he was in complete and utter shock. He realized there was only one way to deal with Jay. So Demetri went to his father, and together Demetri's dad went to Jay's dad. They then came to Amy and David, the eyewitness to Amy's push, and all of them got Jay arrested. It was interesting to meet Jay's dad. He is a hard man. It seemed he almost took pleasure out of seeing Jay fall. Since Jay's arrest girls have been coming forward against him. I heard two days ago from Demetri's dad that he is going to take a plea deal and plead guilty to lesser counts to get less jail time. Gotta love the justice system. But we haven't heard from Demetri since. Charlotte said he quit the play and moved to London."

It was exactly what Sam had said in my dream about Demetri. My mind then slipped to what Evan had said about Jay. I smiled a huge smile, "God is good, Evan. God is so good. I don't care about the jail time. Jay is being taught the lesson he needs. I will pray that maybe God will open his eyes and he will come to know and love the Lord and repent of his ways."

"Seriously?" Evan said surprised at my response.

"Oh, definitely. Evan you have no idea where I was during my coma. I know it wasn't real but it felt real to me. I learned more about God and who He is during this whatever dream I was in, then I have the whole year in school. I can see it plainly now Evan, how He takes care of us even in trials. Trials might not go away, but His love never will either. It doesn't matter what happens in my life because God's plan will be fulfilled regardless. If I can be a servant of Christ in any way I will be happy to do it. He died for me, for all my iniquities. That is the greatest and most powerful thing I will ever know. God *is* in control. He was taking care of me even when I didn't see it. Like how Jay never was able to fully accomplish his evil task with me that night at the frat party. How He brought me you, although I messed that up myself, how He brought me Amy and Charlotte. How even when I had decided to give Jay what he wanted to save those I loved from being hurt, He sent me you, even when you didn't know it. He has been taking care of me and guiding me, I had just been ignoring Him."

"You were going to meet Jay that night?" He looked shocked.

"Yes," I said looking down. "I am sorry, Evan. I felt like I had no other option, and it is because you came, and I got you away from there and didn't go through with it that he went after Amy."

"Amy had told me he had pushed her in retaliation for you being defiant, but she didn't tell me that."

"Well it is good that she kept her promise to keep my secret then," I said.

"Kate, don't ever think you have to give up yourself to protect me. We could have handled it together."

"Yes, I know that now. Another lesson learned I guess right?"

"One I hope you will remember. I promise to do my part to make you know you can trust me."

"I already know I can. It was never you I thought I couldn't trust. I actually never trusted God or myself. I leaned on false knowledge and sin. That never gets anyone anywhere."

"Yeah, like in the hospital."

"You know I don't really mind being here. In fact, I am thankful. God has taught me a lot being here. Not only that, but He accomplished so much through the accident, how could I wish that it never happened. I wouldn't have you."

"Well, I can't guarantee that I would have gone through with going to Italy. I was already thinking of ways to get the courage to tell you I loved you and to pick me instead of Demetri."

"Little did you know, there was no choice that needed to be made."

With that he leaned down and kissed me again, this time a little longer and with more passion behind it.

"I love you more every minute, Kate."

I blushed. I knew I would never get used to him saying he loved me. It would always be like a dream come true.

"Evan, there is one thing I need you to help me with, though," I said.

"Anything!"

"When I was in my coma, not only did I learn more about the greatness of God, but the power of the devil and of the monstrousness of hell. I am blessed to wage the war in my own life to fight the devil and live for Christ, but I was so scared, Evan. It is hard to explain how real it was for me and how scared I was. I know what I was feeling was real, and I know that what I was seeing does really exist. I think in some way it was a call for help. A message for me to not only run to God and fight the war that is happening within me every day, but to also help others to fight as well."

"Yes, very true and it is not always easy, my love, we will fail so many times and that is what is wonderful about the grace of God, but what do you want me to help you with?"

"I need to find Sam."